HAND

DI RITA GUPTA MYSTERY
BOOK 2

Sam Carter

CHAPTER 1

Seventeen-year-old Sarah poised herself over the windowsill, balancing with one hand on the ledge, and both feet. Then she jumped. The grass landing was less than six feet as their council flat was on the ground floor. She landed on her feet and a sharp pain lanced up her left ankle. She rolled on the grass and then got up.

Gingerly, she tested her foot, and found she could weight bear on it. The pain got easier after a few steps. She stopped and crouched by the fence to look back. The windows of her flat were dark. Her mum and brother were fast asleep.

She felt a stab of pain in her heart when she realised she might not see them again. It was for the best. One day, they would understand. As the Keeper said, the world would be a better place if more people reset their lives.

Then the adrenaline and fear took over, a lethal cocktail that injected energy into her limbs. She climbed over the fence, and dropped lightly to the other side.

She heard her phone buzz, and her heart beat faster. She pulled her phone out to check the latest message.

She was hypnotised by the words. The Keeper wanted to see her tonight. She was the chosen one. She couldn't believe it, but it was true.

Are you ready to be free?

Sarah's mouth opened as she gasped. She had waited for this day for so long, and finally, it had arrived.

Yes of course, she wrote quickly.

Then come to the designated place. Everyone is waiting.

I'm on my way.

Good. See you soon.

Sarah had long legs, and she was a fast walker. The summer moon was round and yellow in the sky, showing her the way. It was a long walk, and she stopped a few times to catch her breath. Every time she stopped, thoughts of her family returned to her mind.

Her mother, Jill, had a new boyfriend. Andy wasn't Sarah's dad, and Sarah didn't like him. She was seventeen now, and not little anymore. She could read the look in Andy's eyes, not that her mother ever saw it. A couple of times, Sarah had thought of telling Jill, that Andy was creepy. But after many years, Jill seemed to be happy. Sarah didn't want to spoil that.

She had never known her dad. Jill and her brother David were her only family. She wished Andy wasn't settling himself into their lives, but as the days passed, it seemed inevitable. Andy had brushed past her a couple of times in the kitchen. It wasn't accidental, and it wasn't nice.

Sarah started walking again, going up the hills now, leaving the city behind. She tried to leave the bad thoughts alone, but they kept creeping in. Andy at home. The bullies at school. Sarah wanted to wash the dirt away. When she started to cut herself, Jill found out, and took her to the doctors. Sarah hated seeing the psychiatrists. They knew nothing, only gave her tablets that made her sleepy, and feel weird.

Since she found The Gathering her life had changed. The voices in her mind had stopped. The boys and girls of the Gathering had suffered, just like her. Led by their enigmatic leader, the Keeper, many of them had reset their lives. Tonight, it was Sarah's turn.

She leaned against a tree, sweat covering her forehead, trickling down her face. Beyond the trees, she could see the triangular outline of the warehouse. Excitement flickered in her heart, blotting out the fear and pain. She climbed with renewed energy and crested the top of the shallow hill.

Light spilled out from the closed doors of the warehouse. It wasn't bright, as only candles and phone lights were allowed. It was meant to be secret, after all, and although the location was remote, they couldn't make much noise.

She heard the chanting of hymns from inside. The nightly prayers, led by the Keeper. Sarah opened the side door, and stepped inside. Several people stood close together, facing the stage. A smell of burning incense filled the air. It was stuffy inside, but no one seemed to care. The Keeper was chanting softly, and the others read from the pamphlet in their hands.

The Keeper stood on the makeshift stage. He wore a white hood over his face, and his body was covered in a loose white robe. No one but the ones who had reset themselves had seen his face. Sarah's heart thrummed with nervous energy. Like the other Reset candidates, she had the chance to be intimate with the Keeper. She had seen his face, admired his strong, muscular body. Now, she had to keep her promise to be Reset.

The chanting stopped as the Keeper raised his head to look at her. One by one, the Gathering turned as well. In silence, they stepped aside as she walked through them, a river parting to make way for her.

Sarah felt special. In their faces, she saw tears and smiles of joy. Several of the teenagers reached out to touch her. She held her hands out and soaked in their adulation. The Keeper stood with his arms aloft, guiding her onto the stage. A couple helped the Keeper lay out the table where she would lie. Her heart beat faster.

As she climbed on the stage, the soft chanting started again. The Keeper gripped her shoulders gently. She couldn't see his face due to the hood, but she knew his eyes were roaming over her body. She had seen him without any clothes. He pressed close to her, and she could feel his excitement.

"Drink this" he whispered. Sarah took the offered earthen cup. There was a dark liquid inside, and she hesitated. The Keeper touched her arm, and his head rose, and she saw his calm, sky blue eyes. She felt hypnotised by them.

"Do it now," he said.

Sarah put the cup to her lips. The liquid tasted sweet and thick. She drank the whole cup. The chanting was louder now. Sarah closed her eyes and slowly, her body started to sway with the chanting.

She started to feel dizzy, and her eyes blurred. The candlelight swam in a sea of blackness, round, floating objects. She took a step forward, and her feet felt nothing, like she was walking on air. She would've fallen unless the Keeper grabbed her by the hand and guided her to lie down on the table.

The couple behind the Keeper were now chanting louder, and that had been picked up by the Gathering. Sarah saw the glint of the long knife in the Keeper's hand. He towered over her, as she lay there helpless. He raised the knife above his head, chanting. The sight of the wicked blade, vicious and curved, made Sarah gasp. Reality burst in through a crack in her drug addled mind. She didn't want to feel that knife on her body. She didn't sign up for this.

Suddenly, panic rushed over her like a tsunami.

She didn't want to do this anymore. She wanted to go back.

She tried to get up, but her legs were made of lead, her arms seemingly weighed down with stones. Her mouth opened, but she couldn't utter a word. She felt only the sudden, ripping pain as the knife plunged into her abdomen. She screamed then, her voice rising like a black tidal wave, turning her world into endless night.

CHAPTER 2

"Don't go too far," Rita's mother, Clara, called out. It was a bleak winter's day. Rita was out walking with her mother, and a harsh wind tugged at her jacket. The cliffs were jagged and sharp, and the North Sea was restless, spitting angrily at the rocks far below. The foam from the pounding surf thundered like a demon's growl, far below.

"Rita, come back here," Clara shouted.

"I want to see the waves," Rita shouted back, getting closer to the cliff edge.

"Stop it, you silly girl! Come here, now."

A magnetic force seemed to pull Rita away from her mother, into the howling wind, and the menacing cliff edge.

"Rita!" Clara screamed. Rita turned from the edge, and saw her mother like a faint smudge, as if rain was wiping her image from the landscape. Clara waved her hands, and her voice was loud, but she seemed to dissolve, fade into the rocks.

"Mummy?" Rita shouted back.

"Come back here," Clara's voice was insistent, but suddenly Rita couldn't see her mother anymore. Panic bulged in her throat, and she shivered.

"Mummy!"

The wind seemed to push her over the edge, and suddenly she was falling, arms cartwheeling in the howling wind as it battered her body.

"Mummy!"

Detective Inspector Rita Gupta screamed and woke up. She sat bolt upright in the bed, sweat pouring down her scalp.

The strident alarm cut through her slumber. She slapped a palm over the offending device, sending it tumbling to the floor. The whining didn't stop. Rita cursed and got out of bed.

Her flat was cold, she needed to sort out the central heating. She silenced the alarm, then flopped back on the bed. Her palms dug into her eyes. Her forehead throbbed with the lack of sleep. It was 6.00 am, and she had to get ready for work.

Wearily, she rose and stumbled into the bathroom. She blinked as she stared back at the mirror. She had taken her make up off before going to sleep, which was lucky, as she was a bit hung over. A pub dinner with her team and Jack Banford to celebrate their latest case was a success. One drink had turned into a few, and her alcohol tolerance was low to say the least. Jack had called her a cab, and she had fallen asleep as soon as her head hit the pillow.

But the nightmares remained, as did the aching loss in her heart.

Rita brushed her maudlin thoughts aside and got in the shower. She felt much better after washing her hair. It was growing past her shoulders – long, the way she liked it. But she would need a trim soon.

As she dried her hair, she wondered about the events of the last few weeks. It had been a whirlwind, to say the least. Finding her mother's remains, and then unlocking the secret of her disappearance – the closure Rita had sought her whole life – had driven Rita to the jaws of death.

She had escaped with some scratches, and the bruise on her left cheek was just starting to settle. She wore that injury with defiance. Blusher hid the mark now, but for the first few days, her swollen cheek and black left eye was a reminder of what she had endured.

She would go through it again, regardless of the cost. She would've done anything to find what happened to Clara. Coming back to Scarborough, wandering the streets and town she knew as if from another life, had also been a revelation. It was the same small, remote town by the seaside it had always been. Famous only in the summer, forgotten for the rest of the year.

The radio was playing that song about the boys of summer, and she couldn't help feeling how apt it was.

Scarborough was nicer in the fall and winter, when the crowds had gone. The endless sea, the long arc of light and sand, the desolate cries of the seagulls – it was all as Rita remembered it.

She had never thought it possible, but a part of her now wanted to stay. It was so different from the bustle of London. After she had solved her mother's case, the only excitement was a spate of burglaries by a gang of teenagers. Her days had been relaxing, and she found herself loath to send the email back to her boss in the London Metropolitan Police Force, asking to arrange her transfer back.

It was also nice to have her own spacious flat. It had two bedrooms, and from the kitchen plus diner, the long windows looked down the hill to the sea. She could definitely get used to that. It was on North Marine Road, a location that seemed exclusive to holiday lets. She was grateful to North Yorkshire Police to get her a place here. When she stood in front of the sea view windows, she could see the castle looming on the hills to the right.

The icing on the cake was the one third rent compared to her cramped one bed flat in North London. Jack had already mentioned she should buy somewhere if she was planning to stay any length of time. His expression was serious, but the gleam in his eyes, before she looked away, was unmistakable.

She tried to ignore the warm, fuzzy feeling in her stomach when she thought of Jack. He was her first boyfriend, and he had stood by her side in those terrible years. She lost her mother, her home, her sanity. Somehow, she had survived the council care homes and the foster parents.

Jack had been a constant during that tumult, her harbour in the storm. Then they left for university, and like all young lovers who promised to stay in touch, their lives led them further, and further away. Distance had blinded her memories, and we like to forget the bad times, don't we?

Rita had built herself a new life down in London. But now that she was back, she was finally grappling with the past, still closing the doors and shutters of the empty home she had left behind so long ago. And it was strange that Jack was helping her just like he had done thirty years ago – as a lawyer, he had done her power of attorney papers.

She switched off the drier and stood, checking herself quickly in the mirror. She picked up her warrant card and purse and went out the door.

She walked down to the bus stop, enjoying the sunshine on her face. The wind carried the forlorn scream of sea gulls in the distance. Her work phone beeped, and she answered.

It was Maggie Long, her detective constable. "Guv, we have a problem," Maggie's normally effusive voice was subdued. "IC1 female, teenager, found in an abandoned warehouse. Dead from knife wounds, it looks like."

Rita stopped, frowning. "When was it reported?"

"Half an hour ago. Three schoolkids were taking a detour, and saw the body. Uniforms are on scene, and we're on our way. Rizwan and me. I've informed the skipper." The skipper, or detective sergeant, was Richard Staveley. A short, barrel chested, pugnacious veteran of the North Yorkshire Police force.

"It doesn't look good, guv," Maggie said quietly. "Signs of a ritual killing."

"Send me the location," Rita said. "I'll see you there."

CHAPTER 3

The abandoned warehouse was on a shallow hilltop, not far from the town centre. As the taxi got closer, Rita saw the flashing blue lights on the hill, and the outline of the rusting hulk of the warehouse and huts. If memory served her correctly, this was a disused mining quarry. The taxi curved around the hill, and the buildings disappeared from view. Rita craned her neck, watching the green hills rising up on either side of the road. She patted the driver on the shoulder.

"Pull over."

The man did so, and she paid him quickly, then got out. The road had traffic on either side, but Rita was on the opposite end of the cars headed into town. She crossed over when there was a break in the traffic.

A path snaked up the hill, and above, the warehouse was visible again, this time with several of the uniformed officers milling around. The taxi had come around the wrong way, there was nowhere to park here. Or else, the police vans would've been visible. The path was dry, thankfully. The rains had stayed away, but Rita knew the thunderclouds could gather in the twinkle of an eye, and flash summer storms were common in the coastline. She climbed quickly, her rubber soled feet gripping the path.

She was panting when she got to the top. A uniformed constable approached her, and she showed him her warrant card. Rita stopped at the perimeter, and signed her name on the clipboard, which another constable held out for her. The same woman gave her shoe covering, and Rita pulled out gloves from her pocket.

The warehouse loomed in front now, a blackened gap where the gates used to be. It looked like the scarred mouth of a giant, the sharp edges of rust steel around it like grotesque teeth. A white space suited figure stepped out from a van, and walked inside the mouth, disappearing into the darkness.

Soon, lights were switched on inside, and she heard the soft hum of generators. Shola Adebayo, the head of forensics, had just entered the crime scene. Rita recognised her in the space suit, and she was followed by Henry, her lanky technician, his sterile suit tight and oddly worn, as if the suit was trying its best to cover his scrawny, tall figure.

"You alright, guv," a male voice said behind her. Rita turned to see Rizwan, the detective constable, with Maggie walking up behind him.

"Where's Richard?" Rita asked.

"Skipper's on his way. He had to drop his kids off," Rizwan said. From the evasive look on Rizwan's face, she could tell there was more to it. Richard was going through a difficult time separating from his ex-wife.

The two children were caught in between, and it wasn't easy for any of them. Rita nodded, pulled out her phone, and sent Richard a text to tell him he didn't have to rush back. She would catch up with him back at the office.

Rita turned her attention to the rest of the crime scene. She wanted Shola and Henry to get their bearings first.

"This is an old mine quarry, right?" She asked the two constables, and they looked at each other, then blinked in surprise.

"How did you know?" Maggie asked.

"I grew up here, in case you've forgotten," Rita raised her eyebrows. She pointed behind her, down the hill. "I went to Castlecombe Sixth Form school way down there. Some kids came up here to smoke pot and all the rest of it."

"You were one of them, were yer?" Maggie grinned.

"Aye," Rita smiled back, her Yorkshire accent returning, like it often did these days. "I was well bad back in the day." She looked at the ground. It was brown dirt, with soft patches of grass around. "Any footprints? Blood drops? Have you two looked around?"

"We just got here," Maggie said. "The old quarry's that way. It's been silted over now to stop accidents from happening."

“Yes, there was talk of it back then,” Rita said. They started to walk, Rita urging them to fan out, and observe the ground for any clues.

“Some footprints,” Rizwan called out, as they walked past the forensic and police vans. Rita nodded, she had seen the same. Were these prints made by the school kids, or others? Judging by the number of prints, it seemed like a crowd had descended here. The quarry was still at least a couple of hundred yards away, with two smaller wood cabins close to it. The wood was rotten and the rooves had caved in.

To Rita’s right, there was another path, that led down to a dirt track. The track was wide enough for cars, and that was the road used by the vehicles that had come up here. Rita got closer to the path and then crouched down. More boot prints, but these were hidden by the dust from the cars, and she couldn’t rely on them. Indeed, the cars had destroyed a lot of boot prints.

Maggie and Rizwan joined her. Rita stood. “These boot prints aren’t the standard police boots. Look at the depression. Many of them were made by lighter feet. Not children, but I’d say some were teenagers and young adults.”

“Or women,” Maggie added. “The smaller trainer marks, like these, could belong to teenage girls.” Maggie crouched and pointed at a couple of prints.

Rita nodded. Her gaze fell on the derelict warehouse at the crest of the hill. It seemed to her a lot of people had gone straight to the warehouse recently, maybe last night. It was a mercy it hadn't rained, or she wouldn't have found these prints.

With the constables, she looked around the quarry and the smaller buildings. There were no boot marks there.

"Take photos and send them to our boot print analyst. Is she in Sheffield today?"

Rizwan nodded. "I can't see anything else, guv. No clothes, blood drops, nil on the ground."

"Not true," Maggie sniffed. She held up a specimen bag, with a card and a matchbox inside. The card seemed like an advertisement, a flyer for a nightclub. The matchbox had a logo on it. She winked at Rizwan.

"I think you need to brush up on your detective skills, DC Jaffer."

"Shut your face," Rizwan retorted.

"Liquid," Rita read, squinting as she read the logo on the box. "Where's that?"

"It's a nightclub in town, quite new," Rizwan said. He glanced at Maggie. "Only the cool people go there."

“Not you then,” Maggie scoffed. “You should spend more time looking for evidence, and not in nightclubs, Riz.”

Rita grimaced. “Well, it seems at least some young people were here last night. Which ties in with our victim.” She shook her head once and took a deep breath. “Come on then. Let’s go and see her.”

CHAPTER 4

The halogen lamps cast strange shapes on the corrugated iron walls of the warehouse. Rita walked carefully on the sterile boards that were laid out, leading to the crime scene. The body was laid out on the floor.

The girl lay on her back, eyes staring up in frozen shock. A large gash of blood congealed around her abdomen. Her blonde hair lay like a halo around her face. She was dressed in a white robe that covered her to knee level. She wore blue jeans underneath, and her shoes were removed.

Rita noticed bits of wood lying around the perimeter. Shola was kneeling over the victim, taking fingerprints. Rita watched as Shola clipped the girl's nails, which were polished red. Shola put the nail clippings in a specimen bag. She noticed Rita looking over her shoulder. Not much of Shola was visible, covered as she was in her sterile suit. She nodded at Rita but didn't lower her mask. Rita nodded back and moved towards the head of the victim.

She noted the undyed, natural blonde hair, and the lack of make-up. Only the nails were done. This girl wasn't dressed for going out. There wasn't any sign of trauma to the scalp. With a gloved hand, Rita carefully touched parts of the scalp.

No swelling, and her fingers didn't have any dried or sticky blood. The face was similarly clear of any injuries. Rita lowered one lower eyelid. She was looking for the jagged black marks of conjunctival haemorrhages. They were telltale marks of increased pressure in the neck blood vessels, a sign that the victim was strangulated. Rita couldn't see them, but Dr Das might find something else.

On the neck, she didn't see any bruise marks or fingerprints. The trachea, or windpipe, wasn't deviated. Another sign that strangulation didn't take place. Shola was cutting the white robe with a pair of scissors. Rita helped her to gently separate the blood matted clothing below to expose the wounds. When the abdomen was sufficiently exposed, she took the pair of tweezers that Shola held out for her. She murmured her thanks and lifted the ripped pieces of clothing.

Only one, long wound, that traversed the abdomen from left to right. It was deep and had cut through various structures. Bits of tissue and blood had macerated on the surface. Rita was so absorbed in the detail she didn't hear anything until the voice startled her.

"That probably bisected the abdominal aorta, the main artery that takes blood from the heart to the groin and legs."

She looked up, startled. Dr Das was standing there, briefcase in hand. He was wearing a white apron over his dark blue suit. His salt and pepper hair were closely cut, and his black framed glasses were low on his nose. He had a smile on his face as he looked at Rita. The smile vanished as his sombre eyes looked at the rest of the victim. His eyes closed once, and he sighed.

Rita had worked with Dr Das in only two cases, but she trusted him. His medical knowledge was extensive, and he knew his way around a crime scene. He was in his sixties, and a veteran pathologist for Yorkshire Police.

"Terrible thing, eh?" He said, bending to the floor on one knee. "So young. Not seen anything like this for a long time."

"She died from this wound, didn't she?" Rita asked.

"Without looking at the rest of her, I'd say, yes. That wound alone would cause massive, and fatal haemorrhage."

"Sorry, Doc, didn't mean to put you on the spot," Rita said. "I'll let you be."

"No, that's fine." Dr Das laid out a blue rubber mat and put his instruments on it. With slow precision he assembled the rectal thermometer and asked Shola and Rita to help him. He took the body's core temperature, and then checked the temperature in the warehouse. Once he was done, Rita helped him and Shola to put the victim back in her original position.

Dr Das started examining. He inspected the hands as they were closest to him. He took swabs and talked to Shola about the evidence she had collected already. Rita stood and stepped back. She was at the back end of the warehouse, and even with the police being present, she couldn't help but think the body had been placed like a sacrifice at a shrine. She saw several small pieces of wood, and dust on the floor.

The dirt on the ground was disturbed by several boot prints. She called Maggie and Rizwan, and they joined her.

"Is the boot print analyst coming anytime soon? I want her to see if there's a match with the prints outside." Rita pointed at the floor and the constables bent down to see and take photos.

"What are these wooden chipboard fragments?" Rizwan said, picking up a piece of wood. "Looks like there was a pallet or something here."

"I was wondering too," Rita said. "You think they came from pallets? The wood platforms used to store bricks?"

"And various other things in builder's warehouses," Rizwan nodded. "But they could be from wooden storage boxes as well."

"Was the body carried here in a box?" Maggie asked.

"Not sure," Rita said, stroking her cheek, looking around the warehouse. "Maybe the wood was used to make a platform, and she was laid on it. The poor girl was part of a spectacle, strange as that sounds. Like a ritual." She shrugged. "Just a thought. I don't know."

"One thing we did notice," Rizwan said, glancing at Maggie. "Lots of footprints inside that don't belong to the police. Henry has circled some of them."

"Perhaps the people outside came in, and joined this ritual?" Maggie said, spreading her hands.

"Perhaps," Rita frowned, thinking. "If they did, how did they arrive, and get back home? Have you seen tyre tracks?"

"It's difficult on the road, and they might have walked, or taken public transport."

"Which means they couldn't have lived far," Rita said. "And even if this happened late at night – which is only my guess – chances are we might find a witness who saw something. Like a car passing by on the road below."

She walked over to the crime scene, and the constables followed. Dr Das was looking at the legs, having cut through the blue jeans at the ankles.

"Time of death, doc?" Rita asked.

Dr Das grimaced and stood. His knees clicked and he shuffled on his feet, his expression painful.

"Ouch. Don't get old, whatever you do." He smiled at Rita. "Rigor mortis is only starting in the bigger muscles like the legs and chest. Which means less than twelve hours since death. It's now ten in the morning. And given her body colour, or livor mortis, I would say just after midnight." He shrugged. "Between midnight and two in the morning."

"Thanks. Anything else?"

"I can't see any other signs of trauma, like you said. No tattoos, but I did find these." Dr Das bent on one knee, grimacing again. He lifted the sleeve of the left wrist. On the underside, there was a series of straight lines, one after the other.

"Self-harm," Dr Das said sombrely. "Cuts with a blunt knife, like a paper knife perhaps. This girl suffered with mental health issues."

Rita inspected the wounds. They were all dry but didn't look very old. Some of them were still reddish, indicating recent harm. The lines were straight and symmetrical, indicating the victim had done them carefully. Rita shook her head in sadness. Who was this poor girl, and what happened to her?

"She's got similar marks in the left ankle," Dr Das said. Rita had a look, and she thought she saw faint marks on the right ankle as well. She showed them to Dr Das, and he agreed.

"She's just starting there, I think. She would have a medical record, if these were brought to her doctor's attention. Something to look out for."

Rita thanked Dr Das and turned to the constables. "Where are the boys who found her?"

"Outside, waiting. Uniforms have taken a statement, but they know we're going to question them."

"Let's do it, before they get other ideas."

CHAPTER 5

A uniformed constable was standing opposite the three boys who were sitting on the steps on one of the huts. The boys were teenagers, aged about sixteen, or seventeen, Rita thought. They were growing into adulthood. The oldest boy seemed the leader of the pack. He was taller, and sat with his back straight, glaring at the constable.

The constable seemed nervous. He pulled on his chest rig, and shuffled on his feet, frequently turning his back on his charges, pretending to listen to the radio. He was thin and reedy, with a head that seemed too big on his scrawny neck, like a pumpkin face on top of a scarecrow. Rita hadn't seen him before, and she knew most of the uniformed constables in Scarborough's small force.

"Hello," she said, getting close to him, while watching the boys from the corner of her eyes. She was behind the constable, and he jumped in fright. His name badge said Dixon.

"Hello PC Dixon. I'm DI Gupta."

"Ey yup, alright, guv. Yes, yes, I know who you are." His wide blue eyes scanned her face, and he looked like a fish out of water.

"When did you join the force?" Rita asked.

"It's been three months, like."

That made sense, but he still should be better at his job. "First murder scene?"

Dixon scratched his head. "Aye, yes."

"Never turn your back on suspects, okay? I'm not saying these lads did it, but we need to keep an open mind, and be careful."

"Aye, yes, guv. Got that, like."

Dixon itched his neck and pulled on his chest rig again. Rita wondered if the rig was too heavy for him.

"Have the lads said anything?"

"No, but they used their phone a couple of times."

Rita frowned. "Did you tell them not to? What if they sent photos of the crime scene on social media?"

Dixon looked so lost she wondered how he got the job. "Who's your guv, by the way?"

Dixon's eyes darted around like he was looking for support. His eyes met Maggie and Rizwan's and he coughed, then looked at his feet. Rita sighed.

"Inspector Bennett," Dixon finally blurted out.

"Thanks," Rita said. "Stick around and wait for my instructions."

Dixon stared at Rita as if she had two heads, then nodded vigorously.

Rita stepped up to the three boys. The tall boy in the middle looked at her suspiciously, anger plain in his eyes. The other two were scared, and gaped at Rita, their eyes flicking to the constable on either side of her.

“What’s your name?” Rita asked the boy in the middle.

“Karim,” the boy said. He was olive skinned, and his black hair was longish at the back. Rita couldn’t guess his nationality. Middle Eastern, perhaps.

“And yours?” Rita asked the boy to the right.

“Mark,” came the answer. The other boy was called James.

“What are you doing here?”

The boys looked at the floor, but Karim answered. “We’re on our way to school.”

“What school is that?”

“Sedgley Hill.”

Rita racked her brains, because the name was familiar. Then she remembered. There was a school on the west of Scarborough. It wasn’t close to the industrial estate. She glanced at Rizwan and asked him.

"About three miles from here, down the hill," Rizwan said. He looked at Karim. "You don't live far from school, do yer? Isn't this out of the way for you?"

"Actually, it's on the way, if you bother looking at the map," Karim said insolently. "The hill happens to be on the way. We stopped down there for a bacon butty. Didn't we, lads?" He glanced at Mark and James, both of whom nodded.

"No need to get shirty, lad," Rizwan said back. "You sure you're not up here to score some drugs? What if I searched you, now?"

Karim grimaced, but Rita could see his earlier confidence was wavering. He didn't like what Rizwan just said.

"Go ahead. You won't find nowt."

Rita indicated at Rizwan to stop. She didn't want to get distracted. "Walking this way to school is a detour. You can't just be here for a bacon butty. Why are you really here?"

Karim glared at her. "I just told yer, didn't I?"

"No, you didn't. It makes no sense to come to an abandoned warehouse for breakfast, when you could walk on the road around the hill or take the bus like everyone else. If you don't tell us the real reason you're here, then you become suspects to a murder. Do you understand?"

Mark and James looked like they had been slapped across the face. Karim was also taken aback, but he recovered swiftly.

"We called you as soon as we found the body, didn't we? Is this how you thank us?" He snarled. Then he muttered something under his breath and looked away.

"Tell us what happened after you got here," Rita tried a different track. "You went into the warehouse and saw the body?"

Karim's face changed. His eyes lost the hostility, and he took a deep breath. Colour faded from his cheeks.

"Aye," his voice was lower. "We went in, and it was hard to miss, like. She was lyin' there, just like that. I knew she was dead. I called 999."

He looked down to the ground. Karim had the option of running away, Rita realised. Mark and James would've followed him. He didn't because he was scared, despite all the bravado he was showing now.

"Did you recognise her?" Rita asked. Karim looked at her, then shook his head. Rita asked the other two and got the same response.

"Are you sure?" Rita looked at all of them in turn. "Be honest. Are you sure she didn't go to your school? Or you didn't see her elsewhere?"

One by one, the boys shook their heads. Rita didn't think they were lying. They looked at her, and the shock and fear were evident in their faces. Her eyes lingered on Karim, and she didn't think he was hiding the girl's identity, either.

Rita lowered herself down to her haunches, now at eye level with the boys. "So, tell us why you come here, then? And don't lie, because we can find out."

"There's CCTV everywhere," Rizwan added. "Know what I mean?"

Karim glanced at him sharply. Mark nudged Karim with an elbow. "Go on. Tell them."

"Shut your face," Karim hissed at him in a low whisper, but Rita picked up on it.

"He's right," James said. "Just bloody tell them."

Karim closed his eyes, then shook his head in frustration. "All right. We came up here to smoke a spliff, alright? That's all."

Rita could understand that. Teenagers smoking a little pot, or cannabis, wasn't exactly the end of the world.

"Anything else?" She asked. She thought a wariness remained in Karim's face. He shook his head, and the others followed.

Maggie spoke up. "Do you lads do any dealing here? Sell some pot?"

They denied it, as Rita had expected, but she didn't trust Karim's expression, again.

“So, you came up here to smoke a spliff, and then you were going to school. Is that correct?” Rita asked. The boys nodded.

Maggie leaned over to Rita. “I’ve got their home addresses, guv. We can check up on them. They live with their families.”

“Okay.” Rita said. She turned to the boys. “Don’t leave town. I will want to speak to you again.” Her eyes rested on Karim as she said the words. He nodded once and looked away.

CHAPTER 6

Richard was waiting for them back at the station. His eyes were fixed on his laptop, and his face brightened when he saw Rita. Maggie and Rizwan were at the canteen, getting coffee and breakfast.

"Now then, guv," he said. Rita detected a tiredness in his features but decided not to mention it for now.

"I went up to Traffic and asked for any relevant CCTV footage around the crime scene from last night. Just in the off chance we find something. There are no cameras around the warehouse, obviously. It's a derelict site. But there is on the roads leading up to it, and Traffic found something interesting."

Rita pulled up a chair and Richard turned the laptop towards him. The screen was divided into four boxes, and it showed the black and white image of a street at night. Streetlights glowed above, and some cars went by. Rita noted the time stamp, it was ten to midnight.

A figure appeared at the right corner. It was a slim, tall ish woman with long hair. She climbed the fence over the road and jumped on the road. Then she crossed the road quickly and disappeared.

“That’s all we have on this feed, unfortunately. This is one of the roads that lead up to the hill, and the warehouse. The other roads show nothing,” Richard said. “But I asked Traffic to look for a woman of similar size and shape. As it happens, around the same time, they found this.”

Richard clicked on the keyboard, and another CCTV box appeared. It showed another tall woman walking down a street. She turned to look behind several times. She vanished from view into a park, then appeared again, climbing the park fence, leading to the film Rita had just seen.

Rita leaned back, frowning. “Do we have an ID on this woman? Our victim is a teenager, or a young adult. She can’t be any more than eighteen or nineteen years old.”

“No, we don’t. I zoomed into her face, and Traffic did some clever image manipulation.” Richard showed Rita the close up of the woman’s face. She was indeed very young, just about the age of the victim. Her facial features also looked similar, Rita thought. A tingle of excitement passed down her spine.

“This might be our victim. She looks like her. Ask Traffic to circulate her image and do a facial recognition with anyone on CCTV. She must’ve been out and about in the day. If she went to school, or college, we should be able to find her.”

The door opened and Maggie entered, carrying a tray of coffees. Rizwan followed with a packet of biscuits and croissants. Rita explained the CCTV findings to them and accepted the coffee with a murmur of thanks.

"Did we ask Dr Das when he can do the Postmortem?" Rita asked. She had forgotten, and from the blank look on the faces of both the constables she knew they had as well. She took out her phone and sent the pathologist a text.

"Get in touch with the gait analyst please," Rita said, and Maggie gave her a thumbs up.

"I want a door to door in a five-mile radius of the crime scene," Rita continued. "Do you think this woman is our victim?" She pointed at the laptop and both the constables agreed.

Maggie said, "The close up of her face is very similar. Who else will be crossing the road to go up the hill late last night? That area is normally deserted."

"Good. I want that image circulated widely. Put it in all the schools, colleges, the council, bus stops, wherever you can. We need a positive ID ASAP."

Rita walked up to the white board. Richard handed her a photo print out that had the victim's face on it. Rita attached it on the board with blue tack.

"So far, what we know is that this unknown girl went up to the warehouse, where she was killed last night, after midnight. If she is indeed the woman on CCTV, then she walked up there. Which means she can't live far, or she drove up to the park. But CCTV hasn't picked up a car, have they?"

Richard shook his head. "No. And now Traffic will look for more of her images with facial recognition, so hopefully we can pick her up further out."

Rita added, "She might have been in CCTV black spots last night as well, that's why she doesn't appear till she gets to the park. In any case, our working assumption now is that she walked here. Hardly any buses around that time. That's why I want her poster up in a five-mile radius. She must live within that distance."

Rita wrote down the possible location and put that as number one.

"The manner of her death is disturbing. I think there is a ritual involved here. She might have been on a wooden platform. And there might also have been an audience, judging by the number of fresh footprints we saw there."

"A cult?" Richard said. "A secret society? Now that is weird. Scarborough's strange, but not that strange." He smiled, then became serious. "I've not heard of anything like that, but we can look around."

"Best to search in social media," Rizwan said. "If there is a secret society of weirdos, they're going to be online."

"Look on the dark web," Rita said. "A good place to start. That's where all the kiddy fiddlers and criminals hide."

Rita took a sip of her coffee. "OK. Did we find a phone on her? A purse or keys?"

"Nothing so far, guv," Rizwan said. "But she had a tattoo on the back of her left calf. I took a photo. Sorry, I forgot to tell you." He held out his phone, and Rita showed it to Richard as well.

The tattoo was a black rose in a red circle. Drops of red liquid, presumably blood, were arranged inside the circle. The rose was wilting, the petals separated from the stalk. The tattoo was about the size of a golf ball.

"Never seen anything like it," Rita said.

"It's a sad image," Maggie said. "The flower's drying up. I don't like the blood inside the circle though."

"Neither do I. Let's do a search for this image. We might find something online." Rita looked at Rizwan. "Anything else?"

"Shola did mention her feet were naked but it didn't look like she had walked barefoot. We didn't find shoes anywhere."

"I saw that, too. Did Shola mention a murder weapon?"

Rizwan and Maggie shook their heads. "OK, let's ask Shola for a report asap," Rita said. She went back to the whiteboard and wrote Karim's name. Below it she wrote Mark and James.

"I thought there was something dodgy about Karim. I don't mean the cannabis he smokes, or perhaps deals in. Does he have a PCN?"

Richard answered. "His full name is Karim Ahmadi. He doesn't have any convictions, but he did receive a caution for possession of a narcotic. It was MDMA, a popular drug in nightclubs. This happened last year, in July, and at a nightclub in Sheffield. Nothing else apart from that."

"And what about the other two?"

"Nothing on them. Mark Oakham and James Aspinall. Neither of them had any contact with the police. All three are sixth form students at Sedgley College. It's a co-ed, so there is a chance our victim was a student there."

"A tempting assumption to make, but let's not get ahead of ourselves. Contact the school and set up a meeting with the principal. I also want to meet Karim's parents."

Rita's phone buzzed. It was Dr Das, and she answered.

“I should have the PM done later this afternoon,” the elderly pathologist said. “Would you like to pop around four pm today?”

“Thanks, doc, see you then.”

CHAPTER 7

The Keeper watched the black-haired female detective from a distance. She was strutting around like she owned the place. Her two lackeys, the short guy and the blonde woman, followed her around, listening to her.

The detective stopped to point at something on the hill, and the Keeper felt a thrill pass through him. The finger was pointed almost directly at him. But she couldn't possibly see him, he knew that. He had mastered the art of staying invisible a long time ago.

He smiled to himself. The detective had a nice shape to her body, slender hips but full in the right places. She didn't have a jacket on, and the white shirt strained at her breasts. He felt a stirring in his pants, and a heat low in his belly. This detective liked herself, didn't she? Thought she could walk around giving orders. Arrogance dripped off her like water from a duck's back. Who the hell did she think she was?

The Keeper's smile turned to a snarl. He didn't like strong women. But the thought of bringing DI Rita

Gupta under his control was a tantalising one. He would enjoy subjugating her, making her his very own. She would carry the scars for life and become his submissive.

As submissive as Sarah had been. His mind clouded over, and the sunlight turned to rust. Remorse gathered like a shroud over his heart. Sweet and tender Sarah – so innocent. He would never taste her again or feel the sweet touch of her skin. True, they had only been together briefly, but that was enough to bring her under his control.

She was weak, just the way he liked them. She had a troubled family life, she suffered with terrible moods and sadness, and she had no one to love her. All the ingredients that the Keeper looked for in his submissives – he had found in Sarah. He had kept their affair a careful secret from the Gathering. His own community who would now do his bidding.

A sense of power rippled through him, dispelling his sadness. He had developed the community with help from Robert McFarlane – the Guardian of the Brotherhood. The same Robert that DI Rita Gupta had destroyed, put behind bars for the rest of his life. Little did Rita Gupta know that the Brotherhood might have gone, but many of the players had helped to set up the Gathering. That would continue, no matter what Rita Gupta did. Most importantly, the Keeper would make sure that DI Gupta got what she deserved.

Oh, he was going to make double sure of that.

He watched again as DI Gupta strolled inside the warehouse. He had been careful to remove any identifying documents from Sarah. He had waited after all the men and women from the Gathering had gone. Then he had swept the place as best he could in the darkness. He had hidden his car in a CCTV dark spot, at the bottom of the hill. He knew no one had seen him drive away.

Now, the real game would begin. The cat and mouse, or as he liked to call it, the hunter and the hunted. DI Gupta thought she was hunting the killer? He laughed silently. He was the hunter, not her. And he would show her exactly what he had in store.

Anger flared in his heart, spreading like fire into his limbs. DI Gupta had taken Robert away from him – his precious friend.

Now, she would pay.

CHAPTER 8

Rita arrived at the station early the following morning. The breeze blowing in off the sea left her feeling scoured clean, on the outside, but an uneasiness was settling in her gut about this case. A familiarity she didn't want to acknowledge because of the demons it would drag up from the bottomless well she had tried to drown them in.

As Richard had pointed out, this kind of thing didn't happen in Scarborough.

But it had happened thirty years ago.

Turning her face to the slate-grey sky, she closed her eyes briefly and concentrated on the chill of the wind on her cheeks, tugging her hair around her face, the finest salt particles collecting on her eyelashes. She parted her lips and poked out her tongue to taste the sea and breathed deeply, expanding her diaphragm and holding to the count of three. It didn't help. The exhale was still shaky. So, that was how today was going to go.

Entering the station, she greeted the uniformed officer on the front desk and made her way to the canteen to grab a coffee. She eyed up the chocolate biscuits, was almost tempted, but changed her mind. She didn't need it staring at her all day, and she reminded herself that a decent breakfast would do her good.

The first sip of coffee at her desk scalded her tongue. She enjoyed this quiet moment to herself before the others came in as much as she enjoyed the banter, and the bouncing off each other. The slotting together the pieces of the puzzle.

What had happened to the victim's shoes? The killer hadn't disposed of the body, but they had gone to some lengths to clean the place up, dispose of any evidence that would ID the young woman. She couldn't shake the feeling that this had been some kind of ritual killing – *sacrifice?* – and it didn't sit well with her that the body had been discovered by three schoolkids. Did the killer know the place was frequented by kids wanting to smoke some pot? Had he planned for one of them to discover the corpse?

"Penny for 'em, guv." Maggie came in and sat at her desk, a wrapped bacon sandwich in one hand, and a coffee in the other. She was closely followed by Rizwan.

She smiled at them, wondering if they realized how quickly they'd become her new family, the foundations upon which she steadied herself when she strayed too close to the precipice.

Swivelling around to face the whiteboard, she wondered about the young woman's family.

Memories of herself at eleven years old, wandering from room to room searching for her mother, knowing somehow that she wasn't coming back, replayed behind her eyelids like a movie preview.

The familiar ache blossomed inside her chest. It was the ache of a child who needed her mum. Did the young woman live at home with her parents? What about brothers and sisters? Had she left home? If so, Rita would've been surprised if she could afford a place on her own. Someone must be worried about her, wondering why she hadn't come home.

Rita's phone rang and she answered. It was the uniformed officer on the front desk. Rita answered the call, noting that Maggie was already on her laptop, prompted by Rita's comment.

"Guv, there's someone down here I think you should speak to. A woman by the name of Jill Collins. Wants to report her missing daughter."

Rita's pulse began to race. "I'll be right down." She glanced at the constables, busy with their breakfast, but still eyeing her with interest.

"A woman named Jill Collins has come to the station to report her missing daughter. Want to come with me, Riz? Leave Maggie to her bacon sarnie."

Rizwan was already on his feet.

Jill Collins was waiting inside the interview room when Rita and Rizwan entered. Her face was pale, her eyes red-rimmed and swollen with unshed tears as she peered up at them, sniffing loudly. She dabbed her nostrils with a damp tissue and swallowed hard.

"I'm Detective Inspector Rita Gupta," Rita said softly, taking a seat opposite the woman, "and this is Detective Constable Rizwan Jaffer." She put the manila folder bearing the photos on the floor.

The woman nodded at them. Her fingers clutching the shredded tissue were trembling. Her hair was scraped back into a mousy ponytail, the roots darker than the rest. Her skin was stretched tight across her cheekbones, flushed with emotion, fear evident in her pale grey eyes. It had taken her until today to come forward. Chances were, her daughter had stayed out overnight before, but this was the first time she didn't wander home the next day.

"I understand that you want to report your daughter as missing," Rita began.

"That's right." The woman's chest heaved with the effort of keeping her emotions in check, and she released shallow breaths through her mouth. "She hasn't been home for two nights. She never stays out this long. She didn't even come home to change her clothes yesterday."

Rita nodded, keeping her face impassive. As much as she wanted a positive ID on the victim, this was the toughest part of her job, seeing the distress of a loved one when their fears morphed into the worst kind of reality imaginable. "Can you please tell us your daughter's name?"

"Sarah. Sarah Collins."

Rizwan made notes while Rita did the talking.

"How old is Sarah, Mrs Collins?"

"Seventeen." Her voice caught in her throat, and fresh tears spilled over her bottom lashes. "She's only seventeen."

Rita discreetly slid a box of tissues across the table towards the woman. "I understand how difficult this is, but I need to ask you some questions about Sarah." Rita waited for Jill to nod before continuing. "Has Sarah stayed out all night before?"

"Yes." The woman swallowed the lump in her throat. When she spoke, her voice was barely more than a whisper. "She's been staying out more frequently lately."

"Do you know where she stays, when she doesn't come home?"

"A friend's house." Another loud sniff. "At least, that's what she says."

"You don't believe her?"

"I don't know what to believe." Jill's lips were swollen with tears, and it was obvious to Rita that she didn't want to get her daughter into any trouble if it turned out that she hadn't been staying with a friend.

“Does she tell you which friend?”

“No. She’s seventeen,” Jill said, as if that explained everything. Rita didn’t have children, but if she had, she wouldn’t let her seventeen-year-old stay out all night like this.

“Mrs Collins, can you please describe Sarah to us?” Rita leaned forward and rested her elbows on the table.

“She’s tall, taller than me anyway, blonde, slim.” Jill squeezed her eyes shut. “She’s beautiful. I know all parents say that about their own kids, but she really is beautiful. Did a bit of modelling when she was younger.”

“Mrs Collins,” Rita kept her voice even. “I’m sorry, but I have to ask, does your daughter have a history of mental health issues? Self-harming? Substance abuse?”

The woman blinked furiously like she had grit in her eye from the wind. “Yes.” Rita could barely hear her. “She-she sometimes cuts herself. Her arms. She’s been seeing the school counsellor since she was thirteen. I tried to get her an appointment with CAMHS, but the waiting list is ridiculous, you know. It’s impossible to get a referral anywhere these days. Even with the history of self-harming.”

“I understand,” Rita said. She got lucky when the Met referred her for counselling. She already knew how difficult it was for anyone outside the force requiring mental health advice. “What about drugs, Mrs Collins?”

“She smokes cannabis. All the teenagers do, don’t they?”

“Does Sarah have any brothers or sisters?” Rita asked. She was already convinced that Sarah Collins was the name of their victim, but she needed to get as many details as possible from her mother before she showed her the photographs taken at the crime scene.

“David, her brother. He’s only ten.”

“Are they close?”

“As close as any brother and sister can be. Sarah doesn’t have much time for him these days.”

“Does anyone else live at home with you, Mrs. Collins?”

“Andy. My boyfriend. He moved in a few months ago. Sort of.”

The way she said it suggested to Rita something wasn’t quite right. “Sort of?”

“He hasn’t officially moved in, but he stays over most nights.” Tears caught on Jill’s lashes, glistening in the stark light from the ceiling bulb.

Rita nodded. She had more questions, but they would have to wait. She reached down for the folder on the floor and placed it on the desk, resting both hands on it. “Mrs Collins.” Deep breath. “I’m going to show you some photographs that you may find distressing.”

“Photographs?” Jill Collins seemed to visibly shrink in her seat as though she could make herself so tiny that she wouldn’t be able to see them on the desktop.

“A body of a young woman was discovered yesterday in a disused warehouse near the centre of town. From what you have told us, the victim fits the description of your daughter, Sarah.”

“No.” Mrs Collins shook her head. “No, no, no. Not my Sarah. No. It can’t be my Sarah.” Her mouth kept working around the words, but no sounds came out, and Rita’s heart ripped open for the woman sitting in front of her.

“I’m really sorry, Mrs Collins, but I need you to look at the photographs and tell me if this is your daughter.” There was no easy way to do this, no possible way to soften the edges of the pain that was going to puncture this woman’s heart if this was Sarah.

Rita spread the photographs across the desk and studied the woman’s face.

It took a couple of beats for Jill to make sense of what she was looking at – a typical reaction when someone was asked to identify a body. It was nothing like the movies. A corpse, especially once discovered some time after death, took on an unnatural quality that threw most people, like showing them a rubber mask from a Halloween shop.

When she did finally see through the blue lips and discoloured skin, her expression crumpled. Her breathing became shallow, and she curled into herself, banging her chin on the edge of the table.

Rizwan was on his feet in an instant. He crouched beside the distraught woman, and without touching her, spoke calmly, his voice soothing. “Breathe, Mrs Collins. That’s it, deep breath, in through your nose.” He inhaled, waiting for Jill to mimic him. “Out through your mouth, that’s it.”

When Mrs Collins had recovered enough for Rizwan to fill a plastic cup with water for her and resume his seat, Rita cleared her throat. Good cop, bad cop. She’d take it.

“Mrs Collins, is the young woman in the photographs Sarah?”

Jill nodded. It was all it took for the dam to crack. Her body juddered with heaving, violent sobs as she covered her face with both hands.

Rita gestured for Rizwan to notify the Family Liaison Officer, while she waited silently with Mrs Collins. She put an arm around Jill’s shoulder, and held her. From experience, she knew that all she could do was be here, a solid presence, a gentle glow from the awful darkness that had consumed the poor woman’s world.

CHAPTER 9

Rita and Maggie pulled up outside St Cecilia Academy, the high school Sarah attended. They sat in the car and peered at the unremarkable building through the windscreen. It was a modern, two-storey construction, made with the prefabricated slabs used to build a lot of contemporary buildings. The kind that seemed to soak up the rain and end up looking tea-stained and weather-worn too soon.

"Depressing place," Maggie said.

They'd arrived during lesson time, having called ahead, and the grounds were empty.

"Didn't you like school?" Rita asked.

"Nah. Couldn't wait to get away from my school. I preferred getting my hands dirty outside, guv. What about you?"

Rita didn't recall much about her schooldays. They'd been overshadowed by the loss of her mum, care homes, foster homes, people she knew she didn't want to stay in her life. It had been a constant battle, one in which she needed to stay one step ahead of the system or drown. Although school had been a haven of sorts, a place where she could glean information without looking over her shoulder, she'd compartmentalized the memories, filed them under EDUCATION, and rarely brought them out to inspect.

"Best days of my life," she said, opening the passenger door.

Rita caught glimpses of students staring at them through the classroom windows as they approached the reception, no doubt trying to work out which educational organization they were from, and whether it would buy them some time away from lessons.

The young, dark-haired woman in reception directed Rita and Maggie to a row of seats while she called through to the pupil liaison officer. Moments later, an older woman appeared and introduced herself as Iris Branson.

With the introductions over, Rita and Maggie followed Iris along a hushed, carpeted corridor and into a room with the sign Pupil Liaison Officer printed in bold black font on a gold plaque.

"How can I help you?" Iris said, sitting behind her desk and pushing a pair of silver-rimmed spectacles higher up her nose. "You mentioned this was about Sarah Collins? Sarah hasn't been in school for the past couple of days."

"I'm sorry to inform you that Sarah's body was discovered yesterday at a disused warehouse." Rita saw the woman's eyes blinking behind the thick lenses. She picked up a pen, clicked it on and off several times, and put it back down again. "Oh my god," she said before clearing her throat. "I… I don't know what to say."

"Did you know Sarah well?" Rita asked.

"I… We spent some time together. Sarah is – *was* – a troubled young lady."

"Troubled?" Rita pressed. She wanted to hear it from Iris without putting words into her mouth.

"She suffered from depression and…" Iris's hands fluttered towards her chest almost like she was tapping out a beat with them. "Oh no." Her voice altered; became laced with something Rita couldn't quite put her finger on. Despair? Guilt?

"You don't think… She didn't do this to herself?"

"We're treating this as a murder investigation," Rita said. "Did Sarah ever talk to you about why she was depressed?"

Iris stared at the window, blinking behind her glasses. "Depression doesn't always need a reason, Detective Inspector. It's an illness, although I often wish we could go back to an age before social media got its claws into this generation."

"What kind of student was she? I mean, was she popular? A loner? Somewhere in between the two?"

"She was quite popular, despite her low self-esteem. Girls are particularly good at masking this kind of thing. It's almost like it's bred into us not to complain or make a big deal out of how we feel."

Rita didn't glance at Maggie, but she sensed the tension in her shoulders. Low self-esteem could lend itself to some kind of cult – those fanatics preyed on the weak.

"She had a small group of close friends. Jackie Maynard was her best friend though – they'd been through primary school together, used to have sleepovers when they were younger, go to the arcades together at weekends."

"What about boys?" Rita pressed. "Did Sarah ever speak about a boyfriend?"

"Yes. She was seeing a young lad in her year called Matt. Lovely kid. I had high hopes for the two of them together."

When Iris didn't elaborate, Rita pressed, "Meaning?"

"I thought that Matt might help to keep Sarah grounded, make her realize that she was worthy of his attention. Matt is a real star. He usually ends up with the lead role in the school productions, he's on the football team… Well, you get the picture."

"Thank you." Rita nodded. "We'd like to speak to Sarah's friends if we may. We'll see Matt separately."

"No problem, Detective Inspector." Iris rose, straightened the documents on her already immaculate desk, and left the room.

She returned with four students – two boys and two girls – who filed into the room and sat down in pumpkin-coloured couches with frown lines creasing their foreheads. Iris closed the door behind them and left them to it.

Rita introduced herself and Maggie, and noted the tallest girl's eyes darting around the room as if searching for an escape route.

Maggie jotted down their names in a notepad. Jackie was the tall blonde – Sarah's best friend according to Iris. The others were Ashley, Callum, and Scott.

"We wanted to speak to you about Sarah Collins." Rita paused

Jackie's eyes narrowed briefly. "I haven't seen Sarah for a couple of days. She hasn't been in school."

"When was the last time you saw her?"

"A couple of days ago," Jackie answered quickly. "She was here all day."

"Does that mean she sometimes left early?" Rita pressed.

"Sometimes." Jackie shrugged.

"Where did she go when she was supposed to be at school?"

"I don't know. Hung around town, I suppose. The beach. Got a chippie."

"Did you ever go with her?"

"Yeah."

"It's okay," Maggie said, "this conversation is strictly confidential."

Rita addressed the group. "Did any of you see Sarah after school two days ago?"

There were murmurs of 'no' from the others.

"Jackie?"

"I walked her way home. We split up at the bus stop on the corner of her road."

"Did Sarah tell you if she had any plans for that evening?"

"It was a school night. She wouldn't have been doing much."

Rita's gaze skipped to the others. There was something about Jackie that was abrasive, rubbing her up the wrong way. A healthy dose of teenage attitude probably, but whatever it was, she was surprised she hadn't toned it down given the present company.

"She never mentioned what she was doing outside of school anymore," Ashley said.

Scott added, "I've not seen her in the arcades in a while either."

"So, she didn't really socialize with you guys outside of school?" Rita asked, her eyes on Jackie.

Again, the other three said they hadn't seen Sarah around town in a while.

"I saw her last weekend," Jackie offered. "We walked around the shops, got a coffee, nothing much."

"And how did she seem to you?"

"Fine." Another shrug.

"What is this about?" Ashley asked. "Why isn't Sarah in school?"

"Sarah's body was discovered yesterday," Maggie said softly, taking over. Maybe she still remembered what it was like to be an impressionable teenager at school, Rita thought.

Ashley's hands covered her mouth, her eyes wide. The two boys didn't seem to know how to react. If they were anything like the boys Rita knew in high school, they probably saw emotion as a sign of weakness. And yet, their bodies were rigid, faces taut.

"Her body?" Jackie whispered. "Where was it found?"

"In a disused warehouse," Rita said. "Did Sarah ever mention to any of you about going to the warehouse to smoke drugs?"

"No." Jackie squeezed her eyes closed, tears trickling from the corners of her eyes and down her cheeks. "Is this true?"

"Unfortunately, yes."

"I can't believe she's … dead."

Ashley burst into tears then. Maggie offered them some words of comfort, and Rita went to the door. Iris was outside, speaking to a male teacher in a suit. Iris and the teacher came inside, and took the children away.

"The safeguarding team will look after them now," Iris said, before she left. "And the counsellors."

"Thank you," Rita said. "We still need to speak to Matt."

*****

Rita and Maggie waited a while, then Matt, Sarah's boyfriend, was shown into the room by Iris. She shut the door when she left, informing Rita she would be outside if needed.

Matt looked nervous, and ran his hand through his several times. He sat down, fidgeting.

"When did you last see Sarah?" Rita asked Matt.

She understood what Iris meant when she'd said the kid was a star. He had the looks, the charm, the floppy fringe that would've driven teenaged Rita to write his initials in her diary with a huge red love heart around it, and a cupid's arrow through the middle. Despite this, he gave the impression that he was just a regular kid who happened to look like a young Tom Cruise.

"Monday, I think. We had drama together."

"You didn't see her outside of school this week?" Maggie asked. Rita wondered if her voice had suddenly risen a notch.

"No. Why's that? I don't think she's been in school since then."

Rita delivered the news about Sarah's murder.

"What the hell," he muttered under his breath. That's more like it, Rita thought. "I mean… I'm sorry, I shouldn't have sworn, but, what the hell, man. Am I allowed to ask how she died?"

"I'm sorry, we can't give you any more information than that right now," Rita said. "Did you and Sarah text each other since Monday? Did she tell you where she might've been going or who she was hanging around with?"

"No. We don't talk that much since we split up." He used present tense, and Rita didn't correct him.

"When did you split up?"

"A couple of months ago. She was seeing someone else."

"Does he go to this school?"

"No. That's all I know. I don't have a name, sorry."

That would tie in with Sarah dropping her other friends outside of school. "Did you ever see Sarah using drugs?" Rita asked.

"Yeah, she smoked cannabis. We both did." Matt lowered his head and rubbed the back of his neck. "I've seen her using speed and amphetamines. I tried to stop her, but she said it made her feel better about stuff."

"Stuff?"

"Yeah, about herself, life, you know."

Rita did know. She gave Matt a level stare. He lowered his eyes. Rita saw him for what he really was – a sad, confused boy who had just been hit with bad news he couldn't handle. His mind was turning over, and he didn't know how to deal with it.

"Did you miss her after you broke up?"

He shot a look at her, then his eyes dimmed with sorrow. "Yes," he whispered. "She had issues, but I thought we could work them out. Guess I didn't realise how deep her issues were."

"I don't think anyone did," Rita said, wondering if Sarah's mother had known. She must have, in one way or the other.

Matt's handsome face was now heavy, his jaws clamped together. "Look at me," Rita said gently. The young man did.

"Can you think of any reason Sarah would want to do this?"

Matt shrugged. "Well, she did like taking drugs. I told her she shouldn't, and for a while, she did listen to me. She was getting counselling as well, and seeing her doctor. But soon, she went back to her old ways."

Rita scribbled on her notebook, planning to meet up with Sarah's GP.

"Did Sarah ever talk of suicide? Or self-harm?"

"I know she cut herself. That's why she got help. And yes, she was good for a while, like I said. She took less speed, smoked less, and she was better. But then she relapsed. I don't know why. That's when we started to get distant, 'cos I kept telling her to sort herself out. She said I wouldn't understand."

Something in Matt's voice made Rita frown. "What do you mean? What was she trying to say?"

"I don't know. She stopped me from going to her house and that. She wanted to hang out with other people, outside school. With her new bloke, clearly." Matt grimaced at the last words, and regret, mixed with anger, spasmed across his good looks.

"And you're sure you have no idea who this new bloke was?"

Matt closed his eyes and sighed. "No, I don't."

Rita stared at him, and he met her eyes. She believed him. She gave him her card, and he took it, reluctantly.

"If there's anything else you remember, anything at all, get in touch with me. Okay?" She gave him a smile, and his lips twitched in response. Then he got up, slung his bag wearily over his shoulder, and left.

*****

The bell for mid-morning break sounded as Rita and Maggie were leaving. Groups of kids flooded the corridors, reminding Rita of the scarab beetles in *The Mummy* movie. She imagined them climbing the walls, clinging to the ceiling, and covering every available surface, and shook her head to clear the images. They were just kids.

None of them paid any attention to the two detectives waiting near the entrance, until Rita spotted Jackie.

Stepping into the moving crowd, she caught the girl's eye before she had a chance to turn around and walk the other way. "Jackie, sorry, I have one more question."

Jackie sidestepped a couple of tall boys and waited for Rita to catch up with her. She had stopped in front of a doorway, and Rita peered through the glass to check the room was empty. It was a small gymnasium. She ushered the girl inside, and took a deep breath, relishing the silence.

The girl looked uncomfortable, holding onto the straps of a shiny pink bag slung over her shoulder. Or maybe that was just how kids carried their bags these days.

“I spoke to Matt,” Rita said. Silence from Sarah’s friend. “He said that he and Sarah split up a couple of months ago.”

“Yeah.”

“Apparently, Sarah was seeing someone else. Did she talk to you about him?”

“No.”

“She never mentioned a new boyfriend?”

Rita had lost contact with her friends from school now, but she remembered the other girls always mentioning their new boyfriends and their latest crushes. Girls still did that, right? It was as natural as brushing your teeth twice a day and combing your hair before school in the morning.

“No. I knew she and Matt split up. There was no one else she was interested in. Not enough to hook up with, anyways.”

Hook up. That was like making out, Rita thought, remembering the YA romance books of her teenage years. She suddenly felt very old.

"What about outside of school?"

"Nope." Jackie shrugged again. "She never mentioned anyone." She peered back at the door as if she had another way more pressing engagement.

"Look, I'll be late for basketball practice. Can I go now?"

"OK. But we will want to speak to you again."

Jackie shrugged again, and Rita watched her leave. She wasn't entirely sure that she believed the teenager.

CHAPTER 10

Max Drake, the headmaster of St Cecilia school, greeted Rita and Maggie with a firm handshake. He was younger than Rita had expected him to be. Her only comparison was the headmaster of her own senior school, an aging man with greying hair above his ears, a shiny bald spot on the very top of his skull, and a silver suit with permanent creases. This man was smartly dressed in a navy pinstripe suit, pink shirt, and a tie that combined the two colours with a starry night pattern. Rita quelled the impulse to ask him who his stylist was.

"Please take a seat." Max sat in the expensive leather seat behind the desk and offered his visitors coffee from a machine perched on top of a wooden unit. They both declined. "How can I help you?"

Rita spotted the framed photograph on the desk. From her seat and the slanted angle, she could make out a young couple on a beach with two little boys between them.

The headmaster followed her gaze and flipped the frame around. "My wife and sons. This was taken on holiday in Corfu a few years back."

Maggie beamed at the photo, and Rita continued before her colleague started gushing. "We're here about Sarah Collins. A Year 12 student at St Cecilia."

"Sarah Collins." The headmaster nodded, and regret made his face heavier. He sighed. "Yes, I know. Her referral to CAMHS crossed my desk. She's a bright student. Or was, rather. I often saw her with Ms Iris Branson. Iris informed me." He blinked once. "How did this happen?"

Rita filled him in with a summary of the murder investigation.

He sat forward, the leather seat swinging forward with him. He turned to face the wall, blinking while he processed the information. "That's… Wow, that's not what I was expecting to hear about one of my students when I drove into school this morning." He puffed up his cheeks and sat back again. "How? I mean, am I even allowed to ask you what happened?"

"Sorry, there's not much more I can tell you right now," Rita said. "Procedures, I'm sure you understand."

"Of course, Detective. How can I help? What is it that you want to know about Sarah?"

"Were you aware that she had a history of self-harming?"

"I saw the details on the referral application. Sarah would not have been alone in that, unfortunately. You might be surprised how many kids find relief from hurting themselves."

Maggie winced.

Rita inhaled deeply. This case was different to other kids. Something had set Sarah apart from other teenagers who might've been self-harming, and she needed to find out what it was.

"Did you ever speak to Sarah personally? Did she ever come to you with concerns about anything? Friends. Grades. Relationships."

"No, I'm afraid not," the headmaster said. "There are almost a thousand children in this school, and while I do make a point of knowing them all by name, it's only the repeat offenders who usually find themselves in my presence."

"Repeat offenders?"

"The kids who repeatedly truant or demonstrate aggression towards other students or their teachers. The ones who end up in trouble with the police. Children are not born this way, Detective Inspector. They are moulded this way by outside influences, and if I can help to reshape them into someone who they, *and this school*, can be proud of, then I will give it my best shot to help them on their way."

"So, Sarah wasn't a repeat offender?"

"No, as I said, she had a history of mental illness, and Ms Branson supported her as much as she could. I really wish there was more I could tell you."

"You've been very helpful," Rita said. It was the standard response to an interview that yielded next to nothing. "What about Sarah's form tutor?"

"Mr Logan. I can ask him to pop in and speak to you. You're welcome to use my room."

"Has Sarah ever been in trouble in school?" Rita asked.

Mr Drake inclined his head. "Depends how you define trouble, Detective Inspector. She has been given detention a few times, but never for anything major. It was usually just for turning up late for classes, or not handing in homework. Never for anything that had to be brought to my attention." He paused, his gaze flitting between the two detectives.

*****

Sarah's form tutor, in complete contrast to Mr Drake, looked as if he'd rolled out of bed and grabbed yesterday's shirt and trousers off the floor. His grey shirt was creased, but clean, no tie, his pants hung loose around his slim waist. Rita thought she detected tears in his eyes when she gave him the grave news about Sarah.

He shook his head and slumped back in the headmaster's seat. "So sad." He blinked several times, his Adam's apple bobbing in his throat. "Jesus, that's the worst news I've ever received at work." He swiped his eyes with his thumbs.

"What can you tell us about Sarah, Mr Logan?" Rita pressed.

"Sarah is… Jesus, it's going to be hard getting used to this. Sarah *was* a great student. She was in my form from Year 7 through to now. Middle to top level grades, when she applied herself academically. I've watched her grow into a beautiful young woman."

His eyes flashed at Rita, and his shoulders slumped even further. "I mean that as a solely professional observation. I can't believe I even have to consider that when talking about a student, but such is the world we live in."

Rita recognized that tone. It was defeat being beaten out of the ballpark by a guy who loved his job. She guessed him to be early thirties – younger than the headmaster by at least a decade – still teaching because it was what he wanted to do. Still. After all this time, and no doubt having experienced several of Mr Drake's *repeat offenders*. She admired him. She felt a kinship with the man – they were both just trying to do a decent job and help people along the way.

"Thank you, Mr Logan." She rose and shook his hand. On second thoughts, she removed a business card and passed it to him. "If you think of anything else, anything at all, please don't hesitate to call me."

"What do you think, guv?" Maggie asked as they were driving away from the school.

"I think Sarah's best friend was holding back. Would you know if your best friend was seeing someone new?"

"I'd want all the sordid details over a bottle of wine and a doner kebab." Maggie grinned at her as she indicated left and pulled onto the road to head back to the station.

"Classy," Rita said.

CHAPTER 11

Rizwan and Richard climbed out of the car outside the school attended by the boys they'd spoken to at the crime scene. Richard beeped the lock. The barbed wire around the high walls of the school made it look like a prison, not a place of education. The foreboding grey walls mirrored the roughness of the streets around them.

"What's up, skip?" Rizwan narrowed his eyes at the building, the hairs on the back of his neck standing on end. He knew what was up – he sensed it too, only he wasn't giving in to it.

"They expect kids to make something of themselves when this is what they give them."

It was unfair. There was plenty Rizwan could say on the matter, but he'd learned to keep quiet about stuff like this. His own childhood had been tough, but he'd made something of himself. Or had he?

Turning his back on the school momentarily, he faced the street. Litter. A boarded-up window. A car with its wheels missing. Kids are chameleons. Stick them in an environment that requires them to survive, and that's what they'll do. These kids needed trees, open spaces, a step on the ladder, not a dingy basement outlook with a sign saying, '*Watch yer back'*.

At the entrance, Richard glanced back at the car. "Think it'll still be in one piece when we're done?"

"Only one way to find out, skip."

Richard pressed the buzzer. They waited several beats before the door jolted open and they stepped inside.

The woman in reception greeted them with a smile that didn't quite materialize. There were puffy pouches under her eyes, and red veins appearing on her nose. She looked like she hadn't had a decent pillow to sleep on in years.

"DS Staveley," Richard said, showing the woman his warrant card. "We spoke on the phone earlier."

"Aye." The woman swallowed and shuffled some papers around the desk in front of her as if worried that he would go nosing around in them. "Mr. Hunt isn't available to see you, I'm afraid."

"Did he know that we were coming?" Richard demanded.

Rizwan recognized that tone. The skipper had never been the most patient person to work with, but these days, he was growing more tightly wound, like a spring waiting to pounce.

"I did tell him." The woman's gaze shifted between the two of them. "But something came up."

"Something more urgent than a murder investigation?" Richard snapped.

The woman winced. Still no apology. Perhaps she was bored with making excuses for the headmaster. Rizwan could only imagine what the kids nicknamed Mr Hunt.

A small group of lads sauntered past on their way out of the building. They didn't seem to care it was during lesson time. A couple wore black masks over their faces, but they all wore the unmistakable swagger of aggression bordering on violence. Rizwan's fists instinctively clenched when he sensed the lads stop walking and form a semi-circle behind them.

"Whaddya think?" one said to the others. "They here to shut the place down?"

"Nah. Pigs more like."

"Okay, lads." Richard turned around to face them head on, his cheeks flushed pink. "Don't you have classes to get to?"

"Nah. We're done for the day." This came from a tall beefy lad with a buzzcut and a tattoo on his neck. He had beady eyes. Rizwan felt almost certain they'd be crossing paths again at some point in the future unless something drastic changed in this kid's life.

"Robbie, did you clear it with your form tutor?" the receptionist asked him. She already knew the answer. She was just ticking a box.

"Course I did."

"What are the pigs doing in a place like this?" Another kid this time. Blonde. Blue eyes. Looked like he'd attached himself to the bad kids to avoid getting picked on. "We're all squeaky clean here."

There were snorts of laughter. Robbie clapped Mr Blue Eyes on the back. The kids in masks just stared at the detectives, taking it all in. They were the ringleaders, Rizwan thought. Probably supplied the others with drugs and got them to do the dirty work.

"Okay, I suggest you keep moving unless you fancy a trip down to the local nick." Richard's tone was clipped.

"You can't arrest us," Robbie said. "We ain't done nothing."

"Robbie, time to go." The receptionist buzzed the door open and glared at the lads until they were outside. Then she turned back to the detectives, the same weary expression on her face. She probably dealt with that crap every day and had long ago given up trying to prevent it.

"When will Mr Hunt be free?" Richard asked.

"It won't be until later this afternoon." Her tone was abrupt, but Rizwan guessed that was a repercussion of working in an environment where the kids did what they wanted, and the headmaster hid in his room.

"We need to speak to a couple of lads," Richard continued. "Mark Oakham and James Aspinall." They'd already discussed separating these two from Karim on the drive across town from the station.

The woman didn't ask what it was regarding. She pressed a button beside her computer screen and spoke into a mic requesting that the two boys report to reception immediately.

When the boys arrived and saw the detectives, they hesitated, looking around as if ready to bolt.

"This way, lads." Rizwan gestured for them to follow him and Richard into a room located next to the reception, and they sat down, eyes on the floor.

"Tell us what you were doing at the warehouse yesterday," Richard said.

"Already told you," James answered first.

"I have a short memory, so humour me." Richard raised his eyebrows, waiting for them to elaborate.

"We were smoking some puff." Mark refused to make eye contact. "That's all."

"And what about Karim?" Rizwan directed the question at Mark, the one he thought was most likely to blab under pressure.

"What about him?" James stepped in.

"Does he supply the drugs?"

"He ain't a dealer, if that's what you mean." James shrugged uncomfortably inside his hoodie like it had shrunk a couple of sizes in the wash.

"Did he tell you what goes on inside the warehouse?" Richard asked.

Both boys jolted, their eyes finally meeting the faces of the detectives. "Don't know nothing about it," James said.

"But you do know what I mean," Richard pressed, his eyes narrowed.

"Nah, man. We just hang out there sometimes."

"Mark? Anything you want to add to that?"

Mark shook his head. "Nah, like James said."

"Okay." Richard stood up, towering over the seated boys. "Just a friendly warning, lads. If I find out you've been withholding information pertaining to a murder investigation, I'll haul you both straight down to the nick before you can blink."

James rose, shoulders hunched. "Can we go now?"

"Scram," Richard snapped.

Karim's form tutor met them in the corridor outside his classroom. He was a scrawny man, with hollow cheeks and collarbones that protruded above his sweater. His hair stood on end, and there was tape holding the arm of his glasses together.

"We're looking for Karim Ahmadi," Richard said after presenting his warrant card.

The teacher, Mr Patel, rotated his shoulders like he was trying to clear a crick in his neck. "He isn't in class right now." His voice was weak, and Rizwan almost felt sorry for the man. He didn't stand a chance.

"Do you know where he is?" he asked, trying to soften the edges of the question.

"He asked to use the bathroom five minutes ago."

Tipped off by Mark and James no doubt.

"Are you expecting him back?" Richard asked.

The guy seemed to flinch at the question.

"I'll take that as a no," Richard said. "What do you know about Karim Ahmadi dealing drugs?"

"I've never seen him with drugs."

"That wasn't what I asked."

"I…" The teacher peered left and right along the corridor as though expecting Karim to lynch him from behind. "The boys sometimes smoke off the premises."

Richard changed tack. "Would you say that Karim Ahmadi is a troublemaker?"

The guy blinked behind his glasses. “He … can be quite vocal … at times.”

“About what?”

“About… Karim doesn’t like being disrespected.”

Richard and Rizwan exchanged glances. “Which way is the bathroom?” Richard asked.

The teacher pointed left. “Around the corner, on your right.”

Rizwan waited outside the boys’ bathroom, while Richard went inside to look for Karim. He came back out moments later and shook his head. “Surprise, surprise. No one there. Looks like our boy doesn’t want to speak to us.”

They continued along the corridor, peering through classroom doors for a glimpse of the boy, and there was no sign of him. Until they reached the fire exit at the far end of the corridor and saw that it hadn’t quite latched properly.

Outside, they scanned the school grounds. Rizwan spotted a wisp of smoke curling out from behind the almost empty bike sheds and gestured towards it. “Original,” Richard muttered under his breath.

They were almost there when Karim, alerted by their footsteps, appeared from behind the shed. He took one look at the detectives, flicked the end of a spliff at the ground, and bolted.

"Stop, Karim!" Richard yelled.

But the lad had no intention of stopping. He ran across the playground, away from the entrance and towards the rear of the ugly squat building.

The two detectives gave chase. "We just want to ask a few questions," Rizwan shouted out, gasping. He was faster than the shorter and heavier, Richard, who was struggling to keep up.

Karim shot a glance over his shoulder but didn't slow down. The school was surrounded by tall metal railings. The back gates came into view as Rizwan chased the boy, but they were shut, and he could just about make out a padlock securing them together. Keeping people out, or keeping the students in?

Richard was lagging. Rizwan picked up speed. He'd been fast at school, even competed in the district four hundred metres a couple of times, but he was out of practice. Too many hours spent in the office sitting behind a computer screen. The distance between them closed. Karim would never be able to scale the railing – not without getting caught – and Rizwan couldn't see that there was anywhere else for him to run.

"Wait, Karim," he shouted again, giving the lad the option to cooperate. "We only want to talk to you." Damn, he was short of breath already.

Without warning, the kid shrugged his faded Nike backpack over his shoulder and slung it over the metal fencing. It landed on the pavement with a thud, narrowly missing a parked car. Karim hoisted himself up into the lower branches of a tree that Rizwan had barely registered, climbed until he was high enough to scale the railings, and then lowered himself down on the other side. He dropped the last few feet, crouching as he landed.

"Stop right there!" Rizwan yelled. He knew it was useless.

Rizwan began to climb. He hadn't done this since he was a kid, and he forgot to test a branch which snapped beneath his weight, his chin scraping bark as he fell.

Richard caught up and kept going towards the gates. He yanked on the padlock. Locked.

A bus trundled slowly past and halted at a stop on the other side of the road. Rizwan watched, both hands gripping the branches of the tree, as Karim darted behind the bus and climbed aboard. He saw the lad staring back at him through the grimy windows.

Jumping down, he slid a notepad from his pocket, jotted down the number of the bus and the registration plate, and called through to Maggie in the station. "Check out this bus route, Mags. Karim Ahmadi didn't want to speak to us, apparently."

"On it," Maggie said. "I'll check out CCTV along the route, see if we can find out where he got off. What did you say to him?"

“Nothing. His mates warned him that we were there, and he didn’t hang around.”

“I’ll let guv know.” The line went quiet, and then Maggie spoke again.

“Karim found the body, and now he’s on the run. He just moved into main suspect position.”

“That’s right,” Rizwan said, a grim note in his voice.

CHAPTER 12

Jill Collins' ground floor flat was in an unattractive three-storey building, in a part of Scarborough that Rita had never visited before. The building was drab and grey, built in a forgettable art deco style that belonged in the seventies. There was no intercom entry. Rita opened the door, aware of something sticky beneath her fingers before she could remove them, and she and Maggie stepped inside.

Inside the building there was a strange boiled-cabbage smell – not quite urine, but certainly not pleasant – that seemed to linger around a lot of communal blocks of flats. Graffiti was sprayed across the walls and windows.

Donkey woz ere

Run while you still can

Elvis is still alive in flat 33

Rita tried to place the victim in this context. According to the pupil liaison officer, she'd been a popular student. Her friends were happy to talk about her and seemed genuinely distressed when informed that she was dead.

Did they ever come here and visit Sarah in her own surroundings? What about Matt, Sarah's ex-boyfriend? Somehow, Rita couldn't place him here. She didn't like to think of herself as judgmental, but Matt looked like he came from an entirely different background to Sarah. Perhaps she was wrong. She couldn't shake the feeling, though, that Sarah had been trying to escape this life. Look where she had to live, through no fault of her own.

Jill opened the door to the detectives, clinging to the handle as if it were a lifeline, the only thing holding her up. Her eyes were still raw and puffy, fear dancing behind them.

"Mrs Collins," Rita said softly, her heart contracting at Jill's sad appearance. "Do you mind if we come in? We have a few more questions regarding your daughter."

Jill peered beyond her visitors, checking there were not more police lurking in the shadows, and stepped aside, opening the door wider.

Rita stood inside the gloomy hallway, the dated wallpaper peeling at the corners, a mould stain blossoming in the corner of the ceiling. She smelled damp and fabric conditioner. The stale smell of cigarette smoke.

"Through here." Jill led the way to the end of the corridor and into a square living room.

A man was sitting on the grey two-seater sofa, hunched over, knees spread, a game controller in his hands. Rita caught a glimpse of movement on the TV screen. A racing car – she couldn't be sure – it was moving too fast and making her eyes go fuzzy. She had no idea how anyone spent hours on end playing games like this.

There was another sofa, this one pale green, grubby, with once plush cushions scattered across the seats. A coffee table, ringed with stains. A stack of magazines on the floor at one end of the sofa. DVDs on the stand housing the TV. A bog-standard painting that looked like something out of the 70s hung on the wall. There were no family photographs, nothing personal that might've belonged to Sarah or her mother. No holiday memories, no school pictures, no images of baby Sarah.

"Please, sit down." Jill rushed past them and plumped up the cushions on the spare sofa, making no difference to the shape or size of them. She straightened; hands clasped in front of her. "Can I get you tea? Or coffee?"

They both declined and sat down facing the man with the controller in his hands. He was still focused on the game. "Andy," Jill said, hovering between the two couches. The boyfriend she had mentioned in the station.

"Almost done." The guy didn't even look at her.

"Andy, please." There was a note of pleading in Jill's voice, and Rita willed her to snatch the control from his hands and switch off the game. She didn't. "This is the detective I saw in the station earlier."

A boy came into the living room then, took one look at the telly, and said, "He's playing my game."

"It's okay, David." Jill shook her head briefly at her son like she didn't want him to cause a scene. Was that because Rita and Maggie were there, or because she knew it would descend into an argument between them? "Andy is just finishing."

Rita watched the boy's expression crumple. From what Mrs Collins had told her, she knew that the boy was only ten. He'd just learned that his sister had died. It would be some time before the gravity of the situation fully hit him, but in the meantime, all he knew was that this guy – someone who should've been a protector – was sitting there playing his video game. His comfort. His safety blanket.

"Detective Inspector Gupta." Rita rose and formally extended a hand to Andy, forcing him to take his eyes off the game. With her free hand, she took the controller and handed it to David. "We're here to speak to you all about Sarah."

The man glared at her like she'd materialized in the front room from outer space. Finally, he dragged his eyes away from her, and said to David, “Gained you some more lives.”

Rita sat back down as the kid slunk out of the room. Her hackles were raised, and she felt as though her shoulders were up around her ears.

Andy didn’t even acknowledge Jill as she sat beside him, taking up as little space as possible at the far end of the small sofa. A woman used to taking less than everyone else around her. She studied Andy. He was thin, bony beneath the oversized hoodie bunched up around his neck. His head was too large like it belonged to someone else, and she wondered if he’d suffered with anorexia at some point. His eyes bulged like a goldfish, as if they too, didn’t quite belong to the same person.

“Best off speaking to her.” Andy went to stand up, and Jill’s eyes widened, as she shrank even further into the corner of the seat.

“Sit down, please, sir,” Rita said, surprised at how calm she sounded.

“Can I take your full name?” Maggie asked, producing the little notepad and pen she carried around with her. Thank heavens for Maggie Long, Rita thought.

“Andrew Robson.” He sat back down and focused on Maggie. Rita didn’t like the way he was looking at her, a smile twitching at the corners of his mouth, but kept quiet.

"When did you last see Sarah?" Maggie asked sweetly.

"The weekend."

Rita watched Jill carefully. She didn't react to the answer, but there was still something about the guy that didn't sit right with her. "How did she seem to you?" she asked.

Andy shrugged. He flicked a glance Rita's way, and then averted his eyes to a spot on the worn carpet somewhere near Maggie's feet. "Same as usual."

"Could you tell us what that means?"

"Mopey," Andy said. "Face like a slapped arse. Anyone would've thought the girl had it hard."

"Did you ever ask her if there was something bothering her?"

Another shrug. "She wouldn't have talked to me about it if there was."

No surprises there. "Why do you think that is?" Rita asked.

"She didn't talk much." Andy fidgeted inside his clothes like they were irritating his skin. "Bottled it up. It's why she was so moody."

A spark of anger coursed through Rita's veins. She would never understand why men like Andy Robson got involved with women with kids if they were not prepared to learn the first thing about what made them tick.

She turned her attention back to Jill. "We spoke to the pupil liaison officer at Sarah's school. She said that Sarah struggled with low self-esteem and lack of confidence. Was that always the case. Mrs Collins?"

Jill closed her eyes briefly, rubbed her face with both hands, and shook her head as if bringing herself back to the moment. "It all seemed to change after David was born. I … was struggling. David's dad didn't stick around, pissed off before he was even born. I had post-natal depression. I couldn't cope, so they took Sarah into care for a while, until I could sort myself out."

Right about now, Rita thought, was where Andy should've offered her some comfort. He didn't. She wondered if he was good in bed, but even that seemed highly unlikely.

"That must've been tough for you all," Maggie said.

Jill nodded and swallowed hard, the back of her throat clicking. "It was. When Sarah came back, she was never the same. You never stop blaming yourself, you know." Her voice was little more than a whisper.

"Never the same how?" Rita pressed.

"She was quiet. My bouncy little girl was gone. Instead, she was, I don't know, always watching me like she blamed me too."

Rita made a mental note to check out Sarah's records with social services, find out which care home or foster families she'd spent time with. "Maybe she was scared that she'd be taken away again."

"I know. I tried telling her that I wouldn't let it happen again, but the damage was already done. She started playing up when she went to senior school, got in with some other girls who bunked off most days. Stayed out late at night."

"Was Sarah still friends with Jackie?"

Jill smiled. "She and Jackie were always thick as thieves. Ever since they were little. Couldn't keep them apart."

From Jill's wistful smile, Rita sensed that this wasn't still the case as the girls grew older though. "What about recently, Jill? Did you see much of Jackie?"

"Not so much." She peered at Rita as if this had only just occurred to her. "I guess they were growing older. Boyfriends. You know."

"We spoke to Matt too. Were you aware that he and Sarah had split up?"

"I guessed they had when he stopped coming to the house. Sarah didn't say. Not until I asked her."

"Didn't say much of anything to anyone," Andy added. "Miracle getting two words out of her." Without the game controller in his hand, he kept rubbing his nose every few seconds like he had an itch that wouldn't go away.

Rita ignored him. "Matt thought that she might've been seeing someone else, someone outside of their school. Did she ever mention a new boyfriend, Jill?"

"No. But she was different the last couple of months. Brighter. Like she'd finally found something to look forward to, you know. A reason to get up in the mornings."

"She didn't mention a name? Or tell you where they used to meet up?"

"Sorry." Jill sucked on her bottom lip as if this was another failure she would have to live with—not finding out where her daughter spent her free time.

"Andy?" Rita watched the man's go-to expression of boredom morph into incredulity that she expected a response from him. "Did you ever see Sarah and her new boyfriend outside of the house?"

"Nope. Not that she'd have spoken to me if she did."

"How do you know?" Maggie stepped in.

Andy furrowed his brow. "How do I know what?"

"That she wouldn't have spoken to you?"

The nose-rubbing became more frantic, and he started tapping his heel against the floor. "It's what kids are like. Don't wanna associate with the grownups in their life when their mates are about."

Rita thought that the word grownup was a bit of a stretch, but she didn't let it show in her deadpan expression. "Thank you," she said standing up. "If you do remember anything else, please call me at the station."

Jill followed them back along the dingy corridor. The door to David's bedroom was ajar, and she spotted the boy on his bed, the controller in his hand, staring at a small flatscreen TV perched on top of a cardboard box. She pushed the door open and peeked inside.

"Hello, David," she said. "I'm Detective Inspector Gupta. May I come in?"

David glanced at her, nodded once, then turned his attention back to the game.

Rita went inside. She didn't ask why he wasn't in school – he'd just lost his sister, he was allowed time to grieve although she sensed that he would mask it for as long as possible, hiding behind his video games. "How are you feeling?" She sat beside him on the bed.

"Okay." He didn't pause the game.

"I want to ask you an important question, David." Rita kept her voice low but firm. "Did Sarah talk to you about her new boyfriend?"

He shook his head, his eyelids flickering across the screen.

"Did she tell you where she was going the last time you saw her?"

He peered at her then, his eyes large with tears. "No. She was in her room with the door shut. I was never allowed in when the door was shut."

Rita smiled at him. "Thank you, David." He didn't even watch her leave.

Outside, between the apartment blocks, three youths in logoed hoodies sat on tired rusting swings, smoking rollups. They eyed up the two women like they'd just descended from the mothership. An old woman in a faded raincoat, wispy hair somewhere between mauve and grey, approached Jill's building.

"Excuse me, ma'am," Rita said, sliding her warrant card from her pocket, "do you have time to answer a couple of questions?"

The woman squinted at the ID, and it wrenched at Rita's heart that she didn't have a clue what she was looking at. "What's it about?"

"Do you know Sarah Collins?" Rita asked. "She lives in the ground floor flat here."

"Aye. Pretty lass." Her face became animated. "Always helps carry my shopping. What's happened? Escaped, has she?"

"Escaped?"

"All the good ones get away." The woman's shoulders slumped inside her oversized raincoat. "If they're lucky."

"Do you ever see Sarah with her friends, ma'am?" Rita continued.

The woman shook her head, her mouth turned down at the corners, her face fitting into its natural grooves. Not much to smile about here, Rita thought. "Kept to herself, that one."

Rita smiled. "Thank you, ma'am. You've been most helpful."

It was the kind of area that weighted you down – Rita could feel the pressure on her shoulders already, forcing her head down, preventing her from looking up and forward. Had Sarah been looking for an escape? Bright girl, popular in school, getting help with her mental health problems, which was half the battle. Who'd have blamed her for wanting more?

Two girls, barely out of school, both with bottle-blonde hair and dark roots, rounded the corner pushing buggies. Rita swallowed. Wisps of smoke curled from a fag in one girl's hand while the other raised a plastic bottle of neon-blue liquid to her lips.

Maggie took the lead. "Hey, girls," she said with a wide smile. She flashed her ID card at them, holding it still so that they could get a good look. "This won't take long. Do either of you know Sarah Collins?

Ground floor flat." She hooked a thumb over her shoulder at the Collins home.

They both peered over her shoulder, eyeing up Rita at the same time. "Aye. What about her?" asked the girl with the blue drink.

"Do you know her well? Ever hang out together?"

"Nah." The girl wrinkled her nose. "She don't mix much."

"What about her boyfriend? Is he from around here?"

They both shrugged. The little boy sitting in one of the buggies started swinging his feet and arching his back. The girl rummaged behind him for a dummy and stuck it in his mouth. "Didn't know she had a boyfriend."

"What's this about?" her friend asked. "Has something happened to Sarah? I've not seen her about since the argument."

Rita's skin prickled, and she exchanged a quick glance with Maggie. "What argument?"

"Her mum's boyfriend was following her. I heard 'em last week. Sarah yelled at him to leave her alone and then she stormed off. Not seen her since."

"Okay, thank you." Maggie crouched down and smoothed the hair away from the little boy's forehead. "You're a real cutie, aren't you, eh?"

"He's a little shit," the girl replied.

Back in the car, Rita fastened her seatbelt and stared at the windows of the Collins flat. “What do you think Jill sees in Andy?”

Maggie started the engine and stuck the car into reverse. “We accept the love we think we deserve.”

Rita smiled at her colleague’s profile. “Very profound. Where did you dig that up from?”

“It’s a quote from a book. You don’t read much, do you, guv?”

CHAPTER 13

The Keeper was parked at a discreet distance outside Jill's house, keeping watch. He saw the Detective and her sidekick emerge from the grimy block of council flat's. He knew they had been to see Jill.

DI Rita Gupta thought that she had the whole world at her fingertips like one of those photoshopped images you can find on the Internet: the planet Earth between two slender hands. He saw it in the set of her shoulders, the way she peered all around, her nose wrinkling when she saw something she didn't like.

She thought that she could change the world, didn't she?

Ha! There was only one person who could change the world, and that was the Keeper. His fingers tightened around the steering wheel, his lips bending in a snarl.

They all came to him eventually. The weak. The hopeless. The lost and the troubled. They recognized in him the power to make everything better. It was a gift.

Robert McFarlane, the man who was his Guardian, had helped him hone this gift, had shown him how to tap into it, embrace his destiny, wrap it around his shoulders like an invisible mantle.

But it was all his now.

The Keeper chuckled to himself from the passenger seat of his car. No one could take this away from him now. Especially not DI Gupta. Since Sarah's death, he'd felt his power coursing through his veins as though her blood had merged with his own. It was exactly as he'd promised her – promised them all at the Gathering – they needed each other. They were weak. He was strong. Stronger now, of course. Stronger even than the Guardian had been.

Oh, how he relished this sense of power. It was the best feeling in the entire world, and now that he'd had a taste of it, he was eager for more. He knew that he must be patient, that Rita would come to him when the time was right, but every part of him twitched to feel her submit to him. He could almost taste her. Not as sweet as Sarah, but she would be something to be savoured for the rest of his life. More exotic. More memorable.

DI Rita Gupta scanned the area before she climbed into the passenger seat of the car. He resisted smiling at her. How much more exciting would it be to know that she recognized him when the time came? To know that he'd been right there, within touching distance all along, and she never even knew. One step ahead of her. Pulling the strings.

How would she react? She carried an air of arrogance around with her now that she'd destroyed Robert, the Guardian. She was yet to learn, though, that the Keeper was a whole different ballgame. The Keeper would not be so careless.

Yes, part of him regretted having to lose Sarah so quickly. He missed her vulnerability the way a traveller would miss water in the desert. But her death was not in vain.

Reset a new life by leaving the old one. That's what his followers believed, and it was true, because he taught them that. The Keeper had *also* been reset by Sarah's death. He was stronger, bolder, more powerful.

He followed their car with his eyes as they drove closer to the Keeper's vantage point. They drove right past him, and didn't even bat an eyelid. He had dark sunglasses on, and a hoodie pulled over his head, just in case. He saw their faces as the police car flashed past his window.

A smile tugged at the corners of his lips. Macabre fantasies filled his mind, driving strength into his limbs. He wanted to hear Rita beg for mercy, wanted to see the fear behind those dark eyes when she realized that he was the one with the power in his hands. He wanted her to bend and buckle beneath him like an empty soda can trampled underfoot.

Only then, would the Guardian be avenged, and the Keeper's power be complete.

CHAPTER 14

"Why do you think Karim ran?" Rita asked. "What's he hiding?"

"Drugs, first guess." Richard sat back in his seat at the station office. "His mates were giving nothing away, but they went back and gave him the nod, little bastards."

"Are they scared of him?" Rita had seen kids like Karim more times than she cared to remember. They always followed the same pattern: placed themselves at the top of the pecking order by doing something that wowed the weaker kids, and then gradually turned the awe into fear, so slowly, no one even realized it was happening until they were at his beck and call. Karim could be on his way to becoming a gang leader. That's what happened in this impoverished schools – they were a breeding ground for crime.

The real tragedy, Rita knew, that Karim would be excellent in a real job if only his skills could be turned in the right direction.

"His followers are scared of what will happen to them if they rat on him." Riz was glued to his computer screen, checking out the CCTV footage of the bus route. He glanced up at Rita. "I've got Karim's home address from the lady at reception."

"Any sign of the headmaster?" Rita asked.

"Didn't ask. I think we'd be better off rocking up unannounced. Corner him in his office before he can escape."

"You'd think he'd relocate somewhere quiet." Richard shook his head. "Like the Outer Hebrides." He seemed to be in a good mood despite having lost a suspect earlier in the day.

It was this case, Rita thought. Something about Sarah's murder had got a hold of them and was clinging on tightly. Pretty vulnerable teenager, grisly death, abandoned warehouse.

Whatever Sarah had done, she deserved better than the world had given her, and as cops, they took on a sense of responsibility for society's failures. They couldn't bring Sarah back, but they could see the killer brought to justice. It was the best they could offer, and they would all give it their best shot.

"You and Riz care to do the honours and pay Karim's home a visit later?" Rita asked.

"On it, guv." Richard, for all his personal problems, seemed to be thriving on the case. It was offering him a distraction from everything falling to pieces around him, and she like that. Rita had a lot of time for people who could build on the bum deals in life and rise above them.

"Guv, you might want to see this." Maggie widened her eyes at Rita from across the room, her eyebrows dancing independently.

Rita walked around the desk and peered at Maggie's screen. She was staring at an image of a younger Andrew Robson, only the names didn't match up.

Maggie said, "Riz, run a check on a guy called Derek Eastell."

"Jill Collins' new partner, Andrew Robson, changed his name two years ago," Maggie said to the room in general. "Born, Derek Andrew Eastell in Filey, Yorkshire. It's a seaside village not far from here. Attended Filey Academy. Dropped out with no qualifications. In and out of trouble with the law for shoplifting, possession, driving without a licence. Usual stuff."

"Changed his name more than once by the looks of it," Rizwan added.

"Let's put a timeline together." Rita walked back to the whiteboard and added the names Andrew Robson and Derek Eastell, connecting the two with a black line. "Find out any other aliases this guy had had and why. He might not have travelled far, but he doesn't want to be found."

"Doesn't want his past catching up with him more like," Maggie said.

"I want to know where he works, what he does in his spare time, who his friends are. This guy scratches his balls, I want to know about it."

Rita's landline buzzed and she picked it up. She was distracted by a mental image of Andy Robson following his partner's daughter into a disused warehouse. "DI Gupta."

Nicola Perkins clipped voice answered. "My office, now."

Rita inhaled deeply. Her boss, The Detective Superintendent didn't sound happy. Then again, she never did.

Leaving the buzz of the office behind her, she tried to focus on Andy Robson. Something about the man had made her feel uneasy. It wasn't just his attitude towards Jill – which was bad enough – but he didn't seem to care that her daughter had just been murdered. Like it didn't affect him because she wasn't his daughter.

True, he didn't hide the fact that he didn't care about Sarah, but that might simply be down to arrogance. Or stupidity.

Hesitating outside the Detective Super's door, Rita took a deep breath and knocked.

"Come in," was the reply.

Rita went in and took the seat across the desk from her boss. Nicola was pint sized, dark eyed, with sunken cheeks and a pinched nose. Her exterior was as tough as an old beer barrel, and she had a rough attitude to match.

Nicola sat back in the leather chair, which engulfed her like a throne, and studied Rita, tapping the end of a ballpoint pen on the desk and flipping it. Tap-flip. Tap-flip. Tap-flip. "I hear you're working on a new case."

"Yes, ma'am." Rita maintained eye contact.

Nicola Perkins had never tried to conceal the fact that she didn't particularly like Rita. It was okay – they'd been stationed at opposite ends of the country until now. Unfortunately, now they had to work together. Or rather, Rita worked, and Nicola took the glory.

Was it a power thing? Did Nicola feel threatened by the new DI who'd wriggled her way into her cosy station? Was she afraid that Rita might steal her job? A younger, punchier, more driven version of herself? Or was this personal?

"When were you going to tell me?"

"Apologies, ma'am. I'm still preparing my first report on our findings so far."

The chair jolted forward, and Nicola rested her forearms on the desk in one fluid movement. "When are you planning on returning to London?"

There it was. Not really a question – Nicola had already assumed that Rita was heading back.

"I have no concrete plans," Rita said. "The sabbatical was left open because we didn't know how long it would take to solve my mother's murder."

"And now that you have?"

There was a cold glint in the older woman's eye. The D Sup back at the Met could be a cold-hearted bastard when he wanted, but even he had felt the Clara Winters case personally. He'd shown emotion when Rita broke down, stayed behind to talk to her when going back to her flat felt like slamming a prison door, given her time off when the hole in her chest threatened to rip her in two.

But this woman… She must've achieved her position by sheer determination and strict adherence to the book.

"Now that I have, I can go back whenever it suits." Rita refused to cave in to that steely glare. "How about now? You can get someone else to handle the Sarah Collins case."

She went to stand up. She'd made her point – she wasn't stepping on anyone's toes; she was simply doing her job.

"Sit down, detective inspector," Nicola said. Rita did as she was told. Not that she'd planned on going anywhere. She'd long ago learned how far to push her bosses and which battles were worth pursuing.

Nicola clenched her jaws once before relaxing slightly. "Tell me about the case."

Rita explained the fatal injuries that Sarah Collins had received and her concerns that it might've been some kind of ritual killing. The D Sup's eyebrows slid upwards, but she didn't interrupt.

"Any suspects?"

"The victim's mother's new partner, Andy Robson. He has previous convictions, none of which resulted in a prison spell. Also has a couple of aliases under his belt. And one of the kids who discovered the body, Karim Ahmadi. When we tried to question him at his school earlier today, he managed to escape over a fence."

Nicola nodded. "I want daily updates. Last thing I need is the press knowing more than I do, understand?"

"Yes, ma'am."

Nicola looked down at her papers, and Rita knew she was dismissed.

Rita stood up and went to the door. She glanced back at the D Sup before she left, but the woman was already engrossed in whatever paperwork she'd been reading before she'd summoned Rita to her room.

Heading back to the office, Rita replayed the brief meeting in her head. She'd called Nicola's bluff, and it had worked. This time. The truth was, she wasn't ready to leave. She hadn't realized until she'd been a hair's breadth away from being forced out, but she would miss Scarborough if she left now.

It was that kind of place. The grumpy sea, the changeable skies – the moodier the better as far as Rita was concerned – the majestic houses lining the seafront. They'd snuck back under her skin with no effort from herself, and she knew that the town had never really left her.

She'd been running with no finish line in sight. And now she could slow down. When the wind howled over the clifftops, and sea salt clung to every available surface, Rita felt a sense of serenity inside that no amount of therapy and mood music could ever bring her. While Scarborough blustered, she felt calm.

Rita stepped outside for some fresh air and to soothe the thoughts whirling around inside her head.

She wanted to solve this case too. She wanted to find Sarah Collins' killer, wanted him to know that she was responsible for seeing him behind bars. They were taught in Police Training College to detach themselves from cases – first rookie mistake was allowing a case to become personal – but Rita was doing this for every other Sarah Collins.

This murder was brutal. She could almost feel the killer's bloodlust when she'd stood over the teenager's body inside the warehouse. If she could prevent it from happening again, it cemented everything she'd ever wanted from a career on the force.

Rita tipped her head back against the wall, filled her lungs with fresh salty air, and her eyes fell on the taillights of a BMW waiting to pull onto the road. She realised with a start it was Jack Banford's car. She followed the car's journey until it was out of sight and then closed her eyes. Poetic that, Jack fading from her before her eyes, just like he had more than twenty years ago.

A new morass of emotions assailed her now. Had she done the right thing by pushing Jack away…?

She felt a pang of something sharp inside her chest. Did she simply have fond memories of Jack as her first boyfriend or was it more than that? She expected her heart to tell her the truth – but her heart was more confused than her mind. Misty, like the shadows over the sea.

Telling herself she'd always done what felt right at the time – wasn't that how everyone got through life?

Everyone made choices, and then they had to live with them. Rita shook her head, as if that would dispel the heaviness in her heart. She went back inside, and back to her usual refuge – her work.

CHAPTER 15

Rita faced the team inside the office, hands on her hips. “Any luck?”

Rita had returned to the office, the last traces of her conversation with Nicola lingering just beneath the surface of her skin. She wasn’t going to let the Detective Super distract her from the case. She’d dealt with worse situations in the past – a little bit of friction between them wouldn’t see her on the first train heading back to London. Rita was far too stubborn for that.

“Traced a mobile phone to Karim’s address.” Maggie peered at her from her desk, with the focused look of a cop on a mission.

“Can we get uniforms on it?” Rita asked. “We’ve got the location of the school and the bus route.”

“Already thought of that, guv.” Maggie wrinkled her nose. Whenever she did that, Rita got a glimpse of a younger version of her colleague, frowning over an exam paper in school, eager to get out into the big, wide world, and leave her mark. “Little sod has been clever and not used his phone since he did a runner, so triangulation won’t work.”

"What about previous records? Last twenty-four hours. Any calls made, text messages sent, repeat numbers contacted?"

"Leave it with me, guv." Maggie tucked a strand of hair behind her ear and smiled at the laptop. For someone who enjoyed getting her hands dirty on the streets, she also got a lot of pleasure out of the nitty-gritty legwork.

"Riz?" Rita turned her attention to the DC. "Any joy with Karim on CCTV?"

"Nothing yet, guv. Not a peep."

"Our boy is riding around town on the bus, scratching his balls, and getting his kicks out of terrorizing old ladies." Richard itched behind his left ear.

"Great visual," Rita said. "Proper set me up for the rest of the day."

"Sorry, guv." Richard smiled at her. "Kids like Karim Ahmadi always start somewhere. Bet he's already reaching out for the next rung of the ladder."

Rita understood. Dealing with youths like Karim scrubbed away at your belief in the next generation.

But this young team had a buzz to it that she liked – mostly generated by Maggie and Riz to be fair – and she had no room for negativity. They worked well together, and that's how she wanted it to stay. Even if she had to stand behind Richard and blast a klaxon in his ear whenever he gave off defeated vibes.

"Hold up, guv." There was a hint of excitement in Riz's voice. "Our boy's gone back to school."

Rita went and stood behind Rizwan's desk. She studied the CCTV footage in the bottom left corner, leaning closer so as not to miss anything.

The grainy image of Karim Ahmadi showed him jumping off the bus, his backpack still slung over his shoulder. "Did he have the backpack when you saw him?" Rita asked.

"Aye. It went over the fence before he did." Riz kept his eyes on the screen as the youth approached the school gates and then kept on going. Neither he nor Rita spoke.

Rita glanced at the clock on the wall. 12.15 p.m. If Karim wasn't going back into the building, he was there for another reason. He couldn't use his phone, so he had to show up in person. She knew she'd guessed correctly when he stopped beside a car parked on the kerb and rested his elbows on the open window of the passenger door.

"Can we zoom in?"

She didn't need to ask. Riz was already navigating the footage to get a closer look at the vehicle. A black Ford Focus, basic model. Riz screenshotted the licence plate and zoomed in on Karim Ahmadi. From the camera angle, he couldn't get a clear shot of the driver, but they could see that he was wearing a hoodie – hood up – and sunglasses.

"Not that bright," Riz muttered to himself. "Come on, man, look this way."

Before the driver could oblige, Karim opened the door and climbed in, stowing the backpack in the footwell between his legs. The car sped off, almost before the door had closed.

"Richard, can you trace the owner of a black Ford Focus?" Rita recited the vehicle registration.

To Rizwan, she said, "He had to come back to school to meet whoever was driving that car. Supplier maybe? My guess is this is a regular occurrence. Driver parks on a busy street, Karim bunks out of school early to beat the rush, job done. Can we follow it?"

Rizwan skipped to the closest CCTV, following the direction of the car, but there was no sign of it. "Using the routes with no cameras. Clearly has something to hide."

"Aye," Rita said, "an underage kid with a stash of drugs, most likely."

"The Focus is a rental car. Enterprise," Richard said, one hand already on the landline. "Olympian Trading Park."

"Where's that?" Rita asked.

Riz typed the rental car company into the search engine and enlarged the map of Scarborough. "Across town, about fifteen minutes in the car."

Richard was speaking to someone in the office at Enterprise, his back half-turned to the others so that he could concentrate. He jotted down a name and thanked the person on the other end of the line. Swivelling his seat back towards his desk, he carried out a search on the name and driver's licence number supplied when the car was collected.

He inhaled deeply, his mouth a thin line. "False name – what a surprise."

"Driver's licence?" Rita asked. Richard was looking at the government website for driver vehicle licencing authority, or the DVLA. He shook his head.

"Fake."

"Okay." The familiar excitement buzzed through Rita. Some people got an adrenaline rush from action movies, others from driving too fast, or climbing mountains, or deep-sea diving with sharks. But this was Rita's buzz. Always had been. That moment when she knew she was on to something.

"A fake licence good enough to fool people at the rental agency points to some expertise," Rita said.

"Are there any local suppliers of fake ID's?" she addressed Richard. As the senior detective, he should know better than the constables. "Someone good, who supplies local crooks. This can't be the first counterfeit you've ever heard of in these parts."

“Dickie Slingo,” Richard said, grinning. “Memorable name, I know, but I’m sure even his name is fake. He’s been keeping a low profile, but he’s still around.”

“If that’s a real name,” Rizwan said, glancing at Maggie, “He might be Maggie’s boyfriend.”

Maggie lifted the paper weight on her table and threatened to throw it at Rizwan, who covered her his head with his hands.

Rita was on her feet and grabbing her jacket from the back of the seat. “Where will I find this Dickie Slingo?”

Richard said, “Maybe Riz and I should go.”

Frown lines appeared between Rita’s eyebrows, but she still wore a half-smile. “Almost sounded to me like you don’t think Mags and I can handle it.”

Colour rushed from Richard’s neck to his cheeks. “Sorry, guv. It’s not that.” Rita waited for him to elaborate. “Dickie’s a real charmer.”

“Ah.” Rita chewed her bottom lip, suppressing a smile. “So, you think that we’ll succumb to his good looks and the promise of a good time if we don’t ask questions.”

A strangled sound somewhere between a giggle and a stifled cough escaped from Maggie before she could stop it. Even Riz was shaking his head at his computer screen, a grin on his face.

"Go on then! Ink Heart tattoo parlour. Seafront. Tucked in between the casino and the pizza place." Richard shooed them towards the door with both hands. "Forget I said anything."

Rita was laughing now. "Can you get a description of the guy who rented the car from Enterprise? Long shot but check if the car is tracked. And there must be CCTV on the industrial park. Riz, keep trying to locate the Focus." She reached the door and turned back around to face Richard. "Meanwhile, we'll try to stop our knees from trembling in Dickie Slingo's presence."

She was still chuckling to herself when Richard's stress ball of elastic bands hit the back of the door.

"Harsh, guv," Maggie said as they made their way outside. "But funny. He's always kind of taken on the paternal role with me and Riz. I think it's worse now with what's going on at home."

"I know. And he probably thinks he's doing the right thing, trying to be protective. That's sweet." Rita said, "But one day his daughter's will also grow up, and he'll need to let her fight her own battles."

They were quiet in the car on the way to the seafront. Maggie seemed to understand when Rita needed space and sang along to a song on the radio that Rita had never even heard before. Boy was she out of touch with today's music.

She'd only been messing with Richard. If she was honest, he wasn't the only one who'd stepped into the family role within the team. It took two to tango, as the saying goes, and she hadn't realized until today how easily she had accepted Richard's instinctive paternal shield. It was like having a cosy blanket wrapped around her shoulders on a winter's evening.

Rita thought about her father, Jay. She spent a lifetime not being in touch with him, but now that freeze was starting to thaw. Jay called, and wanted to come over. To see her, and to visit her mother's grave. That meant something to Rita. Exactly what, she didn't really know, but it was a good enough reason to stay in touch with her father.

Losing her mum when she was so young, she'd developed a tough external shell that she kept tucked safely around her like a snail. She didn't need protecting.

If she'd ever had a daughter, she'd have brought her up to give as good as she got, or better still, get in first to keep the wolves at bay.

Had she changed since solving the mystery of her mum's death? Had the resolution softened her around the edges?

Hell, no.

She peered out of the passenger window at the foamy waves decorating the sea like frosting on a cake. But she did feel more at peace inside. Or was it the unexpected sensation of having come home?

CHAPTER 16

Ink Heart was a narrow-fronted shop on Foreshore Road. The window contained laminated images of real tattoos and piercings, scattered amongst tissue-paper flowers. Inside, the front desk was unmanned, and Rita could hear the buzz of a needle staining a client's skin with ink. It smelled clean – she didn't know why this made her feel better. Maggie rapped on the door, hard enough to make the glass panelled structure shake.

"Give us a sec," a man's voice called out from the back room. "Gina's just popped out."

Maggie's eyebrows slid upwards. "What do you reckon?" she whispered. "I'm going Aaron Taylor-Johnson. You know, good-looking with a rough edge."

"I have no idea what you're talking about," Rita said with a shrug.

The buzz ended abruptly, and a tall, slim guy appeared. He had a mop of brown curls, wide brown eyes, and a smattering of freckles across his nose and cheeks that gave him a boyish appearance despite the lines fanning from the corners of his eyes. He was lanky – all arms and legs – but the smile was … charming. This had to be Dickie Slingo.

"Hello, ladies," he said, his eyes appraising them both. "What can I do for you?"

Rita produced her warrant card. "Detective Inspector Rita Gupta. We want to speak to you about a fake driving licence."

Dickie smiled at them, and Rita could see what Richard meant. "Sorry, can't help you. But if you want a tattoo, I'm your guy."

"A guy wanted in connection with the murder of a seventeen-year-old girl is walking around with a fake driver's licence probably supplied by you. Now—"

"Not me." Dickie didn't let her finish. "Have you ever considered getting your dimples pierced?" He reached out to touch Rita's cheek, and she pulled away. "It would suit you."

Rita grabbed his hand and twisted it around his back in one fluid movement. The speed took him by surprise, and he stumbled as she pushed him forwards, pressing him against the counter. Maggie helped her as she slid a set of cuffs from her pocket and clipped it around Dickie's wrists. He resisted, but then realised the futility of his actions.

"We could've done this the easy way," she said.

Dickie leaned closer, so close she could smell his shampoo and sweet fizzy breath, and murmured, "Where would be the fun in that?"

"Okay, you're coming with us." Rita went to walk back to the door, but Dickie wasn't budging. He was stronger than he looked, and jerked backwards.

"I've got a customer through there, and Gina isn't here to take over." He paused. "Look, if I answer your questions, what happens to me? I'm legit these days. I'm getting away from all that."

"We only want a name." Rita released the door handle.

A youth with a purple Mohican tried to come in, and Maggie flipped the sign on the door to show that the parlour was closed. He gaped at the sign, glanced at the shop again, then moved on.

"Carry on," Rita said, folding her arms across her chest.

Dickie was in a talkative mood, no doubt helped by the handcuffs pinning his wrists together. "I've only supplied one licence this year. I couldn't exactly say no." He held her gaze like he was telepathically trying to connect with her to avoid spelling it out.

"Go on," Rita said.

"Guy named Barry Alders."

"Why couldn't you refuse Barry Alders?" Rita could give it a good guess.

Dickie lowered his voice. "Everyone knows Barry." Rita didn't, and none of her team members had thrown the name into the mix, so she kept quiet. "Drug dealer. He works for a big, organised crime network on the east coast."

"Where can I find him?" Rita mimicked his low tone.

"I dunno. Barry usually finds you."

"Does he live in Scarborough?"

"Like I said, you don't find Barry."

Rita nodded and unlocked the metal restraints around their wrists. "If you think of anything else, you know where to find me." It sounded way more suggestive than she'd intended, and she felt the heat rising in her cheeks.

Dickie's smile hadn't gone far. "Don't forget the dimples," he said as Maggie opened the door. "I'll give you a discount."

"Before or after you're rotting in jail?" Maggie shot back as she slammed the door shut.

Rita called through to Richard in the office. "I want a warrant put out for the arrest of Barry Alders. Name mean anything to you?"

"Nope."

Rita could almost hear the chugging of Richard's brain cells. "Dickie Slingo here supplied Barry with a fake licence. Said he's part of an OCN. I want to know where he dropped Karim off, and what Karim's role is within the network. I also want to know if they use the warehouse, and how often."

"Got it, guv." Richard paused. "Dickie not your type then?" His chuckle reached her through the phone.

"Piss off." She ended the call.

"Fancy some chips, guv?" Maggie gestured to the chippie just past the casino. "Best chips around."

"Go on then." Rita had skipped breakfast again, and her stomach growled, a warning that she'd better agree.

Rita couldn't remember the last time she'd eaten chips from thick white paper, salt clinging to her fingers, and the smell of vinegar filling her nostrils. The sun peeped out from behind a fat white cloud as they walked, and she tipped her head towards the sky. "I could get used to this."

"This, Scarborough," Maggie asked, "or this, chips drowning in salt and vinegar?" She popped a gherkin into her mouth and crunched it between her back teeth.

"Both," Rita confessed.

The longer she stayed, the harder it was going to be to leave. But right now, the thought of swapping this for an overcrowded London street with its drab buildings and grey tired faces, left her feeling hollow.

She knew that when she went back – *if* she went back – she'd settle straight into her regular routine, and Scarborough would fade into a pleasant interlude. But her heart was balking at the idea like a horse frightened by a rodent.

"Did you hang out at the seafront when you were a kid?" Maggie asked.

"Aye, I'd come and sit on the Southside beach and people-watch in the summer. You could always tell a tourist by the bags they were lugging around."

"And the camo shorts." Maggie giggled. "And the guys with flash cameras hanging around their necks."

"The cameras…" Rita nodded. "I forgot about them. And the poor donkeys. I always wished someone would come along and set them free."

"I think they're more well looked after than you imagine."

Rita popped a chip into her mouth and savoured the tang of salt. "I always loved the doughnuts. It was a Saturday treat for me and … well, for me and my mum." She swallowed. The lump was still there in her throat, but it was shrinking. Slowly. "Do you ever think about moving away?" she asked, diverting the attention back to Maggie.

"Nah I like it here. I'm Pisces. We're home bods."

Rita smiled. Her phone vibrated, and she checked the caller ID. Rizwan.

"Where are you, guv?" His tone was full of an urgency that made her sit up.

"Seafront. What have you got?" Rita felt the hairs on the back of her neck stand on end.

"Positive ID on Karim Ahmadi at the harbour."

Rita's eyes instinctively shifted to the harbour up ahead. "We're almost there." She slid her phone into her pocket and scrunched up the paper around the last of her chips with a pang of disappointment. "Karim's been spotted at the harbour."

Maggie didn't waste a beat. She tossed the remains of her meal into the closest bin and started sprinting towards the boats moored along the jetty, Rita struggling to keep up with her.

Pedestrians dodged out of their way, but Rita hardly noticed. She was scanning West Pier, the warehouses and industrial buildings, the carpark which was almost full.

She and Maggie turned into the Pier, picking up speed. Rita scanned the carpark while Maggie took in the buildings, the small forklift trucks shifting pallets onto vans, the workers in greasy overalls, the delivery drivers hanging around smoking fags before they set off.

Rita called Riz back. "We're on West Pier. Did you see where he went?"

"Sorry, guv. Lost him near the carpark."

If Karim was part of the same OCN as Barry Alders, there was a chance he'd got into another car. Rita stopped to catch her breath, her eyes skimming the tops of the vehicles, searching for a glimpse of a kid in a pale grey hoodie carrying a backpack.

She almost missed him. A figure in a hoodie snuck behind a white van and reappeared the other side, walking quickly towards the pedestrian walkway. He looked back once, and that gave him away.

Rita followed. She slid her phone out of her pocket and alerted Maggie to turn around and head back to the seafront.

Slipping into a steady jog, Rita kept her eyes fixated on the youth and almost collided with a car pulling out of the parking lot. She winced as the driver slammed on the brakes. The tyres squealed. Karim, hearing the abrasive sound, looked around and spotted Rita as Maggie caught up with her.

Then he ran.

Back to the seafront buzzing with people as usual, Karim turned right and sprinted along the pedestrian walkway towards the jetty. He glanced over his shoulder, saw that the detectives were giving chase, and picked up speed again.

He was fast, but Maggie wasn't bad. She was striding ahead, keeping up her pace. Rita was lagging far behind, her lungs wheezing. Rita felt a stitch burning in her side from where she'd just eaten and tried to ignore it.

The kid had something to hide. Drugs, aye, but he'd scarpered from school when Richard and Riz wanted to talk to him about the Sarah Collins case. He clearly didn't want the cops getting too close.

Onto the jetty, and Rita suddenly clocked on to what he was going to do. There was only one way off, and that was via water, so Karim was either going to swim away from them, or he was taking his chances on a boat.

"Stop!" Rita yelled. "Karim, stop!"

Karim didn't even glance backwards. He ran along the jetty, close to the water's edge, eyeing up the boats and yachts moored up in a row like smart, white soldiers.

Rita's footsteps thudded across the jetty, jolting her ribcage and vibrating inside her skull. He was gaining distance. Too late to call for backup – he'd be long gone before uniforms arrived. What was he going to do? She saw him glancing at the boats, took her eyes off him for a second to follow his gaze, and then he was gone.

"Where'd he go?" She was still running, her breathing ragged, heart knocking against her ribs.

"Boat!" Maggie gestured ahead of her.

Rita allowed Maggie to take the lead. They slowed down when they reached the spot where they'd last seen Karim. Every mooring post was occupied, and Maggie seemed to falter, unsure which boat he'd climbed aboard.

"Come out, Karim!" Rita yelled. "This will look a whole lot worse for you, if you keep running."

A dark-haired man stood up on the deck of a boat two down from where they were standing. Rita didn't know much about seafaring vessels, but it looked like a small yacht complete with sleek cabin and deck area. The kind of boat where she could imagine posh people with plummy accents drinking champagne while they cruised along the coast. It took her a beat too long to realize that the man was holding a rope in his hands. He returned her stare, a puzzled expression drawing his eyebrows together.

Rita and Maggie ran towards the boat. "Stop!" Rita shouted. "We're looking for Karim Ahmadi."

She heard the purr of the engine as she reached the mooring post. She gave her legs one final burst of energy, prepared to leap aboard if she had to.

"Stop!" She waved her arms above her head and pointed at the man. "Police!"

His expression faltered, and he peered down at the rope in his hands, as if it were stolen goods.

"You're hiding a murder suspect on your boat! His name is Karim Ahmadi! He's wanted in connection with the murder of Sarah Collins."

That did it. The man lunged back towards the post, managing to secure the rope around it with an easy knot, to stop the boat from moving away, a foamy avalanche already building up beneath the wooden jetty. The man went backwards, and flicked a switch on the dashboard, killing the engine.

Maggie grabbed Rita's arm just in time to stop her hurtling headfirst into the water.

They both watched Karim peeped out from beneath a heavy tarpaulin on the floor behind the bewildered man.

CHAPTER 17

Rita started the tape recording in Interview Room 1, and spoke aloud the date, time, and people present in the room. “Detective Inspector Rita Gupta, Detective Constable Maggie Long, and Mr Karim Ahmadi.”

Karim sat slumped back in his seat, legs outstretched beneath the table, hands stuffed inside the pockets of his joggers. He eyed up Rita as if he knew the rules of this game and wasn’t going to divulge them.

“Karim,” Rita began. “Why did you run away when my colleagues tried to interview you in school?”

“I had a dentist appointment.”

“You always climb a fence to get out of school for your dentist appointment?”

“The gate was locked.”

“Why didn’t you leave via reception? Don’t you need a pass for a dental appointment?”

The youth shrugged. “No one bothers checking ’em.”

"But you weren't in a hurry until you spotted my colleagues."

"I was late," he said. "Saw the bus coming."

"Which dentist did you see?" Maggie asked.

Karim's gaze slid her way. Rita saw no fear in his eyes, no anxiety in his casual stance. The kid had either been hauled in for questioning before or he'd been primed by Barry Alders on how to behave if the cops ever picked him up.

Frustration balled inside her gut – she already knew how this was going to go. He would stall them with rubbish, then ask for a solicitor. Rita wanted to avoid the last situation at all costs, but her heart was sinking already.

Karim grimaced. "Dunno. Old geezer with white hair."

"You don't know the name of your dentist?" Maggie persisted. If there was an Olympic event in patience, she'd win every time.

"Don't need to. Nothing wrong with my teeth." Karim grinned at Maggie to provide the evidence.

"I go to the one in Alma Square," Maggie said. "I see Mr Singh."

"So?" Another shrug.

"I just want to confirm your appointment with them."

"Why?" He held Maggie's gaze with the confidence of someone much older.

Rita wished that he would apply that confidence to something worthwhile. Kids like Karim could really go places if only they had the drive and the ability to see beyond the ready cash involved with supplying drugs.

Right now, he didn't care that people got addicted to the stuff they bought from him. He probably didn't care much about anything other than his next iPhone or impressing a girl. Short-term gains. He was a teenager after all, and teenagers felt they were immortal.

Until they weren't, she thought, an image of Sarah Collins popping into her head.

"Because you didn't get off the bus at the dental practice, did you, Karim?" Rita stepped in. "You stayed on the bus until it looped full circle back to your school."

No response.

"Tell us about Barry Alders."

Karim flicked his eyes to her. Then he shrugged, trying to act casual. "I don't know anyone called Barry Alders."

"Strange." Rita sat forward and knitted her fingers together on the table. "Because you were seen getting into a car driven by Barry Alders outside your school at 12:15 today."

Karim swallowed. Was that a flicker of uncertainty behind his eyes?

"No comment."

"How do you know Barry Alders, Karim?"

"No comment."

"Where did he take you?"

"No comment."

"Do you both work for the same organised crime network?"

"I want a lawyer."

Rita sighed; aware she had reached the end of the road. There was a wariness in Karim's face now, and a tautness in his spine.

"You could be going in for a long time, Karim," Rita said. "You could stop that by talking to us. Help us to help you."

Karim swallowed, and blinked a couple of time. Rita saw the indecision hover over his face, and for a few seconds, she almost felt sorry for him. Could he have killed Sarah in a fit of rage? Maybe. But even if he didn't, he knew things about Sarah that could prove vital to finding the real killer, in addition to his links to the crime world. A misguided youth, wasting his life. But at the same time, Rita had to be careful she didn't give him too much rope to play with.

"Don't hide the big boys, Karim. They won't protect you. Don't believe what they say. They'll throw you in the fire at the first chance they get."

Karims's jaws stiffened, his handsome face getting tighter by the second. "I want a lawyer," he repeated.

*****

Rita sent Maggie to get the name of the new duty solicitor from the custody sergeant. They'd pushed Karim, and it hadn't taken much for the first cracks to appear, but once a lawyer got involved, he'd clam up like a dodgy mussel, and they'd get nothing out of him.

Outside the station in her regular spot with the sea in the distance, Rita played out all the different scenarios in her head. They could only hold Karim for twenty-four hours without charging him, and unless they had an airtight case against him, the CPS would dismiss it. He'd already tried to give them the slip today; if they released him on the CPS's instructions, he wouldn't be so careless next time. Especially if the OCN was involved. The bigshots wouldn't risk a kid like Karim snitching on them to the cops – they'd be watching his every move.

Rita needed a charge against him, and she needed it to stick. Which wasn't going to be easy with a duty solicitor breathing encouragement down the lad's neck.

She found herself checking out the cars in the station's bays, disappointment flaring like a weak match when she didn't find Jack's BMW. He might know the new duty solicitor. She could always ask him, just so that she knew where she stood before she questioned the suspect further. Forewarned was forearmed.

At least, that's what she told herself when she found Jack's number in her contacts and tapped the green button with a fingertip.

He answered on the second ring. "Rita?" She could tell by the muffled background sounds that he was driving with the windows down. She also thought that she detected the smile behind his voice.

"Jack, what do you know about the new duty solicitor?" She'd never mastered the art of small talk.

"Peter Watson? I've known him a while." There was a pause, and Rita waited patiently for Jack to navigate whatever traffic signals or roundabout he was dealing with. "He can be a bit of an old dog. Pete wants an easy life, and if he thinks you're pushing the CPS for a case that will increase his workload, he'll make life difficult for you."

"Great." The clouds dispersed almost as if by magic, and Rita closed her eyes, relishing the sunlight on her eyelids. It changed everything – sunshine – apart from a difficult duty solicitor.

"What have you got?" Jack asked.

She summarised the day's events with Karim giving them the slip and his potential connection with an OCN, as well as being one of the kids who discovered Sarah's body and called it in to the emergency services. "So, you think Peter Watson might be obstructive?" she asked.

"As a dam at high tide."

Rita couldn't help smiling. Jack might've gained biceps and a few laughter lines, but his voice hadn't altered at all. She found herself picturing him sitting next to her at the cinema while they shared a carton of popcorn, whispering about the movie in her ear so as not to disturb anyone else in the audience. She reflexively shuddered at the memory, rotating her shoulders as goosebumps popped on her arms. How could a voice do that to a person?

"Okay, thanks for the heads up."

"Look, Rita, would it help if I stepped in as go-between for your case and the CPS? That way, I can make sure that Peter doesn't sway them in the wrong direction."

"Would you do that for me?" Rita chewed her bottom lip and traced her shadow against the wall with her finger.

"Do you really need to ask?"

"I guess not. But thank you."

"I'll give you a call back once I stop driving." Jack ended the call.

Rita, still smiling to herself, was about to go back inside when a text message pinged through on her phone. She frowned as she didn't recognise the name at first, but then of course she did. It was from her father. Jay Gupta.

Call me when you get a chance.

A man of many words, obviously.

A second message quickly followed the first: *Please*.

Deep breath. Slow exhale. Push the misery and the memories back, then let them go slowly.

The sun was still painting the back of the building in shades of gold, but Rita could already feel the clouds creeping back in. She'd had little to no contact from him her entire life, had accepted that as simply the way it was – some people had two parents, some didn't – and now here he was, wanting to speak to her twice in the space of a couple of weeks.

What did he want? Some kind of reconciliation? *Sorry I wasn't around when you needed me, but I'm here now?* And what about what *she* wanted?

Had he even considered that Rita might not need him? He might've been ready to rebuild his bridges, assuage whatever guilt he may or may not have been carrying around with him since he walked away from her, but she was quite happy on her side of the water. She didn't need to cross that bridge to the other side to complete her life.

She went to delete the message, but something stopped her. Despite everything, she couldn't just walk away, cut him off without at least hearing him out. She wasn't looking for answers, she told herself. Just closure.

Her finger hovered over his number. Would this open a whole can of worms that was best left shut? Did she even need this? She'd survived all these years without him, and he was hardly going to waltz back into her life with a bunch of flowers and a promise to stick around. This time.

Squeezing her eyes shut, she hit the call button.

"Hello? Rita?" She heard the faint but unmistakable accent and released the breath she hadn't realized that she was holding.

"Hello," she said.

"How are you?"

"Fine." She swallowed. The silence dragged. Okay, so she wasn't exactly making this any easier, but then she didn't owe him anything.

"Rita, I… I'd like to come and see you. If that's okay with you. I-I realize that, well, that it's a big ask, but, well…" Pause. "I'd like to see you," he finished.

Rita's pulse raced, but she felt numb. This man wasn't a part of her life. This man on the other end of the line with his stumbling words and his polite requests – he didn't exist in Rita's world. At least, he hadn't until she found her mother's killer.

"I'm sorry," he said, filling the gaping hole in the conversation. "I shouldn't have asked. I completely understand if you don't want to see me. It's just that I-I thought, that perhaps it would be good to meet up, you know, after what happened. I'd… I'd like to visit your mum's grave … with you … no pressure to talk about anything that makes you feel uncomfortable."

He was trying. Rita could hear the pleading in his voice. It was almost pitiful, and one thing she did not want to do was pity her father. He'd made his choices. She could be the bigger person now, couldn't she? Wasn't it supposed to be good karma? Give to receive. Be kind. Positive energy.

"When?" she asked before she could talk herself out of it.

"I have some time off work, so I could come as soon as," came the tentative reply.

CHAPTER 18

Back in the office, Rita asked the team if they'd had any luck tracking down Barry Alders.

She was still strangely uncomfortable after the stilted conversation with her father. He promised to text her when he'd booked his train ticket, so she packed his impending visit safely away in the recesses of her mind until then. She refused to allow him to interfere with her job.

"Barry's a slippery one," Richard said. "No fixed address. No employment records, or unemployment records for that matter."

"Dickie Slingo said that you don't find Barry Alders, he finds you," Maggie interjected.

"Let's change the pattern then, shall we?" Rita sat down at her desk and studied the whiteboard. Barry's name had been added to the list of suspects, but they needed to find a connection between the organised crime network and the warehouse where Sarah's body was found. "What about the rental car?"

"Still working on it," Rizwan said. "Our man knows what he's doing, sticking to routes with no cameras."

"He knew the roads that did not have CCTV," Rita was thoughtful. "He did his own surveillance. Medical records?"

"I'll get on it," Maggie offered. "I'll check his aliases too."

Richard took a call from the custody sergeant – the duty solicitor had arrived and was waiting with his client.

"Coming?" Rita asked him. She'd barely swallowed a mouthful of the coffee she'd picked up from the canteen on her way back through. "Let's see what Karim has to say for himself with a lawyer present." She wasn't expecting much, especially after her conversation with Jack. She filled Richard in as they made their way down to the interview room.

This time, Karim was sitting straighter in his seat, like a kid waiting for an exam to begin. When he wasn't slouching inside his hoodie, he looked smart, handsome, like a young, dark-skinned Elvis Presley. She tried to imagine him in a suit and tie, auditioning for a movie role. The kid could cut it on looks alone, if he wanted to.

Peter Watson, on the other hand, wore a tight suit that had seen better days, his shirt buttons straining to contain his paunch. Rita would've placed him around his mid to late fifties, with jowls that were sagging too soon. The hairs on his knuckles were sun-bleached, and she guessed that he spent much of his free time on the golf course with his solicitor buddies, discussing their handicaps over a few beers in the clubhouse when they finished the course.

His gaze flitted between Rita and Richard when they walked in, and then finally lingered on Rita as she sat down. She recognized the look in his eyes. It was the look of a man accustomed to staring down his nose at those lower down the pecking order than himself. The look of a man who knew all the shortcuts and angles to getting what he wanted. She'd bet that his wife rubbed her hands together and mentally opened a bottle of wine every time his golf clubs came out of the cupboard.

Rita recited the date and time, and their names, for the recording.

"Where were you between 10 p.m. on Tuesday 10th September and 2 a.m. on Wednesday 11th September?" Rita began.

"Is my client a suspect in a murder investigation?" Peter asked. He leaned back in his seat, his frame wider than the chair, and cricked his neck from side to side.

"Your client discovered the body of Sarah Collins yesterday in a disused warehouse near the centre of town." Rita eyed him coolly. "When my colleagues tried to question him further today, he ran."

"I told you I had a dentist appointment," Karim said.

"We've already established that you didn't attend a dental surgery." Rita waited for Karim to drop the attitude that was only ever a heartbeat away from taking centre stage. "Please answer the question."

"I was at home that night."

"Can anyone vouch for your whereabouts?"

"My mum and my little sister."

"Do you ever sneak out of the house at night, Karim?" Rita pressed.

"My client does not have to answer that," Peter said. "It has no relevance to the enquiry."

"I'd be surprised if his mum checked on him at 2 a.m., wouldn't you?" Rita arched one eyebrow, noting the narrowing of the solicitor's eyes. "Which means that it would not stand up as a reliable alibi in a court of law."

She smiled at Peter, then focused back on Karim. "Did you make any calls while you were at home, Karim? Message your friends?"

"Nah. I was asleep. It was a school night." There was an unmistakable hint of sarcasm in his tone.

"What were you doing at the warehouse when you discovered the body?" Richard asked.

"My client does not have to answer the question," Peter interjected. "He reported the discovery to the police. It doesn't make him a suspect."

"Does Barry Alders supply you with drugs to sell on to your friends?" Richard continued, unfazed.

"Is this a murder enquiry, or is my client being questioned about an alternative crime?" Peter's expression was smug like he had a whole repertoire filled with objections that he could reel out like tennis balls being fired from a training machine.

"Did Barry Alders introduce you to the organised crime network, Karim?" Richard asked.

"No comment," Karim said, stone faced.

"Are your friends Mark Oakham and James Aspinall involved in the same organised crime network?"

"No comment."

"Do they know that you're dealing with the big boys?" Richard was quick off the mark, trying to chip away at the youth's calm façade.

Peter sat forward, his sausage fingers wrapping around an expensive-looking, gold-lidded pen. "Unless you have any evidence to support these claims, my client has no comment."

"Or do you keep this information to yourself?" Richard asked, ignoring Peter. "Are you worried that they'll want in and take a share of your profits? Or can they not keep their mouths shut?"

"No comment." Karim released a bored sigh.

"Were you using drugs when you discovered the body, Karim?" Rita asked.

Peter opened his mouth to speak, but Karim got in first. "I told you we sometimes go there to smoke weed."

"That you get from Barry Alders and supply to your friends," Richard suggested.

"I don't know anyone called Barry Alders," Karim said.

"You got in a rental car with him." Rita held his gaze, trying to cut the duty solicitor out of the conversation. Karim remained silent. "Is Barry Alders your connection to the organised crime network?"

"I don't know anything about an organised crime network."

"Were you at the warehouse the night Sarah Collins was murdered?" Rita's gaze was enough to cut short the *no comment* from the solicitor. "Do you know who else uses the warehouse?"

"No," Karim said.

"Did you see anyone entering the warehouse or loitering in the area the night Sarah Collins was murdered?"

“My client has already supplied you with an alibi for the night in question,” Peter said. “Unless you can provide any evidence to place him at the scene of the crime, his previous answer stands.”

Rita could feel the interview slipping through her fingers like water. The solicitor knew that they had no evidence. He was biding his time until he could get his client released and go home to a hearty cooked meal and a chilled beer straight from the fridge. But Karim had tried to avoid being questioned for a reason. Time to play her ace.

Rita opened the manila folder in front of her and spoke for the benefit of the recording. “Showing the suspect images of the victim taken from the crime scene.” She slid the photographs of Sarah’s body from the folder and spread them across the table, watching Karim closely.

The boy’s gaze tripped over the graphic images at first, his eyelids flickering. Until he saw the closeup of Sarah’s vacant-eyed, blue-lipped face. He swallowed hard like there was an apple core stuck in his throat. His jaws tightened as his cheeks blanched white.

Even Peter’s face had paled. He wasn’t completely heartless then.

“Do you recognize the victim, Karim?” Rita asked gently.

"I… I might have seen her around town. Not sure." His voice was husky, filled with emotion. He sniffed and swallowed again, but each time he dragged his eyes away from the images, they drifted straight back to them.

"Her name is Sarah Collins," Rita continued. "She was seventeen years old. She attended St Cecilia Academy."

Still, Karim stared at the graphic image of Sarah's sad, vacant eyes as if mesmerized.

"Did you know Sarah?"

Slowly, Karim raised his head. But very quickly, he averted his eyes.

"No," he whispered.

"Are you sure?"

Karim flicked his eyes back to Rita, then nodded. She knew he was lying, and he knew that she could tell.

"No," he whispered again.

"Did you kill Sarah?" Rita asked, trying to shock him.

"What?" Karim looked like he'd just been kicked in the stomach. A wave of crimson appeared on his cheeks.

The lump in Karim's throat swelled and saliva collected in the corners of his mouth. His head jerked back and forth between the photos and Rita. He looked like he was ready to bolt.

"No," he said finally. "No, I would never… No." he sniffed again. Louder. He wiped his nose with the back of his hand, and hunched forward in his seat, his arms trembling violently.

"So, you did know her, then?" Richard spoke up.

"What? No, I didn't say that." Karim glanced at his lawyer. Peter sighed. "Please, can we stick to my client's responses? He said he didn't know the victim."

Rita's voice was calm but persistent. "Karim, do you know who killed Sarah?"

"No." He answered before Peter could give the stock response. He didn't look at Rita.

"Did Sarah tell you where she was going the night she was murdered?"

"I… No."

They were losing him. The initial shock of seeing the images had passed, and numbness was setting in along with the stark reality that he was in a police station being interrogated in connection with a murder.

Karim had recognized Sarah though; of that Rita was certain. From his reaction, she would guess that he had feelings for her, even if they'd never been in a relationship. Was he jealous of Matt? Her new boyfriend? Something in her gut was telling her that Karim Ahmadi didn't kill Sarah, but he knew more than he was letting on.

"Who else uses the warehouse, Karim?"

"Kids."

"Aside from kids. Does it get used by anyone else?"

"I've never seen anyone."

"But have you heard anything on the streets?" Rita persisted. She felt like she was so close to getting something out of him. But she could smell the duty solicitor's aftershave, a reminder that he was still there, the 'no comment' on the tip of his tongue, and if she could smell it, so could Karim.

"A whisper of what goes on inside the warehouse when the kids have gone home?" she asked hopefully.

Karim finally raised his eyes to her, and she saw the debate playing out inside his head. "No. Nothing."

She tried one last push. "Do you know Jackie Maynard?" She'd had the feeling that Jackie also knew more than she was prepared to divulge. A girl had died. Someone Jackie – and potentially Karim – were close to. Who were they protecting?

"No."

"Jackie was Sarah's best friend. Did you ever see them together at the warehouse?"

"My client didn't say that he'd seen the victim at the warehouse," Peter said.

Deep breath. "Okay, you said that you'd seen Sarah Collins *around*. Did you ever see her with her friend? Tall girl, blonde."

"Maybe. I dunno. A lot of girls are tall and blonde."

"Did they go there to do drugs?"

"Uh-hum." Peter Watson clicked his pen and slid it back into his pocket as if he was done with the conversation. He had the smug arrogance of a man who could play these games all day if necessary. His next move would be to remind Rita that she could only detain his client for twenty-four hours without charging him.

Rita ended the interview, announcing the time for the purpose of the recording.

"Can I go?" The numbness had been replaced by impatience. Karim Ahmadi was itching to get out of here, and Rita couldn't help but wonder why. She had to place him under surveillance.

"No." Rita gathered the images together, slid them back inside the folder and rose. "We'll continue this interview later."

She stood, ignoring Karim and Peter's protests.

Outside the interview room, Richard said, "One day we'll find a duty solicitor who's prepared to waver from the script."

"Do you think?" Rita inhaled deeply. "It would shave some time off the golf course later though. They have to get their priorities right."

Richard chuckled to himself. "Anyone ever tell you that you can be a bit harsh sometimes?"

"No, probably too scared to." Rita couldn't help smiling at her colleague.

"Coffee?"

Rita declined and headed outside instead. She called Jack, her pulse instinctively speeding up while she waited for him to pick up. Muscle memory, she told herself. It was how it had always been between them when they were younger, and the prospect of hearing his voice simply dredged up long suppressed memories. But she wasn't sixteen anymore. She was a grown woman with a job to do.

"Twice in one day," Jack said, his voice sounding rosy.

Rita pictured his smile and realized that she was smiling too. "Don't get used to it."

Jack chuckled. "You've met Peter."

"Is it that obvious?"

"Where are you?"

"Outside the station." Rita's eyes instinctively roamed the carpark for Jack's car.

"Be there in five. Got time for a coffee?"

"Alright. Where?"

"I know a good place close by. I'll pick you up. Gimme five minutes."

CHAPTER 19

Four minutes later, Rita climbed into the passenger seat of Jack's BMW. She could smell the fresh, woody smell of his cologne. She didn't know if it was the same one he used to wear, or if his tastes had grown more expensive over the years, but for some strange reason, it felt familiar.

She smiled at Jack once after she got into the car, saying hello. Then she kept her gaze fixed straight ahead.

Jack pulled up outside a small independent café on Eastborough and peered at the quirky blue façade and tall narrow windows, checking it wasn't too crowded. "Best coffee in Scarborough," he said, unbuckling his seatbelt.

"That's a bold claim."

"Trust me, it's not a difficult claim to make in Scarborough." He winked at her and an infectious grin appeared on his lips. "Besides, I'm a bold man."

Inside, Jack chose a table for two by the window and waited for Rita to sit down first. He ordered a mocha, extra-hot, and a slice of lemon and poppy seed cake.

"I'll have the same," Rita said. She didn't have the mental capacity for life's mundane decisions when she was in the throes of a case, and the interview with Karim had left her feeling frustrated, drained. She needed a slice of cake.

The café was small and cosy, the aroma of coffee and cake instantly soothing the tension in her spine and shoulders.

"Let me guess," Jack said. "Standard script and plenty of clock-watching."

Rita allowed herself to gaze into Jack's eyes. "I don't think the suspect is guilty, but he either knows who is, or he has connections that could lead us to the perp."

"You don't have enough to charge him?" Jack asked. "Even on the suspected OCN involvement?"

Rita shook her head and sat back as the waitress brought their coffees and cake. When the young woman had gone, she leaned forward and sipped her coffee. It was extra-hot, as requested, something she found rarely happened with the generic coffee shops. For someone who couldn't finish her coffee once it had begun to cool, this made her happy. Life's little pleasures.

"No. If he had drugs on him in school, he managed to ditch them between getting out of the school gates and being apprehended at the harbour. His mates aren't snitching either."

"They probably get mates' rates." Jack broke a corner off his lemon cake and popped it into his mouth.

"These kids are seventeen. They should be doing homework and playing video games."

Rita swallowed another mouthful of coffee and tracked its heat inside her. It felt so natural sitting here with Jack, that she almost regretted pushing him away when she first came back. Almost.

She didn't know how long she would be here, and there was no point making life any more complicated than it already was. *Don't look back*. She'd spent her whole life looking back – it was time to start looking forward. She owed herself that much.

She said, "Karim knew the victim. I saw it in his eyes when I showed him the photos. Can you imagine being shown that kind of evidence at that age?"

Jack shook his head. "Honestly, no."

"I did feel for him then," Rita reflected. She felt Jack's eyes on her. "Reminded me of myself, in another life." The words slipped out of her before she had realised. She closed her eyes. *What was she doing?*

Jack seemed surprised, but he regrouped quickly. "I'm sorry. But I also know the kind of fear you lived with, Rita."

Rita blinked away the tears stinging behind her eyes. Not here, she told herself. Not in front of Jack. "I don't think they're not talking because they're afraid. I think they're protecting someone."

"They?" Jack watched her intently.

"Her best friend denied knowing her movements leading up to her death."

"But you don't believe her?"

"No. They'd been best friends since primary school. Thick as thieves according to the victim's mother. Her best friend has just been murdered… But she couldn't even tell me the name of the victim's boyfriend. It doesn't sit right with me." Rita was glad the conversation was now back on the case. She had these unguarded moments when she just said the wrong thing. She had to watch herself when she was with Jack.

Jack smiled at her.

"What?" She smiled back at him.

"I remember you getting this invested over a history project on Jack the Ripper. You insisted that the evidence hadn't been recorded correctly. I actually thought that you weren't going to drop it until you'd solved the case."

"It wasn't that it hadn't been recorded correctly," Rita said, "There were too many gaping holes. Too many people protecting the killer."

Jack spread his hands wide. "Should've known then you were destined to be a cop."

"Detective Inspector if you don't mind."

Rita laughed and finally succumbed to the lure of the lemon cake. It melted in her mouth, and she closed her eyes, savouring the explosion of tart flavours on her tongue. "That's good," she said, a crumb flying onto her plate.

Jack grinned at her as if he'd baked the cake himself and was basking in the praise. Then he got serious.

"Can you not release the suspect and put him under surveillance? If he is involved in the OCN, he'll lead you to them sooner or later."

It was a good shout. Rita was loathe to let Karim go, but perhaps it was the best she could hope for in the current circumstances. Maybe, if Jack was right, he would lead them back to the crime scene too.

CHAPTER 20

Rizwan stopped the car in a dead-end road on a council estate near Scarborough town centre. They'd tracked the Ford Focus rented by Barry Alders using Traffic Cameras live CCTV footage, but now that they were here, there was no sign of it.

"What do we do now?" Maggie asked.

"Wait around a bit." Riz peered out of the driver's window, at the rows of square houses lining both sides of the road. The estate was a maze of similar, flat-fronted houses with no distinguishing features. Maggie could see a house at the far end with all the windows boarded up. It was obvious that someone had tried getting in through one of the lower windows – the board was hanging lopsided, nothing but darkness behind it in the fading light.

Grubby curtains hung behind the windows of the house next door. The front door was an indistinguishable colour, the rotting wood peeling in narrow strips. The front gardens were more nettles and waist-high weeds than lawn and perennial shrubs. The gates either non-existent or covered in rust and swinging loosely on what remained of their hinges. A dustbin rolled around on its side in the breeze.

Somewhere nearby, a dog barked aggressively, and Maggie could picture it foaming at the mouth. A shudder travelled down her spine.

She'd grown up in a neat, three-bed semi with a front and back garden surrounded by colourful flower borders, and neighbours who sent them Christmas cards, and did chocolate egg hunts along the street at Easter for all the kids. She wasn't a snob. But she couldn't imagine pulling up outside one of these houses after work, in the dark of winter, letting herself in and feeling safe. Safety and home went together, didn't they? Or was her idea of safety different to that of the people who lived here?

A door slammed, and Maggie jumped. She peered in the wing mirror to watch a youth in baggy jeans and an oversized hoodie walking in the opposite direction from one of the houses. This kind of area must've been a haven for drug pushers. No one asking questions, no one willing to snitch.

"Which house did he go into?" she asked. She wanted to get this over and done with and get away from here before night set in and the shadows grew wings.

Rizwan pointed to a building across the street with heavy curtains pulled across the windows guarding the house's secrets. The front garden was as uncared for as its neighbours', but the door appeared to be newer than the rest. Rubbish spilled from the top of the bin parked near the gate – the house was lived in.

"Shall we?" She unbuckled her safety belt, opened the passenger door, and climbed out. Crossing the road, the hairs on the back of her neck prickled. She saw the net curtains on a ground floor window twitch. They were being watched.

Rizwan tried the plastic doorbell attached to the side of the frame. No sound reached them from inside. The silence was intense, as if the house was holding its breath, waiting for them to get back in the car and drive away. He knocked on the door using his knuckles. The resulting sound was hollow. But the house was giving nothing away. There were no footsteps thumping along the hallway, no voices yelling that they were coming, no subaudible sounds of life.

Maggie stepped back and peered at the upstairs window. Nothing moved. Not even a twitch of a curtain to reveal someone staring back at her. Still, she couldn't shake the feeling that the building wasn't empty. Did Barry Alders live here? Did he have a family, a wife and kids, who were blissfully unaware of his criminal activities? Or was this the kind of forgettable place where those activities were carried out under the radar?

Rizwan tried the door handle. "Locked," he said. Crouching, he opened the letter flap and called out, "Hello! Anybody home?"

Nothing.

"I'm going in," Riz said. "Wait here in case Barry comes back."

"I don't like it."

"That's why you stay here and keep watch."

Maggie peered left and right along the street. To their left was the dead end, a buckled wire fence separating the street from the back end of the industrial park. She could see the warehouses looming like caves in the distance beyond the expanse of scrubby wasteland. She'd bet the local kids hung out in there rather than the excuse for a park they'd passed on the drive in – two swings, chains tied up in knots, and a slide covered in graffiti.

"I'll stay on the radio," Riz said, sliding it out of his pocket. "You don't hear from me every two minutes you have my permission to alert the guv."

"Okay." Maggie waved her own radio in front of him. "I'm holding you to that, mind."

Rizwan tried opening the door using his shoulder, while Maggie watched the other houses. The streetlamps flickered on, casting an eerie yellow glow over the pavements. She thought she caught a glimpse of movement behind an upstairs window across the street, but even though she stared at the pane until her eyes watered, she couldn't see anything.

"Stand back," Riz ordered.

Maggie stepped away from the cracked paving stones marking a path between the weeds and watched Riz raise a booted foot and kick the door. It gave just a fraction. Second kick resulted in a faint crack. The third kick saw the lock lose its grip on the frame, splinters of wood littering the front step as the door swung open with the force.

"Two minutes," Maggie said, her voice low. Riz nodded, and crept inside.

She blocked the doorway by standing in front of it. She couldn't hear Riz. It was as if the house had swallowed him whole, and she had a mental image of the door being yanked open and Riz being spat out.

When the radio crackled two minutes later, she jumped. "All clear so far," came Rizwan's tinny voice.

"Do you think this is where he lives?"

"Maybe. Looks like a regular house."

Maggie lowered the radio and stared at the unused strip of land on the other side of the wire fencing. Too many places to hide. Had Barry Alders seen them coming and done a runner the back way? From the industrial park, he could make his way to any of the major routes out of town, and they'd be too late to catch up with him. Maybe that's where he'd ditched the car.

"Heading upstairs," Riz's voice said through the radio.

"Okay." Pause. "Riz, be careful."

In any other circumstances, she would've smiled to herself that he was keeping his end of the deal by radioing through to her every two minutes, but something about this place was making her feel uneasy.

Barry Alders had picked up a kid outside a school earlier today, and everything about this case was screaming WRONG to her.

How did someone like Karim Ahmadi get mixed up in an organised crime network? Despite what he'd done, he looked too … clean.

Like he should've been at home studying for exams and applying to uni. She knew they'd never be able to stop kids from smoking weed and dabbling in drugs – she wasn't that naïve – but turning to organised crime and selling narcotics for a living meant crossing a line that most people would be repulsed by. Even with the promise of a wodge of undeclared cash. Or was Karim being forced into this line of work?

Maggie heard a sound that sent a tremor down her spine and made her heart race. How long had it been since Riz last checked in? She pressed the button on the radio and murmured, "Riz? Everything okay?"

Nothing. "Riz?"

She moved to the door and listened. Not a sound from inside. She didn't even know if the sound had come from inside the house, couldn't be sure where it had come from, but her gut was twisting. One hand ready to push the door open, she heard more noises from the other side of the fence.

Forgetting that she was supposed to guard the door in case Barry came back, she ran to the fence and scanned the unused land, overgrown with brittle reedy grass and rubbish that the wind had blown in.

It was several moments before she spotted two men sprinting towards the nearest warehouse to the far right of the industrial park. She was too far away to catch up with them. They'd have vanished in the warehouse carparks by the time she'd even scaled the fence or found a way through it. Besides, she couldn't leave Riz inside the house.

Maggie tried the radio again. Still no response from Riz.

She didn't waste a beat. Running back to the house, she went inside and checked the downstairs rooms, kicking each door open before entering. The back door was wide open.

Heart thumping against her ribcage, she made her way upstairs, baton in one hand, radio in the other. The house was silent. All she could hear was her blood gushing in her ears.

She spotted Riz from the top of the stairs. He was sprawled out on the floor of one of the bedrooms. He wasn't moving. The door had been left open, and Maggie waited behind it, her extendable baton now flicked up and raised.

"Police!" she called out.

When there was no response, she darted inside and knelt beside Riz who was unconscious, face down on the grubby beige carpet. Maggie checked his pulse – slow but strong. There was a swelling the size of a tennis ball on the back of his skull. The skin was broken, blood clumping in his hair – whatever he'd been hit with was hard enough to knock him out. But the blood wasn't pouring out. It was clotting already on the surface wound.

Still on her knees, Maggie put out an All Points Bulletin (APB) for the two men she'd seen running towards the industrial park. The early evening light wasn't the best, and she couldn't go into much detail having only seen them from behind. But she knew the man on the right fitted the description they'd been given by the car rental company of Barry Alders.

Turning her attention to Riz, Maggie moved him into the recovery position, one arm outstretched, palm facing upwards. She bent one leg at a right angle to his body, and gently rolled him onto his side, taking care not to roll him too far onto the swelling on the back of his head.

"Riz," she said, lowering her face so that she was almost touching him. "Riz, can you hear me?"

Maggie sat back on her heels and called an ambulance. While she was giving the necessary information to the coordinator, she looked around the room. It was the size of a small double room, she guessed. Bunk beds were pushed up against the far wall, but the mattresses were bare, and there were no pillows or duvets. Apart from the beds, the room contained unmarked cardboard boxes, lids open, and a floor lamp in one corner with no bulb and no shade.

Whatever the two men were doing in here, they weren't getting comfy. This might've been a family home once – stickers were peeling from the bedframe, the kind that came in kids' activity books – but from what she'd seen, it hadn't been lived in for a while.

As she ended the call, Rizwan stirred. A groan escaped his lips, and she bent closer so that he would know he wasn't alone when he opened his eyes. "Riz. It's Maggie." Pause. "Riz, can you hear me?"

Riz's eyelids flickered. He tried to move, and Maggie placed a hand on his shoulder. "Slowly, Riz. I think you might have a concussion."

"Huh?" Riz's face scrunched up as if his alarm had gone off on a day when he didn't have to get up for work. His shoulders slumped again.

"Riz. How are you feeling?" Maggie tried. "Do you remember what happened? You were attacked."

Riz half-opened his eyes, his lids heavy with sleep. "A-ttacked?"

"We were trying to find Barry Alders. You came into the house. Can you tell me what you remember?"

Riz tried to push himself into a sitting position, and Maggie got behind him to support his back and shoulders. She propped him up against the wall, and his head slumped forwards. "Two … men…" he mumbled. "I think…"

"Would you recognize them again?" Maggie asked.

"Maybe." Riz swallowed, his eyes squeezed tightly shut.

"I've called an ambulance. Wait there while I take a look around, okay."

"I'll help." Riz pushed himself off the wall and swayed sideways precariously as if he was drunk.

"No," Maggie said firmly. "Sit back down now and rest."

Riz looked at her with unfocused eyes, and he blinked. "I'm alright, honest. Just a little dizzy."

She frowned at him. Why did men have to be so difficult? "Rizwan Ahmed. Sit back down, right now!"

"You can't order me, I'm the same rank as you." He stumbled forward, and Maggie grabbed his elbow.

"Got ya." Maggie caught him easily and propped him upright. "Take it slowly. One bump on the head is enough."

She helped him onto his feet, trying not to look at his face scrunched up in concentration. He was so young and fit and full of energy, and she hated seeing him wiped out like this.

"You stay here and look in these boxes, and I'll check out the other rooms." She went to the door and waited until he was kneeling beside the carton closest to him before leaving the room.

There was another bedroom, slightly bigger than the one where she'd discovered Riz unconscious, and a bathroom. The other bedroom also contained a bed and no other furniture, and when she checked out the storage boxes, she felt as if she'd won a jackpot payout in the arcades.

Pills. Rolls of cash. More pills.

She went back into the other room to tell Riz and found him staring at the open doorway, swaying on his feet. "You'll never guess what I found," he said groggily.

"Pills?" Maggie suggested. "Cash?"

Riz managed a half-smile. "Add … a couple of guns … and burner phones."

CHAPTER 21

"How is he?" Rita asked when Maggie returned to the office alone. The paramedics insisted on taking Riz to Scarborough hospital to run some tests and carry out a brain scan.

The uniforms had confiscated the drugs and weapons discovered in the house and taped it off as a crime scene.

"Still joking that he got a bigger bump on his head when he was a kid and slipped over running around the local swimming pool."

Rita smiled and shook her head. That sounded like Riz. He'd have probably preferred to go home, take a couple of paracetamols, and sleep it off so that he could be back in the office the following morning with a sausage butty and a canteen coffee.

Even though they'd discussed the incident on the phone, Rita made Maggie sit down and talk them through what happened, step by step.

"What can you tell us about the men you saw running away?"

"One fits the description of Barry Alders. Stocky, wide neck, average height. The other one was a bit taller, lankier, but unfit you know, like he lived on pasta and doughnuts. He was the one lagging behind."

"You think he was struggling to keep up?" Rita asked. She didn't mention that pasta and doughnuts sounded like her kind of diet.

"Seemed that way." Maggie sipped the coffee she'd picked up on the way in.

"Hey," Richard said, patting his stomach, "skinnier doesn't necessarily mean fitter."

"Did you get a look at his face?" Rita asked, knowing it was a long shot given the distance and the time of day.

"Only his profile. Pale skin, dark hair, dark eyes. Not much to go on, sorry," Maggie said.

It was disappointing, but the image of someone lanky and unfit was niggling away at Rita. The haul from the house was currently being examined by the SOC team, and she was hopeful that it would at least yield some fingerprints they could match up to the IDENT1 database.

She was glad that Riz hadn't been more badly hurt. But she had a more pressing concern – she was running out of time to continue holding Karim without formally charging him.

Rita's phone buzzed, and she picked it up. "DI Gupta."

"My office. Now." The line clicked dead.

Rita stared at the phone, her eyes instinctively narrowing. What did Nicola want now?

"Keep checking CCTV," she told Maggie and Richard. "Our friend Barry Alders doesn't just keep vanishing into thin air."

She sensed her colleagues' exchanging glances behind her back as she left the room. She hoped that they would miss her if the Detective Super wanted her off the case and out of her station.

Nicola was pacing her room when Rita knocked and entered. Her mouth was a thin line, making the older woman appear even stonier and less approachable than normal. A sense of foreboding and anxiety was churning in Rita's guts.

Rita didn't sit down until Nicola stopped and faced her, gripping the back of her seat with white knuckles. Her neck was pink and blotchy. She didn't look well, and Rita wondered if there were some underlying health issues that the woman was taking out on her because they painted her as more of a threat than she actually was. Rita wanted to tell her that she didn't secretly want her job.

"I need you to release Karim Ahmadi," Nicola said, "and drop the search for Barry Alders."

Okay, that was unexpected. Until yesterday, Nicola wasn't even aware that Rita was working on the Sarah Collins case.

"May I ask why, ma'am?" Rita asked.

Nicola sat down heavily, her movements slow and measured like she was trying – and failing – to contain her temper.

Rita said, "You are aware that DC Jaffer was attacked last night, at a private property that Barry Alders had been seen entering shortly."

"Yes, I am well aware of that fact." Nicola inclined her head, avoiding eye contact with the DI sitting opposite her. "Is there an update on his condition?"

It was almost the first time since Rita had arrived in Scarborough that the Detective Super had expressed some emotion regarding a member of her staff. It softened the edges of the conversation, just a little.

"He isn't in any immediate danger," Rita said. "They're keeping him in overnight to monitor his concussion. He suffered quite a blow to the back of his head."

Nicola nodded. She was building up to the crux of the conversation. "The National Crime Agency have been carrying out surveillance on both Karim Ahmadi and Barry Alders. So, I need you to back off."

"They're aware of the OCN?" Rita gaped at her, stunned. She was stalling, buying some time to process the big reveal.

"Barry Alders has been on their radar for some time. They – *we* – think that he must've been tipped off somehow. He recruited Karim a couple of months ago. Small-time dealer. Young lad no one would pay too much attention to. No criminal record. Easier to use someone like Karim to smuggle drugs in and out of Scarborough and lay low for a while."

Rita controlled the anger bubbling up under the surface. "You knew about this, and you didn't think to warn me?"

All that time wasted trying to track down Barry Alders. Karim almost escaping, stowed away on a stranger's yacht in the harbour. The interrogation with that smug Peter Watson getting in his twopence worth of '*my client doesn't need to answer the question*'.

"With all due respect, Detective Inspector, I thought that you were investigating a murder case."

"I was. I *am*." Rita's voice was growing shrill, and she didn't want the Detective Super to have the satisfaction of knowing that she was getting to her.

"Then I suggest that you release Karim Ahmadi and continue the investigation." Nicola's tone was cold, dismissive. She would not tolerate any arguments.

Rita had two choices. She could get up, walk out, and do exactly as she had been warned, or she could get to the bottom of what was really eating the woman and clear the air so that they could both move forward.

"With all due respect, ma'am," she said, mimicking Nicola's words, "but what is your problem?"

The older woman blinked at Rita as if she might be able to rearrange the words and inject them with the respect due her position. Her lips tightened to almost a circle, and her voice dropped dangerously low.

"I beg your pardon?"

"You have made it clear from the moment I arrived, that you don't want me here."

Rita could hardly believe that she was doing this. It might result in her walking away from here without a job to come back to, and the promise of a disciplinary hearing, but now that she had started, the words just kept on coming. "I want to know what I've done to make you dislike me so much."

Nicola's eyes narrowed almost to slits. "I suggest that you walk out of that door, Detective Inspector, think about what you're saying, and carry out my instructions."

Rita rose, gripping the edge of the wide desk. She was not a child to be dismissed so easily; she was a grown woman – they both were – and she was not leaving until the woman spoke to her as an equal. "I never had you down as a coward," she said.

"And I never had you down as a troublemaker." Nicola's cheeks were flushed pink with anger now.

"Didn't you?" Rita spat. "I thought that's exactly what you had me down as. The troublemaker with the haunted past. The woman who couldn't move on until she solved her mother's twenty-seven-year-old murder case."

"Enough, Rita," Nicola said. "I want you to leave."

"Or is it because I'm a senior DI, a little too close to your role for comfort?"

"I said *enough*." Nicola was staring at a spot on the desk like it might open up and swallow Rita whole, save her the inconvenience of explaining her attitude towards the younger woman.

But Rita was on a roll, her voice gathering momentum and growing more spiteful. She knew that she was being unprofessional. She knew that there would be consequences, but she'd learned at a young age that things left unsaid festered inside you until they swelled into something toxic and incurable.

"Or is it because the staff here likes me?" The instant the words left her mouth, Rita crumpled inside along with Nicola's expression. It was a low blow. Did she regret it? Maybe she would later, but right now, she was still waiting for an explanation.

Nicola's chest heaved with the effort of containing her anger. "May I remind you that you are here because I agreed to your sabbatical?"

She spoke slowly, enunciating every word so that there was no room for ambiguity. "I agreed to you working on your mother's case because I felt that it would bring you closure, and I also believed that closure would allow you to become the best version of yourself. Both professionally and personally."

Rita opened her mouth to speak, and Nicola shut her down.

"*Let. Me. Finish*. Despite what you might think, I would encourage any member of my staff to grow. I do not feel threatened by you, especially given the recent display of temper. You still have much to learn, Detective Inspector. Including how not to confuse professionalism with cowardice."

Rita massaged her temples with her fingertips. She had crossed a line. She had acted in anger, had forgotten everything that she had ever learned about dealing with senior members of staff, and she had been put in her place quietly and without judgement. Was it more than she deserved? Quite possibly. Could she argue if Nicola demanded that she return to the Met immediately? Not a chance in hell.

She faced Nicola squarely, unpeeling her fingers from the edge of the desk. "I apologise, ma'am. I crossed a line. I've allowed personal circumstances to interfere with my better judgement. I completely understand if you want me to hand over the case to the rest of the team and return to London."

For several long, painful moments, Nicola eyed Rita up, her expression unfathomable. Finally, she said, "Sit down, Detective Inspector. Too much nervous energy going on there. You're making me feel uncomfortable."

"Sorry, ma'am." Rita sat down.

"The drug dealers are not your concern right now," Nicola continued. "Leave them to the NCA."

"Yes, ma'am."

"Your suspect will remain under surveillance, so you can release him when you leave my office."

"Yes, ma'am." This was it, Rita thought. The dismissal would be next, and there was nothing she could do about it. She would barely even get a chance to say goodbye to Jack, not that he should be her main concern after the things she'd said to her superior.

"I don't want DC Jaffer returning to work until he has been given the all-clear from the hospital."

Was that a note of compassion Rita could hear in her voice? She studied Nicola's face, trying to see the woman behind the role. She pictured her as a mother, nurturing her kids like a mummy duck, a chick tucked under each wing. Or a grandmother even, cuddly and patient, reading books out loud and feeding her grandchildren biscuits and treats behind their mum's back. She couldn't see it. Richard had told her Nicola had never married, and apparently, had no family. That, Rita could believe.

"Agreed, ma'am," Rita said aloud.

"Now, don't you have a killer to find?" Nicola's tone was efficient again, clipped, the glimpse of maternal instinct safely hidden beneath the smart suit and the thin-lipped half-smile. Rita actually thought the woman was looking at her with a new found respect.

Rita stood up and tucked the chair neatly under the desk. She recalled her mother once telling her when she was a little girl that if you left a chair out, it meant that you would be coming back one day.

Without glancing at Nicola, she pulled the chair away from the desk just a fraction, enough to let the superstition go. She'd been given a reprieve, this time. She wasn't about to blow her chances again even if it was only an old wives' tale. She wasn't done with Scarborough yet.

"Yes, ma'am. Thank you."

"One more thing, Rita," Nicola said as Rita reached the door. "Just like you, I want to see Barry Alders behind bars too. But don't let that cloud your judgement in the murder case."

Rita held Nicola's eyes for a few seconds, then the D Super bent her neck to look at the papers on her desk, her usual indication their meeting was over.

CHAPTER 22

Jill Collins seemed flustered when she opened the door to find Rita and Maggie standing outside. A hand flew instantly to her throat like she might catch her breath before it got trapped. Her eyes darted behind the two women as if afraid they'd come mob handed.

"Hello, Mrs Collins," Rita said. "We'd like to have a word with Andy."

"Andy?" The woman appeared to visibly shrink, as she had during their previous meetings.

Rita wondered, not for the first time, how a mother of two children ended up with such little confidence that her go-to stance was to make herself invisible and pray that everything would go away. It fuelled her anger against men like Andy who seemed to prey on the weak. It wouldn't surprise her if he was a bed-hopper, the kind of man who used women for a place to crash until a better offer came along.

"Is he here?" Rita asked.

"No." Jill Collins shook her head, relief oozing from her slumped shoulders. "No, he isn't here."

"Is he working?" Maggie asked. "Can you please tell us where—"

"No!" Jill flinched at the sound of her own voice. "No, he doesn't… He's unemployed at the moment."

So, Rita was right. He was scrounging off Jill, living off whatever benefits she received as a single parent with a council house. Eating her food, drinking the beers she probably picked up for him whenever she passed the corner store. She wanted to ask Jill what *she* got out of it, but she was still allowing the confrontation with Nicola to sink in. She'd got off lightly from that one, but was still reeling, even though she was the one who'd jumped in feet first before engaging her brain.

"Can you tell us where we might find him?" Rita asked.

"I-I don't know."

"He didn't tell you where he was going?" Rita furrowed her brow and immediately tried to smooth out the lines.

"No. Sorry." There it was again: the lack of confidence, accepting the blame for Andy not being there when the cops showed up.

"How long ago did he leave?" Maggie asked.

"Ten minutes." Even Jill's voice had shrunk. "You just missed him."

Rita thanked Mrs Collins, and they headed straight back to the car.

"He can't have got far," Rita said, scanning the estate. She'd half expected to find him on the swings, rocking back and forth, a spliff stuck to his bottom lip. She shook the mental image from her mind.

They found Andy two blocks away, strolling past another squat apartment block that was identical to the one in which Jill lived.

Maggie stopped the car on the side of the road, and both women climbed out.

"Andy," Rita called out to get his attention – he hadn't even glanced around when the car pulled up at the kerb. "Detective Inspector Gupta. We met yesterday."

He flicked the end of a spliff into the scraggly grass behind him and stared at Rita. His bottom lip drooped, she noticed now, giving him a permanent air of bewilderment.

"We'd like you to come along to the station," Rita said.

His head jerked like he was trying to dodge a fly. "What for?"

"We heard about your argument with Sarah shortly before she died."

He sniffed loudly, twisting his nose from side to side, and peered along the street. When he finally faced Rita, his tongue was in his cheek suggestively.

"Dunno what you're talking about." He went to walk away, but Rita stopped him.

"Sarah warned you to stop following her, didn't she, Andy?"

He sucked his top teeth. "Not me. Why would I follow her?"

"That's what we'd like to know." Rita faced him squarely. She couldn't quite read his body language. She didn't think that he was about to bolt – if anything, he was prepared to walk casually away as if they'd just apologized for stopping the wrong person.

"Told ya, I dunno what you're talking about."

"Okay, you can either climb into the back of the car willingly, or we'll arrest you. Your choice."

"You can't arrest me. I ain't done nothing wrong."

"Possession of drugs for starters." Rita glanced pointedly at the dead spliff on the grass. "We'll see what else the DNA swabs reveal."

"DNA swabs. What are you charging me with? You can't arrest me for arguing with the damn kid."

Rita's eyebrows instinctively slid upwards. "Right. That's enough from you."

"In the back of the car." Maggie held the door open and did the honours of placing her hand on his head as he climbed in.

CHAPTER 23

"I think Andy was the other guy who attacked Riz, guv."

Maggie was waiting in line for their coffees in the canteen. She'd even tempted Rita to pick up a couple of apricot pastries and laughed when Rita warned her not to say a word.

"I got the same feeling when you described the men you saw running away from the house."

"He's got some chest," Maggie said.

"Chest?" Rita's mouth twisted to one side while she tried to work out which language her colleague was speaking.

"Front." Maggie tapped her own chest. "Attitude to your oldies."

"Hey, less of the lip." Rita frowned. "I can't work out if it's *chest* or the inability to see any further than the end of his nose."

"Bit of both, I reckon." Maggie paid for the coffees and handed one to Rita.

"I think we should keep an eye on him."

Outside, they sat in the car with their coffee and pastries and waited for Andy to be released after his DNA swabs. They hadn't questioned him. Rita thought that it would do him good to be kept wondering what they had on him while he walked free. Twenty-four hours, and he'd tell himself that it was nothing. He was good to go. He'd continue with whatever shady activities he got up to when other folks were working and congratulate himself on staying one step ahead of the law.

That's when they'd pounce.

Sure enough, it wasn't long before Andy exited the station and headed in the opposite direction from the seafront, giving it the same swagger as earlier, like the world owed him something.

They trailed him from a distance and at a snail's pace, stopping frequently, not that he even glanced over his shoulder to see if he was being followed. When he was close to the estate where Jill lived, instead of heading straight back, Andy veered off towards a high-rise block of flats. He skirted around the back of the building, high fiving a guy in grubby black jeans and a Rolling Stones hoodie along the way.

Maggie pulled up out of sight on the main road. They locked the car and watched Andy from the corner of the building, strolling along a row of garages.

His behaviour altered here. A guy was working on a car outside one of the garages, bonnet raised, head and shoulders invisible as he tinkered with the engine.

Andy kept a safe distance. He didn't acknowledge the guy, who peeped around the car as he walked past. He stopped outside a locked garage, peered left and right, his gaze skimming the corner as the two detectives ducked behind the wall.

Andy disappeared inside, closing the garage door behind him.

"What do you think, guv?" Maggie asked. "Drugs?"

"Something tells me it isn't a sports car that he rolls out for cruising the seafront like a boy racer."

"Nah, bit old for that."

They waited. Thirty minutes later, the guy closed the bonnet of the car he was working on, shifted it back inside a garage, and cut through to the block of flats. No one else came or went.

"You reckon he spends all day here and tells his missus that he's been job hunting?" Maggie shifted her weight from one foot to the other. "I'm getting pins and needles."

"Poor circulation," Rita said. "Try jogging on the spot."

Maggie had barely got the feeling back in her feet when the garage door opened, and Andy reappeared.

As before, he glanced left and right to check that no one was about, before closing and locking the door behind him.

Maggie and Rita ducked behind a communal rubbish dumpster and waited for him to reach the main road before they headed over to the garages.

Rita removed a multi-purpose tool from her pocket and used it to manoeuvre the lock open with an easy click. They raised the door above their heads and peered inside.

Both women froze. Instead of cartons filled with packets of white powder or bottles of pills, the garage was setup like a makeshift film studio. In each corner, umbrella lights – the kind used to create YouTube videos or to record podcasts – were set up on tripods, all aimed towards the centre of the garage space.

In the middle, a mattress had been placed on the floor beneath a tall metal frame that wouldn't have looked out of place in a department store, hung with racks of clothes. Only, when they looked more closely, the frame was on wheels. Handcuffs were attached to the top and bottom rails. Heavy silver chains dangled from above with metal clips attached to the ends. Scattered across the mattress were lengths of rope, rubber contraptions with balls in the middle, gimp masks, and whips.

“What on earth…” Maggie leaned against the wall, and turned her head away from the weird collection, taking deep breaths.

Rita entered the garage and crouched beside the mattress. She’d always thought that she was pretty openminded, but some of the items she saw there made her shudder. Double-ended dildos the girth of her upper arm. Cables with clips attached to a battery. More black leather gimp masks, zipped at the back. Contraptions that looked like harnesses.

She peered up at the frame and tried to imagine its uses. Bile rose in her throat. Did Andy bring Sarah here? Or did he get some poor council estate girls to come and do his films?

Maybe he got his kicks keeping it a secret from his new girlfriend, Jill. Did Sarah find out about it? If she threatened to tell her mum, or report him to the police, it would’ve given him a motive to kill her.

Rita swallowed and dragged her eyes away from the sex toys. She was looking for a video recorder. Those lights weren’t set up because Andy was afraid of the dark. The thought of him videoing this stuff and then going home to Jill and her family made Rita feel nauseous.

She saw a sheet thrown across something pushed up against one wall and tugged it off. Plastic boxes stashed with cellophane wrapped flat rectangular boxes. Putting her gloves on, Rita pulled one out.

Maggie, also wearing gloves now, produced a pen knife and perforated one edge. White powder leaked out.

Drugs. Not to the same extent as the stash found in the house where Riz was attacked, but more than enough to charge Andy Robson with supplying.

Crouching, she spotted something else that raised goosebumps on her arms and legs. At first glance they looked like how-to articles printed off the Internet. Spreading them across the floor with the tip of her radio, she discovered that she wasn't wrong – they were instructions for making snuff movies.

"What's this, guv?" Maggie had come up behind her and was peering over her shoulder. Rita sensed the younger woman's eyes scanning the articles. She heard the click in the back of her throat when she swallowed. "Is this for real? People actually write this stuff?"

"People actually read this stuff too," Rita said. "Or in Andy's case, they print it off and hide it in a locked garage for safekeeping."

Rita went back outside and filled her lungs with fresh air. There was a chemical smell inside the garage that was starting to make her brain cells spin. She called through to the station and gave uniforms the location of the garage. She couldn't wait to hear Andy Robson talk his way out of this one.

*****

Jill appeared even more diminished when she opened the door to the detectives a second time. "What is it?" she asked. "Have you found anything?"

Rita was about to ask how she knew about the garage, when it occurred to her that Jill was referring to her daughter's murder.

"Can we come in?" Rita asked.

The woman nodded and stood aside, opening the door wide.

Rita entered, noticing how gloomy the narrow hallway became with the front door closed, even though the sun had made an appearance today and seemed determined to stay.

"Is Andy here, Mrs Collins?"

Jill's gaze flitted between the two detectives. "No. He… He hasn't been back."

"You haven't seen him since this morning?"

The door to David's bedroom opened, and the boy poked his head out to see what was going on. His hair was mussed up, sticking out at right angles to his head, and his cheeks were still rosy with sleep. "What's up?" he mumbled.

"Nothing, David." Jill seemed torn between staying where she was and ushering her son back inside his room. "It's fine. Go back to bed."

"I'm hungry."

"I'll make you some toast in a bit."

David didn't budge, but his mouth turned down at the corners, his expression turning sulky. "I don't want toast."

"I'll make you something else," Jill said. "A sandwich. I've got cake in the cupboard."

Something in her tone must've got through to the lad, because he glared at the visitors and then shuffled backwards into his room, closing the door behind him.

Jill glanced at Rita and Maggie and then proceeded into the living room, out of earshot of her son. "What's going on?" she asked in a low voice. "Why do you need to speak to Andy?"

"Mrs Collins," Rita said, "have you spoken to Andy since he left this morning?"

"No. He probably won't be back until dinnertime."

No surprises there, Rita thought. "Do you have any idea where we might find him?"

Tears welled in the woman's eyes, and she sucked on her bottom lip. "What's he done?" she whispered.

“Mrs Collins, perhaps you should sit down.” Rita gestured to the sofa.

Jill turned around and obediently sat in one corner of the sofa. When she faced them again, her expression had crumpled.

Rita sat next to Sarah’s mum on the sofa. “Mrs Collins, we followed Andy to a garage earlier, just north of here. Did you know anything about it?”

“A garage? You mean for a car?”

“Yes.” Rita glanced at Maggie. “Only Andy hasn’t been storing a car in the garage. He has been making sex videos.”

“Sex videos?” Jill closed her eyes for a long moment. “You mean porn?” she breathed shakily.

Rita hesitated. The woman had been through enough finding out that her daughter had been murdered, and now this. She wished that she could spare her the sordid details. But, from what little she had seen of Andy so far, the man had no redeeming qualities. Jill Collins had brought him into her home with a teenaged daughter and a young boy, without ever stopping to ask herself if she really knew him.

No one deserved to lose a child. Finding out that your daughter had been murdered… Rita didn’t have kids, but she couldn’t even begin to imagine how any parent could move on from that. It wasn’t how the circle of life was supposed to operate. But what was in this woman's control was her choice of partner. And she'd chosen Andrew Robson.

"No," Rita said gently. "We discovered the kind of materials associated with violent sex. Torture. Bondage. S&M." She paused. "Mrs Collins, I'm sorry to have to ask, but did Andy ever hurt you?" At the confusion passing behind the woman's eyes, she pressed, "Was he violent towards you, Mrs Collins?"

Tears spilled over Jill's bottom lashes. "He hit me one time." Her voice was barely audible over the music coming from the radio in the kitchen. "He apologized after, said that it would never happen again. It was my fault. I pushed him too far, and he lashed out."

"It's never your fault," Rita hardened her tone. "Arguments happen between couples all the time. That is never an excuse for him to hit you. Got that?"

Jill sniffed, wiped her nose, and nodded.

Maggie said, "Mrs Collins, did you report it to the police?"

"What? No." Jill shook her head "It was nothing. A little bruise."

"A little bruise the first time," Maggie said. "Mrs Collins, it is never nothing."

"Did he ever hurt Sarah?" Rita asked.

"What? No." The colour drained from the woman's face. "Oh my God. You think Andy.... he might've killed Sarah?"

Rita and Maggie didn't reply immediately, and that was all the answer Jill needed.

Her shoulders heaved with sobs, and Maggie crouched in front of her, one hand on her shoulder while the tears flowed through Jill's fingers.

CHAPTER 24

Riz smiled widely at Rita and Maggie when they entered his hospital room. He was dressed in jeans and a pale grey sweater that suited his dark skin. "Hey, guv," he said. "You're in time to meet my parents."

Rita greeted Mr and Mrs Jaffer, who were sitting on uncomfortable plastic seats, a look of fear on their faces. Rita nodded at them and said hello. Mrs Jaffer rose and came up to the edge of the bed. She had a kind face, and her black hair was streaked with silver.

"Is my son going to be ok?"

"Yes, he will," Rita said. "Please don't worry. His tests are all ok, and I just spoke to the doctors outside."

"Mum, I'm fine," Riz said, getting slowly out of the bed.

"Where are you going?" Maggie perched on the edge of the bed and helped herself to a grape from a punnet on top of the metal bedside cabinet.

"I've been discharged. Just waiting for the doc to come round and lecture me about taking it easy, then I'm heading home."

"Have they signed you off with concussion?" Rita asked.

"They want to." Riz raised his eyebrows at her. He looked like a kid who'd been told to sit out the next football match.

"You know the rules, Riz," Rita said. "If you're signed off, I can't have you in the office."

"And I thought you'd be on my side."

"She is," Maggie said. "How's your head?"

"Feels like I got hit with a cricket bat, but apart from that I'm fine. Brain scan came back all clear."

"Was it a cricket bat?"

Riz's mum's voice was soft, ethereal almost – it floated around the room, and Rita had the urge to catch it and listen to it whenever she was feeling rattled. She'd bet that the entire family listened to that voice and didn't dare disobey her though. For a tiny woman – Rita could tell that she barely reached five foot – she carried a strong presence that would suffer no arguments.

"We don't know," Rita said. "No weapon was discovered at the property. It was a blunt object that's all we know. But it doesn't matter."

Mrs Jaffer eyed her son from beneath lowered lashes. If she could've chosen his career for him, there was no doubt in Rita's mind that it would've been something slightly less dangerous.

"Your son is a great Detective Constable, Mrs Jaffer," she said. "He followed procedures, which meant that Maggie was able to call an ambulance within minutes of the incident."

"Have you caught the culprit?" Mr Jaffer asked. Rizwan had his eyes, but the rest of him was all his mum.

"Not yet, but we have the names of two suspects. We will catch them, I promise."

She didn't add that the deeper she delved into this case, the more her gut twisted. Something about it had sunk its claws into her, but she was the one holding on tightly, and she wasn't letting go until she'd found Sarah's killer.

*****

Rita and Maggie left Riz with his family in the hospital. Riz was ordered to rest for a few more hours by the doctors, and Rita reinforced it in no uncertain terms.

"But I'm getting bored," Rizwan said, flopping down on the bed.

“Better than passing out at work,” Rita said, and Mrs Jaffer agreed. Grumbling, Rizwan shook his head, aware he was out of options.

Maggie drove the car to Jackie Maynard’s house. Rita heard a beep on her personal phone and pulled it out to see a message from her dad. He had texted her before, to say he would be arriving tonight. This was a confirmation.

Hi Rita. See you later this evening. Love, Dad.

It was oddly emotional reading the words. In her heart of hearts, she had missed not being in touch with him. Well, you could only miss something you once had. And she only had her father’s company fleetingly. Whatever, she thought. She had stopped trying to make sense of her heartache a long time ago. It was better to let it go, then trying to make sense of it and hurting herself more.

Could this be a new beginning between them? Her father had made much more of an effort since he heard of Clara’s death. He asked about her life, stayed in touch. He wasn’t happy she was still in Scarborough, but then he laughed about it as well. Rita wanted to see him. She didn’t know how they would get on – but at least they had a chance at making this work. That gave her a strange, warm glow deep in her chest.

See you soon, Dad. What time do you arrive?

20.05 at Scarborough. Send me your address and I'll see you at home.

She hesitated for a while, then wrote back. *I'll pick you up.*

He protested, but she insisted. They could both be as stubborn as each other, and that made her smile.

Rita focused on the road as Maggie drove to Jackie's house.

A guy stumbled out of the corner store as they got closer, and swayed precariously close to the kerb. He was early- to mid-fifties, Rita guessed, dressed in cargo pants and a baggy T-shirt, but he could easily have passed for twenty years older. His entire body shook violently, his teeth chattering as he passed them by.

A couple of teenaged boys laughed and pointed at him as they entered the shop.

"Shouldn't they be in school?" Maggie asked.

"If I could earn a pound for every kid I caught bunking school, I could retire tomorrow," Rita said.

Maggie grinned at her. "You'd miss it too much, guv. All the excitement, the adrenaline rush of solving a case."

"And the canteen coffee," Rita added.

They crossed the busy street and entered another estate not dissimilar to the one where Sarah lived. All these estates looked the same, Rita thought. She understood that the local council's funding was limited, but people would be a lot happier if they had a home that was distinguishable from everyone else's. A place that felt like theirs.

They located Jackie Maynard's home and Rita knocked on the door. A woman came to the door. She wore a leopard-print top that left little to the imagination, tight jeans, and her hair piled on top of her head in a messy bun. Her makeup was immaculate. She waited for Rita to speak.

Rita produced her warrant card. "Is Jackie in?"

The woman's eyes narrowed. "What's she done?"

"We'd just like to ask her some questions in connection with the murder of her friend, Sarah Collins."

The woman winced. "Shocking that. The poor girl had everything to live for." She peered over her shoulder and yelled, "Jacks! Someone here to see you."

Jackie appeared behind the woman, who was still blocking the doorway. She faltered when she saw Rita and Maggie.

"Jackie, we want to ask you some questions about Karim Ahmadi. May we come in?"

"Aye, we're not doing this out here, not where old Mrs Scott can bog at us." The older woman opened the door wide enough to let them in.

Rita could see the resemblance between them, despite Jackie's lack of makeup and the *Friends* pyjamas that she was wearing – and guessed that they were mother and daughter.

"It's about Sarah, love," her mum added. She led them into the kitchen, directed them to a small four-seater table, and filled the kettle with water from the cold tap.

Jackie sat down first. Her eyes hopped back and forth between the two detectives. She looked tired, Rita thought. There were dark smudges beneath her eyes, and her hair was lank and greasy. Her mum remained standing. She didn't offer the detectives a drink but added a spoonful of coffee and several sweeteners to a mug and waited for the kettle to boil.

"How well do you know Karim Ahmadi?" Rita asked.

"I've seen him around," Jackie said. So, Karim had clearly lied about not knowing Jackie.

"What's this about? I told you all I knew about Sarah."

Rita doubted that – the girls had been friends for years, and Jackie hadn't even given them the name of Sarah's new boyfriend.

“We tried speaking to Karim yesterday,” Maggie said, “but he climbed over the school fence and jumped onto a bus. Why do you think he would run?”

Jackie shrugged. “I barely know the guy.”

She was still holding back, Rita was certain of it, so she pushed a little harder. “We know that you and Sarah hung around with Karim. We also know that Karim is involved with a well-known criminal called Barry Alders.”

“I…” Jackie shot a glance at her mum and shook her head. “I don’t know this Barry guy.”

“You’re not in any trouble, Jackie,” Maggie said gently. “We only want to know where you and Sarah used to hang out with Karim.”

“We didn’t. Not really. It’s like all the kids who hang out at the harbour know each other. Don’t mean we’re besties or nothing.”

“Did Sarah know Barry Alders?” Rita pressed. “Did she ever mention his name?”

“No. I don’t think so.”

“Was Karim Sarah’s new boyfriend?” Rita watched her closely.

Jackie shook her head. “No! Sarah never mentioned her new boyfriend, I already told you.”

The kettle stopped chugging, and Jackie’s mum filled her mug, the aroma of cheap coffee wafting towards the table. She took a sip, leaned back against the counter, and then remembered with a jolt that she had visitors. "Can I get you guys a drink?"

Rita and Maggie both declined.

"So, what's this all about?" Jackie's mum asked. "Who's this guy you're asking about. Is he a suspect?"

"Karim Ahmadi ran away when my colleagues tried to question him, "Rita said. "We're just trying to understand why he didn't want to speak to us."

"Sounds dodgy as hell," the woman said, and Rita suppressed a smile.

"How well did you know Sarah, Mrs Maynard?" she asked.

"Known her since they were at primary school. She was lovely. I hope you find the bastard who killed her and see that he gets what he deserves." She rested a hand on her daughter's shoulder and squeezed.

"We're doing everything that we can to make sure that happens."

Rita knew that Jackie was reluctant to tell them anything else – she sensed the girl praying that they would get up and leave. But she also sensed that her mum would want her to speak up. They might even get more out of her than they had in school, now that the shock of Sarah's death had been processed.

“Did you and Karim ever hang out without Sarah?” she asked. “Just the two of you?”

“No.” Jackie chewed her bottom lip and slumped back in her seat. “No. Karim and Sarah had a thing a while back. Before she was with Matt. Girl code, you know? You don’t hang out with your best friend’s ex.”

That was what Rita had been waiting for. “What about after Matt? Could Sarah have been dating Karim again?”

“Dating?” Jackie’s expression twisted into something ugly. “Boys don’t do dating anymore. They’re only interested in hooking up.”

Rita glanced at Maggie – a nod for her to take over. Jackie was angry about something, and she had a hunch that it revolved around a certain good-looking kid.

“Were you disappointed that Karim was out of bounds, Jackie?” Maggie asked.

Jackie shrugged. “What does it even matter?”

“Do you think that perhaps Sarah knew how you felt about him and kept their relationship a secret because she didn’t want to upset you?”

“I never told her.”

“No,” Maggie said, “but you’d been mates a long while. She must’ve known that you fancied him.”

"Maybe."

It would explain why Karim bolted, Rita thought, if he knew that it would come out that he and Sarah had been seeing each other.

"What else is part of this girl code?" Maggie pressed gently. "Can you think of anything else that Sarah didn't want anyone to know about?"

Jackie wound and unwound the cord from her pyjama bottoms around her finger and refused to make eye contact.

"Jackie, love?" Her mum pulled out the seat next to her and sat down. "Whatever it is, you need to tell the cops."

"It's nothing, Mum."

Mrs Maynard glanced at Rita and sucked in a deep breath before turning back to face her daughter. "This is me you're talking to, Jacks. You can't kid a kidder, you know that."

Jackie rolled her eyes and turned away. Her chest was heaving, and indecision rippled across her face. She chewed her bottom lip.

"Jackie, please," Rita said. "If you know anything that might help us to find Sarah's killer, you must tell us. Is this about Karim?"

"No. It's about The Gathering" Jackie whispered.

CHAPTER 25

A chill ran down Rita's spine. Despite the bland name, she couldn't help think something sinister lay behind it. "Tell me about The Gathering."

Jackie squeezed her eyes shut briefly and swallowed hard. "It was this social media group. I don't know how Sarah found it. She was always reading this moody goth stuff."

"Did you join The Gathering with her?" Rita asked.

"No. It was all a bunch of kids talking about killing themselves, like real depressing stuff. Sarah was on antidepressants. She was always reading stuff that made her feel worse instead of better."

"Did Sarah ever talk about killing herself?" Maggie leaned closer, keeping her voice low.

"Sometimes."

Her mum groaned out loud. "Oh my god, this breaks my heart. Why didn't you tell me?"

"She made me promise not to tell anyone." Jackie wound the cord even tighter around her finger until her fingertip started to turn red. Then she released it.

Her mum sat down beside her and cupped her hands between her own. "You'd better promise me that you didn't join this bloody society."

"I didn't."

"What did Sarah tell you about this group?" Rita asked. Now that Jackie had taken that initial leap of faith, she hoped the information would keep on coming.

"Something about resetting their lives. When the kids got really depressed, they could press the reset button and start their life over."

"Did Sarah know what happened after they pressed this button?"

Jackie shrugged. "I never asked."

Maggie was on her phone, searching for the Gathering.

"Did she ever talk to you about self-harming?" Rita wanted to keep the momentum going.

"Aye, kids used to post pictures of their cuts." Jackie shuddered. "That was when Sarah started up again."

"Had she stopped before she found this group?"

"For a bit. When she was seeing Matt."

"So, the Gathering wasn't about making kids feel better then?" Rita was thinking out loud.

"Nah, it was shit," Jackie said. "She showed me a live video once. A girl recorded setting fire to her arm."

Rita winced. What kind of sickos preyed on that level of vulnerability?

Maggie's face paled. "The kids are encouraged to post this stuff online?" She looked at Rita. "How is this even allowed?"

"There's always ways around this stuff." Jackie dismissed the question. "It was like a test. If they were serious about resetting, they had to prove it."

"By self-harming online." Maggie puffed up her cheeks and released a deep breath.

"Fucking sickos," Mrs Maynard said out loud what they were all thinking.

"Did Sarah ever mention who was in charge of this group?" Rita asked.

"There must be a moderator or administrator," Maggie added. "Someone must oversee the posts and approve anyone who applies."

"I don't know." Jackie shook her head. "I didn't want nothing to do with it."

Her mum pulled her close and hugged her tightly, rubbing her back as if trying to warm her up.

"I can't find it on Facebook, guv," Maggie said. "Nothing like it on the app store either."

"I think you have to be invited by another member," Jackie said. "The link is posted on some encrypted channel like Telegram. That link takes you to a website."

"Who invited Sarah? Did she tell you?" Rita asked. "Was it Karim?"

"She never said. Only said that it was right up her street. Like these other kids understood her."

The problem was this society wasn't being run by kids. It was luring them in with the golden promise of a reset and a new life in which they'd miraculously wake up with no mental health issues. Kids like Sarah who'd been self-harming and taking antidepressants would've lapped it up. The image of Sarah's fatal wounds popped into her head. Rita's immediate reaction had been ritual killing…

"Jackie," she said, her voice low and urgent. "Was there anything of a sexual nature taking place within this Gathering?"

Jackie shook her head. "I don't think so. Sarah wouldn't have been into that kind of crap."

"Did Sarah arrange to meet someone from The Gathering the night she was murdered?"

"I don't know. She never mentioned meeting anyone."

"She wouldn't," Maggie said. "These kids would've been sworn to secrecy."

"That's right," Jackie nodded. "It was like ultra secret."

"Did Sarah ever mention going to the abandoned warehouse near the town centre?"

Rita's thoughts were tumbling over each other. Decrepit old building. No CCTV cameras. Perfect place to gather a bunch of kids looking for a way out. She'd seen the statistics.

Teenage suicide was on the increase, and Jill had mentioned during their first interview that she couldn't get any help from CAMHS for Sarah. These kids were desperate. The idea that someone out there had twisted this desperation into something horrific for their own gratification congealed inside her stomach, and she felt sick.

"Did the other kids ever meet up?" she asked. "You know, to compare stories."

It sounded so gruesome that the words clung to her tongue like semolina. She had the urge to down a bottle of ice-cold water and breathe in the sea air for a while. Even then, she wouldn't be able to erase these images from her mind.

"Not in real life," Jackie said. "Not as far as I know, anyway."

"And Sarah never mentioned anyone by name?"

"No." She hesitated, heat suddenly flooding her cheeks. "She did mention someone called the Keeper.

He might've run the group, I don't know. He told the kids how to manage their mood swings and practice mindfulness. I think the Keeper decides when someone is ready to reset."

"Did Sarah tell you if she was going to reset?"

"No. She wouldn't have told me. It was like the greatest thing that could happen to someone in that group. Anyone would've thought they'd been offered a million quid."

"So, she would've kept it a secret," Rita said. "Did Sarah know who the Keeper was? Did she ever show you a picture?"

"No. The Keeper used an avatar. A stag head with antlers. Creepy if you ask me."

CHAPTER 26

Max Drake rubbed a fingertip across Sarah's photograph on his phone screen. She looked so happy. Her smile was so brilliant. So infectious. Only he knew how deeply vulnerable she was behind that gorgeous smile and those beautiful eyes. She'd allowed him in, and now…

He closed his eyes, tipped his head back, his heart lurching sickeningly. When he opened them again, he hit the delete button on the photo.

The crystal tumbler on his desk was empty, a trace of amber liquid in the bottom. He pulled a bottle of brandy from the bottom drawer, added a splash of liquid to the glass, and knocked it back.

The last time he'd seen Sarah, she'd been buzzing. Brighter than he'd ever seen her before. Like nothing could wipe that smile away ever again. And he'd basked in that irresistible enthusiasm, tasted her all over, told her how beautiful she was, how he never wanted to lose her.

"You won't," she'd whispered to him. Max's heart tightened in regret, making his eyes moist.

"Mum!" The voice was upstairs, almost directly outside the door of his study. "Liam hid my stickers, and he won't tell me where they are."

"Liam!" his wife Marissa yelled from the bottom of the stairs. "Give Damian his stickers back!"

The brandy fuzz was already wearing off. He couldn't risk another shot – he had to take the boys out later.

He followed Damian's footsteps back into his bedroom. For a seven-year-old, he sounded like a baby elephant thumping around the house.

A yell followed shortly after. A bang that sounded like the ceiling falling down. More yells and tears.

Max stared at the ceiling, waiting for the noise to go away. This wasn't how he'd imagined his life would turn out. When he married Marissa, he thought he loved her. He truly did. But it was crazy how quickly that love evaporated when the boys came along.

Marissa stopped loving him when Liam was a baby. She didn't have enough love to go around – it was obvious to everyone who knew them – even though she denied it. She stopped *seeing* her husband.

Whenever she raised her eyes from whatever she was doing with the boys, she either looked straight through him, or settled her gaze somewhere behind his left shoulder. When she spoke to him, it was to complain about something that needed doing in the house or to discuss their next holiday, or decorating the bedroom, or getting new bikes for the boys.

And, yeah, he knew he sounded like the classic neglected husband with a nagging wife, but he'd tried. He really had.

Then Sarah wandered into his life one day and flipped it on its axis.

So young, but so wise. Like she'd experienced more than he could ever hope to experience, had learned that the world didn't always treat people fairly, and had still come out of it filled with sunshine.

But he was part of the problem. He knew that. He made things worse for her, and he was too much of a bloody wimp to do anything about it. She wanted him to leave his family and they could elope together. He couldn't leave because of his boys, he'd told her. He couldn't walk out on them, not while they were so young.

He was too much of a coward to admit to himself that it was more than that. He couldn't abandon this way of life. His beautiful five-bedroom home. His job. His status as a headmaster. He couldn't walk away and start afresh *with* Sarah, because he knew what people would say. He knew what they would think of him.

He made Sarah wait for him, and now she was gone.

Tears filled his eyes when he looked at the next photo of Sarah. He'd taken her to a hotel further up the coast. They'd ordered room service. Champagne. They spent the entire night entwined in each other's arms. It was the first time he'd confessed that he was in love with her, and she'd kissed his lips so tenderly…

Footsteps on the stairs. Max hit the delete button, sending the image – his favourite – spiralling into the ether. He barely managed to slide the phone into the top drawer of his desk before the door opened and his wife Marissa peeped inside.

Her dark eyes scanned the desk, taking in the empty brandy glass partially hidden behind a bottle of water. The open laptop. His tie in a coil on the desk's surface. He was still wearing the suit he'd worn to work that morning. He was surprised that she couldn't hear his heart thumping behind his ribs.

His wife would still be attractive if she smiled occasionally. Instead, her mouth was permanently turned down at the corners, and no amount of rearranging the furniture and buying new cushions could make them turn upwards.

"You haven't even changed," she said. There it was – the disapproval. The disappointment. The unmistakable dislike.

"I've been busy."

She glared at the back of his laptop as if it was the third person in their marriage. "The boys are ready for football practice."

"Okay. Just give me five minutes."

A retort was on the tip of her tongue; he could see it trying to emerge like a crab from its shell, all snappy claws and sharp pincers. "A detective rang earlier. Gupta, she said her name was. Wanted to speak to you."

"W-wanted to speak to me?" His heart stopped. He didn't think it was possible. But it stopped, and now it was trying to escape from his chest like that scene in the movie *Alien* when the creature bursts out of the actor's chest. "Did she say what it was regarding?"

"A murder investigation. A student was murdered, and you never told me about it. Made me feel like a right twat when I had no idea what she was talking about."

"I … yeah … sorry." Could she hear his heartbeat? She never missed a thing – eyes and ears like a hawk. "They asked us to keep it quiet."

"They?" Snap, snap. He could feel Marissa's eyes bore into him like a pair of lasers.

"The detectives. They came to the school yesterday."

She nodded then, like she was giving him the benefit of the doubt. This backing down would manifest itself in other ways; Marissa always had to have the last word, no matter how long she waited to get it in. She'd spend money on a kitchen gadget that they'd never use or book a spa weekend with her friends. But it would come back to bite him somehow.

"I have to attend an NEU meeting tomorrow. In Manchester," he said, surprised at how normal his voice sounded. "I'll probably end up staying overnight."

"Told to keep that one quiet too, were you?" Her eyes became cold deadly bullets as she checked out the desktop one last time and slammed the door behind her.

Breathing heavily, fingers trembling, Max slid the phone back out of the drawer and unlocked it. He got the pin wrong first time. Once he was in, he deleted every image of Sarah, every message they'd ever sent, and then removed her number, even though it had been stored under a different name.

Still shaking, he put the phone back in the drawer and locked it, slipping the key inside the printer flap kept on top of the filing cabinet. He had no proof, but he was certain that Marissa came in here during the day while he was at work, snooping around for evidence that he was cheating on her.

Well, good luck with that one. He wasn't going down without a fight.

CHAPTER 27

"I think we'll call it a day," Rita said to Maggie and Richard.

She stared at the whiteboard. She hadn't released Karim, yet, despite Nicola's warning. She was still hopeful that they'd get some information out of him after a night in the cells.

She'd added Barry Alders and Andrew Robson to the list of suspects. Shola and Henry had just delivered the forensic test results on the stash discovered at Barry's house. There was a DNA match with Andy's DNA. It was highly likely that Andy was one of the two men Maggie had seen running away from the scene of the crime.

Rita studied the names. They already knew that Karim was involved with Barry and the OCN. Did he know Andy also? And if Karim was Sarah's new 'secret' boyfriend, had she been introduced to both men?

Her eyes kept drifting to the list of pornographic torture material confiscated from Andy's garage. Was it connected to Sarah's murder? There'd been no evidence of sexual assault, but Rita didn't trust coincidences, not when it involved a murder investigation.

And who was the Keeper? Someone who enticed vulnerable kids into a closed society where he invited them to share their self-harming and 'reset' their lives, was the kind of sicko who would know all about snuff videos. There was a loop going on there – she just needed to figure out where Sarah slotted into it.

"You look done in, guv," Maggie said.

She'd been quiet since their sordid discovery at the garage. Sarah's case had affected them both, and neither of them wanted to imagine Sarah cuffed to a metal frame inside that garage with its chemical smells and harsh lighting. But she'd been overheard telling Andy to leave her alone. Was murder his revenge for her rejection of his sexual advances?

"I'm fine," Rita said, turning away from the whiteboard.

"Need a lift home, guv?" Richard rose, swinging his car keys around his index finger.

"Not tonight. Thank you." Rita smiled at them both. They all missed Riz's laidback presence, but she wanted him fighting fit when he came back, not flinching every time he moved his head.

She waited until they'd left before tidying her desk and flicking off the lights.

Jack had offered to drive her to the train station. Her dad was arriving on the 20:05 train from Cardiff, and she'd been so caught up in Sarah's case she hadn't devoted any thinking time to his visit. If she was honest, she didn't know how she felt about spending time alone with her father. His presence was an unknown quantity in her life. Something she would have to learn to navigate as she went.

Jack was waiting for her in the carpark, his engine running, windows wound down. "Ready?" he asked.

"As I'll ever be, I guess."

She was grateful when Jack left the windows open, allowing the breeze to filter through the silence in the car. She was even more grateful when he didn't attempt to make small talk.

Funny how they'd drifted straight back into this comfortable way of being around each other with no preamble. It was as if their minds and bodies still subconsciously responded to one another. Like animals attracted by scent. Rita smiled to herself. Jack still smelled good.

"What?" Jack's gaze flitted between Rita and the road ahead. "What's got you smiling?"

Dare she ask? Oh, well, in for a penny… "Do you still use the same aftershave?"

Jack's smile was instantaneous. "You remember it, eh?"

"My nose does."

He laughed then, a deep, warm, mellow sound. "Your nose is playing games, I guess. No, I don't use the same aftershave. Moved on from that." He glanced at her and she nodded, smiling.

Rita unfastened her seatbelt when they pulled up outside the rail station and peered at the people loitering in the entrance. She didn't know what to expect and was shocked when she recognized her father instantly.

He was standing beside a small carryon wearing a smart navy blazer, grey trousers, and a white shirt. He was scrolling through his phone, so she had a moment when it felt as if she had him all to herself, and she felt a rush of indescribable emotion in her chest. He wasn't tall. He had a compact physique, his dark-skinned face framed perfectly by thick, silver-tipped hair. Her first thought was that he would look handsome in a suit and tie.

"Is that your dad?" Jack asked, breaking into her reverie.

"Yes." It was all Rita could manage.

She felt a warm hand on her shoulder. "Look, if you need anything while he's here," Jack said, "give me a call. Anything at all. Bottle of wine. A shoulder to cry on." Rita couldn't help smiling at that. "I mean it, Rita."

"Thanks, Jack."

She climbed out of the car and watched her father's reaction as she approached him. He glanced up from his phone, spotted her, looked away and then did a doubletake. A tentative smile stretched his lips upwards, and it was the same smile she saw in the mirror every morning when she greeted another day. She had his lower face, but her eyes belonged to her mother.

"Rita?" Her father came forward, and they stopped within inches of each other. She didn't know whether to hug him, or kiss him on the cheek…or do nothing at all. But the last option didn't feel right. He solved the problem by leaning forward and pulling her into a gentle, brief embrace before letting her go. He smelled of coconut shampoo and spice, and rather than being repulsed by it, Rita felt as if she had come home. Her heart lurched, and she felt tears well up in her eyes. She blinked them away, glad it was night time.

"Let's go outside and call a cab," she suggested. They walked to the cab station, making small talk.

"Busy day at work?" Jay asked.

"On a case at the moment, so yes." She didn't elaborate more. "How was your journey?"

"It's a long way from Cardiff, as you can imagine. But not bad, to be honest. The train connections were all on time."

They found a cab easily enough, to Rita's relief.

It didn't take them long to get to Rita's two-bedroom flat on North Marine Road, overlooking the sea.

Jay stood in front of the sea view windows of the living room. Rita had kept the lights off so they could see better, and although night was closing in, the blue and white cliffs, and the wide sea between them, was just about visible. To the right, lights glowed on Scarborough Castle's ramparts.

"Nice place you have here," Jay remarked.

"It is. I like it."

Rita made pasta for dinner. She tossed a salad, made some garlic bread, and opened a bottle of white wine. Jay had dumped his case in the spare bedroom, removed his jacket, and insisted on helping her prepare dinner.

He talked about his wife, Anna, and their son, Matt, who was at Uni now. Her half-sibling was a scientist, and she wondered if this was down to something in his mother's genes. Rita had scraped through her science exams at school, but that was as far as her relationship with the subject went. Jay spoke about their home in Wales, his newfound love of football and Cardiff City, Barry Island, and the Welsh coast which, he claimed, you had to yourself if you chose the right spots.

Surprisingly, Rita felt no jealousy towards Jay's new family. There was no bitterness, no anger, no resentment towards her father for abandoning her when she was a little girl. If Jay felt any sense of regret, he was keeping it tucked away. Which made it easier for them to slide into a relationship of sorts, even if there was an invisible barrier between them. It was self-preservation.

They both sat on the floor to eat at the coffee table in the living room. Rita played a Celine Dion album on Spotify and swallowed a mouthful of creamy pasta. She'd never mastered the art of cooking – had never needed to as she lived alone, and Uber Eats was a thing – so pasta had been a safe option.

Now, watching her dad's profile, she wished that she'd made a little more effort. Not that she wanted to impress him, but simply because this was an occasion.

"Your mum loved Celine Dion," Jay said, setting down his fork and swallowing a mouthful of wine.

Rita was shocked that he remembered. "She always played Celine Dion on a Saturday morning," she said. "She would dance around the kitchen, singing along badly, and make me dance with her. I think she knew all the lyrics to every song Celine Dion ever recorded."

Jay smiled. “Your mum always loved to dance. She would dance in the garden, even in the rain. I remember she said that people who didn’t like the rain, didn’t like life.”

“That’s right.” Rita sipped her wine, recalling images of her mum in a long floral skirt and navy and white polka-dot wellies. “She lived in her wellies through the winter.”

“Yes.”

They were both silent for a while. When she looked at him, she knew their minds were filled with memories of Clara.

“Rita.” Jay leaned back against the sofa.

“It’s okay, Dad.” Rita shook her head.

She didn’t want or need an apology. If anything, now that Jay was here in her flat, eating pasta on the floor and listening to these songs, she wanted to draw a line under what happened before. Start with a clean slate. Get to know each other at their own pace.

“I just wanted to say that your mother never deserved what happened to her.” His eyes grew large with tears, and Rita hid behind her glass of wine, blinking furiously. “She was a warm and generous person. A shining star in a world that often seems to thrive on gloom.”

Rita nodded. It filled her with warmth that her father had harboured fond memories of her mum.

“Anna says that some people shine brightly because their time on the planet is too short. They have to light up the people they touch while they have the chance. That’s how I remember Clara.” Emotion clogged his throat and the tip of his nose quivered. He dabbed his eyes with the back of his sleeve.

“Me too.”

Even though she’d seen her mother’s remains, had sifted through the evidence, and jailed her killer, Rita had clung to the happy memories of the two of them together. Laughter and music, baking cupcakes, and playing the sugar game with hot doughnuts on the beach - first one to lick the sugar off their lips loses. She always won, and loved the fact that Clara let her win.

“You look like her, you know,” he said. “She would be so proud of the young woman you’ve become.”

Rita was finding it hard to keep her emotions at bay. Her father was suddenly this warm and strong presence, and she hadn’t thought it possible. After all these years of wondering why he left, why he didn’t want to be her dad, she understood that it had nothing to do with her.

Her parents simply weren’t meant to be together. Maybe she could understand that, and perhaps try to forgive him. But she missed her mother like mad, right now, and always.

“I wish she was here, Dad,” she murmured.

"I know, sweetheart. I know."

CHAPTER 28

Rita arrived early the following morning at the office. Her dad had insisted on getting up when her alarm went off. He even made her a coffee and said that he would buy some healthy breakfast while he was wandering around Scarborough today, dismissing her claims that she couldn't eat breakfast.

"You've never tried the right kind of breakfast."

"There's a right kind of breakfast?"

"Yes. Fruits, cereals, yogurt. No bread or croissants."

She'd enjoyed having someone to chat to over a coffee. Normally, she'd be in work mode from the instant her eyes opened and would remain that way until she climbed into bed at night. She had a feeling her dad would have something to say about that too. The strange thing was she didn't even mind if he did. The strong independent woman was starting to accept that it was nice to have someone looking out for her.

She sat down and sipped her coffee – third cup of the day already; she'd be climbing the walls by lunchtime if she didn't take it easy.

Towards the end of the bottle of wine, Jay had expressed his guilt over not staying in touch with Rita. She'd allowed him to get it off his chest, asked no questions, and it had paved the way for the photo album that he'd brought with him. She'd smiled at the pictures of her half-brother, Aaron, at their caravan holidays and Christmases and birthday dinners. That's what people kept in photo albums, wasn't it? Memories of happy times. Celebrations. Vacations.

Jay hoped that Rita and Aaron might get to know each other in time. "You would like Aaron." He was obviously biased, Rita thought. This was his son they were talking about. But studying the photographs, she had been struck by the young man's attractive features, the intoxicating smile, and the kind eyes.

"I bet he's a heartbreaker," she'd said without thinking.

Her dad had rubbed the stubble on his chin. "Quite the opposite. He has already had his heart broken by a girl he'd been seeing since they were fourteen."

"Fourteen? Wow." For some reason, it made her like her half-brother more, knowing that he was already a little bit damaged.

Then, her dad had produced some worn and crumpled photos of Rita as a baby. She stared at them, mesmerized by the plump face, dark curls, and wide brown eyes. He'd kept them all this time. She pictured him taking them out whenever he was alone, tracing the image with a fingertip, and trying to connect with her telepathically.

"Photos of me?" she'd said, unable to drag her eyes away from them.

"You were such a bonny baby, Rita. Everyone thought so."

She hadn't known what to say. But she'd lain awake in bed, staring at the window, at the eerie glowing moon fading in and out of focus as the clouds drifted past, and taken some comfort from the photos. They were clearly well-worn. Her dad had looked at her smiling face hundreds – possibly thousands – of times over the years, and she had never known.

Until now.

Rita took a deep breath, expanding her diaphragm, and smiled to herself on the exhale. She still had a case to solve. She would enjoy what little time she had with Jay while he was here, and yes, this felt like a new beginning with her father. She felt elated, and oddly emotional every time she thought about it.

As a baby she looked so much like Jay. Like a little Indian girl. That's what Clara used to call her – my little exotic baby. She told Jay that, and they both laughed together.

*****

As she sipped her coffee, and stared out over the sea from the kitchen window, her mind returned to the case. Sarah's troubles were floating in her mind, and she felt she needed to get to know the teenager better.

Placing her phone on the desk, she opened the Instagram app and found Sarah's profile.

Her grid was dark and gloomy, the images ethereal and sometimes ghostly. Scrolling through them, Rita read the quotes:

Skinned knees are easier to fix than a broken heart.

Still holding onto something that will probably never happen.

I was never going to be his first choice.

Life is too short to spend it with people who suck the happiness out of you.

There were images of broken hearts, moonlit rivers with half-submerged boats, girls hugging their knees to their chests with their faces hidden or in shadow.

Rita checked out the names of Sarah's followers, friends, girls from school, all around the same age. Their profiles were different. Brighter. Happier. These girls posted selfies of them posing in front of a mirror getting ready to go out. They had pictures with their friends, heads together, pulling funny faces at the camera.

Pictures taken at the beach, tanned legs exposed, toes buried in the sand. There were posts of them with their families, birthday meals, younger brothers and sisters with balloons and at the arcades along the seafront.

She went back to Sarah's profile and scrolled back to the beginning, when the teenager must've been thirteen or fourteen. The contrast between images was unmistakable. Sarah was fresh-faced, smiling at the camera in most of the images. There were still a few where her eyes were downcast, her expression almost pensive, like she couldn't switch off from the bad thoughts in her head, even for Instagram. But they were mostly the posts of a regular teenager combined with pictures of male pop stars and actors.

It broke Rita's heart to think of the teenager caught up in such a downward spiral of negativity that she couldn't see beyond the grey as she grew older. And her recent social media posts wouldn't have helped. She'd have attracted likeminded followers, probably actively sought them out herself, and they'd have all fed off each other's depression.

Then along came the Keeper with his promise of a reset. She pictured the Keeper as a spider, lurking in their web, waiting for the first hint of movement before they pounced on their victim.

And girls like Sarah were ripe for the picking.

Well, not on her watch. It was too late for Sarah, but Rita knew the Keeper would strike again, and soon.

Maggie and Richard came in together. Maggie was missing Riz, Rita could tell, but she'd bounced back after the shocking revelations of the previous day and tucked straight into a McDonald's breakfast, making the kind of noises most people reserved for a gourmet meal. Oh, to be young again, Rita thought to herself.

Rita, grabbing her coffee, stood in front of the whiteboard. "Bad news. We have to let Karim go today."

Richard unwrapped a sausage and egg sarnie and nodded. "Unless we get something on him today."

"The Detective Super sprung a little bombshell on me yesterday." Rita kept her expression neutral. "The NCA have Karim and Barry Alders under surveillance."

Richard paused with the sarnie in his mouth. He removed it again, eyeing it up like it would be cold before he got to take a bite. "Because Karim and Barry can lead them to the top boys of the OCN?"

"Got it in one," Rita said. "We're to back off and let them do their job."

"Even with Barry Alders, guv?" Maggie asked.

"Yes. Have uniforms managed to track him down yet?"

"Not a peep," Richard said. "Traffic is still scouring CCTV in all the local cities: Sheffield, York, Leeds. They're monitoring Whitby, Bridlington and Wetherby too. The last three are smaller, as you know, so should be easier. Less CCTV though, and still no sign."

"What about the car?"

"Must be off-road. Hasn't been picked up anywhere."

"He must suspect we've picked up Karim," Rita said. "Any news on Andy Robson?"

"I'll call Sarah's mother now, guv." Maggie wiped her hands on a tissue and picked up her phone. "Morning, Mrs Collins," she said brightly. "This is DC Long. We spoke to you yesterday about Andy." Pause. "Has Andy been back since we last spoke?" Maggie covered the phone with her hand and shook her head at Rita.

"Richard," Rita said, "I want a patrol car stationed outside the Collins home. Andy won't stay away for good. When he comes back, I don't want him taking out his temper on Mrs Collins and her son."

Rita sat back down. She had a feeling that Barry and Andy had gone into hiding together. Unless Andy had returned to the garage later in the evening and discovered that his nasty little secret had been confiscated, she didn't think that a DNA swab would've driven him to hole up somewhere safe.

Which meant that he'd stayed in touch with Barry and knew that Karim was off the radar.

"Karim's lawyer is here, guv," Maggie said, putting down her phone.

Richard swallowed a large mouthful of breakfast and tossed the packaging into the bin under his desk. "Last Chance Saloon." He grabbed his phone and stood up.

"Is that from a movie?" Rita asked, following him to the door, the sound of Maggie's chuckles chasing them to the corridor.

"I've no idea." Richard shrugged. "Something my grandad used to say."

"You know Maggie keeps a tally of all your old-fashioned sayings?"

"She doesn't." Richard's eyebrows practically met in the middle. "Does she?"

Rita gave him a sideways smile but didn't put him out of his misery. The banter was what kept them going, after all.

*****

Karim and the duty solicitor were waiting for them when they entered the interview room.

The boy looked more dishevelled this morning, his hair flopping into his eyes. There were dark circles under his eyes that had been there the day before but were more pronounced now that he was so obviously out of his comfort zone. He was still a good-looking lad though. Did he revel in knowing that Sarah and Jackie were both attracted to him, using it to his advantage? Or was he that rare breed of young lad who only had eyes for one girl?

Either way, the arrogance had evaporated overnight.

"Those cells are not quite the local Premier Inn, are they?" Rita said, sitting down opposite Karim.

Peter, on the other hand, was as primped as he had been the previous day, the smell of his overbearing aftershave almost cloying in the cramped room.

Rita started the recording and studied the young lad sitting across the table. There was only one way she was going to get through to him, and that was via Sarah, but if she could sow the seeds of his future destroyed by drugs and prison sentences, she had to at least try.

"What sort of life do you think you'll have, Karim, with a police record following you around?"

"You haven't charged me with anything." Karim sat up straighter. Peter Watson's lips twitched at the corners.

“Yet,” Rita said. “Your parents were disappointed when I spoke to them.”

Karim’s eyes flashed her way. For all the bravado, she’d bet a month’s wages that he was the politest, most obedient kid at home. She could even picture him helping his mum prepare food for family gatherings, scrubbed up nice and clean in a new designer shirt and a pair of smart jeans.

“They’re worried about you getting in with the wrong crowd.”

He sat back and wiped his nose with the back of his hand.

“Do you have evidence to support this claim?” Peter stepped in.

Rita ignored him. Instead, she pulled her phone out of her pocket and unlocked it. “DI Gupta is opening the Instagram app on her phone,” she said out loud, “to show the suspect photographs of the victim.”

Karim glanced at the tape recording as if waiting for it to reply in a mechanical voice.

Locating Sarah’s profile, Rita scrolled back to the earliest photos, the ones in which Sarah still looked happy. “Have you seen these images before?”

Karim sat forward and studied the posts, his eyes flickering across the screen. He shook his head.

“Please answer for the recording,” Rita said.

"Nah."

"But you recognize Sarah Collins."

Karim didn't say anything, and Rita thought he was on the verge of coming out with another *No Comment.* But he changed his mind. The light had gone from his eyes. He stared down desolately. Rita knew how hard a night in an uncomfortable cell bed could be. Clearly, Karim had been thinking while he was lying awake.

When he spoke, it was an almost inaudible whisper. "Yeah."

Rita leaned forward, and she felt Richard stir next to her. This was a big moment. Karim was changing his story. He had previously denied knowing Sarah.

"Can you speak up, please?"

"I said, yeah, I do recognise her."

Peter sat stiffly, his face not giving anything away. Rita said, "So you did know Sarah Collins, the victim?"

"Yes," Karim sighed, and rubbed his forehead.

"Was she your girlfriend?"

Karim's Adam's apple bobbed up and down slowly. "Yes."

"When did you last see her?"

"A couple of weeks, if not more. She had this new bloke. We had drifted apart, anyway."

"Who was this new bloke?"

"I don't know."

Rita was silent for a while. Karim's attitude had shifted. His face hung down, and his spine sagged on the chair. When he looked at her, she didn't see defiance any more, only defeat.

She pushed her phone with the social media photos under his nose.

"Sarah looks so happy here," Rita continued. "Do you think it's fair that she died the way she did?"

Karim shook his head again, and muttered, "Nah."

"Compare those images to Sarah's most recent posts." Rita scrolled through the profile, the photos growing darker, gloomier, the higher she went. "What happened to her, Karim?"

She waited for Peter to intervene, but he didn't move.

Karim hung his head, massaging his temples with the palms of his hands. Finally, he looked at Rita with moist eyes. "She had these really bad mood swings. They were uncontrollable. When she was like that … there was no talking to her."

"Was this when you were seeing each other?" She almost said dating but stopped herself, remembering Jackie's reaction to the term.

"Yeah, for a while."

"Why did you stop seeing her?"

"A month ago, or maybe six weeks. I couldn't deal with that shit." Karim flinched. "The moods. She wouldn't listen to anything I said when she was on a downer. Just acted like she'd lost the will to live."

"Did Sarah ever talk to you about killing herself?" Rita pressed.

"In passing."

"How do you mention killing yourself in passing?" Richard asked.

Karim glared at him. "She didn't say it like, 'I want to kill myself.' She just said she understood why people did it."

Rita leaned closer. "Did she tell you why?"

"She blamed it on life. School. Peer pressure. Parents."

"How was her relationship with her mum?"

"I dunno. She never spoke about it." His entire body caved back into the seat. "Some people are sad, and there's nothing you can do about it. But it drags you down, man."

"Did Sarah do drugs?" Rita asked.

"Sometimes."

"Did she buy them from you?"

"He's already answered that question," Peter said.

"Yeah. Sold 'em for me too," Karim said, ignoring the solicitor. Rita gave Peter a sweet smile. She might as well have taken off her shoe, and hit him on the head with it. He stared ahead, his nostrils flaring. Rita turned back to Karim.

"Who was Sarah seeing before she died?"

"Dunno. Someone outside of school. Never saw her with anyone."

"Did she mention a name?"

"Nah, I didn't ask. None of my business."

Rita gave it one final push. "Did she ever mention the Keeper?"

"The Keeper? Like in goalkeeper?" Karim scrunched up his face, confused.

"Yes, that was his name. He was the leader of a secret society called the Gathering?"

"What's that? Like a gang or something?"

"No, like in a secret online society."

Peter's eyes darted back and forth between Rita and his client. He was psyching himself up to step in and shut the line of questioning down if it showed signs of taking Karim down a sordid rabbit-hole he might not climb back out of.

Karim shook his head. “Nah, never heard of it.”

Rita believed him, which meant that they were still no closer to finding Sarah’s new boyfriend.

CHAPTER 29

The Keeper released a steady stream of cigarette smoke through the lowered window of his car and watched it drift lazily up towards the sky. What a superpower that would be, to dissipate like that, mingle with the air, only to reappear elsewhere. Oh, the things he could do if he was made of air. The people he could follow without even a whisper of movement or a hint of body odour.

True, he was adept at making himself invisible. Take right now, for instance. He was sitting in his car, parked under a tree opposite the police station, and not a single soul had noticed him. It was a skill. Something he'd learned at a young age when he managed to slip through the cracks of his caregivers' attention and that of the teachers at school.

Once you'd mastered becoming invisible, the rest was easy.

People were so careless. With their belongings, with the people they loved, with information. But mostly with secrets. They spouted stuff without a second thought as to who might be listening, never for a moment thinking that it might just be their undoing.

That's where he stepped in. He taught kids how to hold on tight to their secrets. When he alerted them to the dangers of revealing their innermost thoughts and desires, they understood how much they needed him. They understood that he was their saviour. That, without him, they were nothing.

He smiled to himself.

The power he experienced, knowing that he was everything to his followers was such a dopamine rush, he felt as if he was flying even when he was sitting there in his car. The invisible man.

No. The invisible *hero* to those who'd been touched by him. His mentor and guide, Robert McFarlane, had taught him that. Gain their trust. Become their emotional crutch. Then you can do with them as you like.

The station door opened and Karim stepped out into the sunshine, turning his face to the sky briefly. The Keeper flicked his cigarette butt onto the grass and slid his phone from his pocket. He snapped a picture of the kid standing on the top step of the police station, tasting freedom on his tongue and through his pores.

The Keeper didn't care about him. The boy didn't know about Sarah and the Keeper. It was a secret, one that Sarah had been only too obliging to keep sacred. She'd been desperate for her reset – there was no way she would ever have let the Keeper down by mentioning him to anyone.

As Karim walked away from the station, the Keeper, head down, checked his website. So many posts and comments about the photos of Sarah's body had appeared now. He scrolled through them, soaking up the comments and the positive energy flowing from his followers. As expected, everyone was enthralled. The live videos that he encouraged them to upload were nothing compared to this. To Sarah's reset.

The Keeper could barely contain his excitement as he commented on every post, asking his followers who else wanted to discover freedom.

Who is brave enough to be rekindled?

He sat back and revelled in the flurry of comments appearing in response to his question.

Me!

I do!

Please choose me next. I can't cope if you don't reset me now!

He licked his lips and read every single reaction. He'd always known that he was special, and now, here was the proof. These kids wanted his help. They were *begging* for his help. They knew the doctors and counsellors and psychologists could do nothing for them. He'd offered them a lifeline, and they'd snatched at it like hungry birds.

Salvation will be coming to one of you very soon, he typed. *Who will it be?*

He imagined his followers crying over his teasing replies. They all wanted to be next, and the power was in his hands. But he was going to keep them waiting a little longer. He was enjoying watching his society grow too much. The more followers he gathered, the tougher the decision, but when he chose his next victim, he would know that the time was right.

Besides, he needed time to savour Sarah's reset. To relive the moment when he had killed her, setting her free from her demons.

He'd seen the fear in her eyes in that final moment, but that was the biggest demon. Fear. Knowing that he had released her from its terrible grip, that she was at peace now, gave him the level of satisfaction that no one else on earth would ever understand.

A glimmer of movement caught his eye, and he peered through the window at the station entrance. Rita was leaving. Alone.

Just for a moment, she belonged to him. He studied her smooth dark skin, her huge brown eyes, the silky black hair. He wondered how it would feel to have her hair pouring through his fingers. To be close enough to breathe in the scent of her. She was nothing like Sarah. But something about her aroused him in a totally different way. He could almost feel her beneath him, feel the thrust of her hips as she struggled to get away from him, and the despair when she realized that it was too late. That his power was all-consuming.

What demons would leave DI Rita Gupta when she was reset?

Maybe she should be next?

His followers would be disappointed, but what better way to keep them hanging on than to reset someone who didn't even know she needed a way out? It would be his proof to his followers that he only chose the most deserving. That freedom would come to those he deemed most worthy.

Rita crossed the street without a glance in his direction. She was preoccupied, speaking into her phone. She barely glanced up in time to avoid a pedestrian walking in the opposite direction.

The Keeper climbed out of his car and closed the door with a gentle click. Rita didn't peer behind her. She was walking at a steady pace. The fact that she was alone told the Keeper that she was taking a brief respite from work, time out to make a personal call.

He followed, moving behind the trees separating him from the pavement and the road. She stopped and stared at the station as if the person on the other end of the call had asked her when she would be finishing work.

The Keeper seized the opportunity and moved closer, ducking behind a wide tree trunk. He was close enough to see her seductive black eyelashes when she showed him her profile. Her high cheekbones. Her smooth jaw. He could almost feel his grip tightening around her throat and realized that his fist was clenched.

"I'd have picked stuff up for dinner, Dad." Rita smiled into the phone.

She'd stopped so close to the Keeper's hiding place that a thrill travelled the length of his spine. He could see her, and she was oblivious.

"Okay," she said. "Thanks, Dad. I'll see you later."

He watched her walk back to the station. Concentrated on her swaying hips, the gentle movement of her ponytail with each step, the confident set of her jaw, meeting the world face on.

She'd said 'Dad' on the phone. She'd said that she would've picked stuff up for dinner. Was she seeing her father tonight? Did he live here in Scarborough?

Oh, this was just too perfect.

Hadn't she destroyed the only family that the Keeper had left? Robert McFarlane, his mentor, would spend the rest of his life languishing in prison because of DI Rita Gupta. Because she figured out the Master had murdered her mother. She'd tried to destroy the Brotherhood. She had ruined Lord Northallerton.

But the Keeper was still there. And she had just played straight into his hands. How did the idiom go: an eye for an eye, a tooth for a tooth? Rita Gupta stole his family. What better revenge than for him to steal her family, show her how it felt to be left all alone before he offered her the freedom of being reset?

Perhaps he wouldn't offer her freedom after all. He would wait and see.

Rita, and her dad's, time would come soon enough.

CHAPTER 30

Back at the station, Rita asked Maggie if she was any closer to locating the Gathering that Jackie had told them about.

"Nothing, guv." Maggie puffed up her cheeks. "I reckon it must be called something else online. Maybe the Gathering is like a codename between the members."

"Did forensics find any of Sarah's personal belongings near the warehouse?" If they had Sarah's phone, they could trace her communication with the society, and ultimately with the Keeper.

"Nothing, guv," Richard said. "Place was cleared out. The killer knew what they were doing."

Rita's phone rang and she felt a tiny frisson of excitement when she saw Jack's name on the caller ID. She felt buoyed having her dad and Jack back in her life, like she was floating six inches above the ground, even if they weren't going to stick around permanently. They were there. They'd given her a taste of how it felt to have someone standing right behind her, holding her up when her knees buckled.

"Jack?" she answered, swivelling her chair away from Richard and Maggie and facing the whiteboard.

"How was last night with your dad?"

"Fine."

"Fine?" She could hear the smile in Jack's voice. "Is that all I'm getting?"

"It was … better than I expected."

"I guess you can't talk right now." Jack was intuitive, she had to give him that.

"That's right. I'll chat to you about that later. But it was good."

"I'm glad. Any developments on the case?"

"Karim was released a short while ago." She didn't mention the NCA. With no evidence to charge Karim, she didn't need Jack's services as go-between with the CPS. "The other two suspects have gone into hiding. Traffic is still trying to trace a rental car hired under a fake licence. On a brighter note, Rizwan has been released from hospital."

"Glad to hear it. Where did the attack happen?"

Rita told Jack what she knew of the estate and its proximity to the industrial park. "Riz and Maggie traced the rental car to the property, caught one of the suspects entering. The SOC team matched the second suspect's DNA to samples taken from the same house."

"Hmm..." Rita could almost hear Jack's brain cells working around like the cogs of an old grandfather clock. "Did you check out the canals?"

"The canals?"

"Scalby Beck's not far from the old industrial park. A lot of the warehouses are empty now since the new park opened, but the canals are still busy."

Of course! Why didn't she think of that sooner? Uniforms have been checking roads, railways, and ferries, but it didn't even clock onto her that there was a far gentler and more sophisticated means of travel out of Scarborough. Probably because she associated the canals with older folks looking for a peaceful retirement away from the hustle and bustle of the towns and cities.

"Jack, you're a genius. Gotta go." She ended the call and turned to Richard.

"We need to search the canals around the house where Riz was assaulted."

Richard understood immediately, a flash of excitement spreading across his face. "On it, guv."

Rita dashed upstairs to the Traffic team and asked them to check CCTV by the canals. She stood behind a young officer with tousled sandy hair and black-rimmed spectacles, and studied his computer screen as he navigated the cameras around the canal banks.

The old Scarborough to Whitby railway shut down back in the sixties, but people still liked to cycle the old route, taking photographs of the abandoned station houses and railway buildings. The canals ran alongside the railway lines – that's how the Victorian railway engineers had designed England's railway tracks.

The officer didn't speak. Rita knew how unnerving it could be having someone breathing over your shoulder, but he worked calmly and methodically until he picked up on movement. He zoomed in. Rita's pulse sped up.

"That's it," she said, pointing to the grainy image of a dark coloured Ford. "Where's it going?"

The officer panned the camera across and followed the Focus's short journey through the entrance of a derelict building. "Old rail yard," he said. "They're all along the canal banks. That's as far as I can go."

Rita studied the footage for a couple of minutes. Barry went there to hide the car, which meant that he either abandoned it and left on foot, or, as Jack suggested, he travelled by water.

"Time on the footage?" she asked.

"18:34 yesterday. I'll print off the report and fire it through to you."

“Thanks. Can you keep watching and let me know if it moves?” Rita was already heading for the door.

She had a feeling that the car was still there. There’d been no trace of it in Scarborough or anywhere else in Yorkshire for that matter. Barry Alders knew exactly what he was doing when he abandoned it in a derelict railyard. He didn’t even need to come back for it – the car was rented under a fake name. By the time the rental agency contacted the police and traced it back to him when the car wasn’t returned, he’d be long gone.

“Traffic located the Focus,” she told Maggie and Richard back in the office. “Left at a derelict railyard, early yesterday evening.”

“Adds up,” Richard said. He had the look of an excited school kid. “Barry Alders owns a canal boat under one of his aliases.”

Rita didn’t waste time. “In that case, let’s go find it.”

CHAPTER 31

Rita, Richard, and Maggie took a team of uniforms to the derelict railyard. The Focus was still there, looking out of place with the decrepit boarded-up building as its backdrop like it was trying to make an artistic statement.

Having checked out a map of the canal routes around the area, Rita guessed that Barry would've made it difficult for them to locate his boat. He'd been one step ahead of them so far, and he had a whole night on them. But thirty minutes later, spread out along the canal paths in various directions, an officer gave the signal via radio that he'd found the boat. Hidden in plain sight.

"He's got some chest," Rita said, and Maggie smiled. "There's a reason he's hanging around."

The foliage surrounding the canal paths was dense and overgrown. In sections, it was virtually impossible to see the water unless you waded through the nettles and brush. But it meant that the team could reconvene close to the boat under shelter of the trees and bushes heavy with berries and weighted down with trailing ivy and sticky-willy.

Rita crouched low as she moved, following behind a uniformed sergeant. Sweat budded in her forehead and stung her eyes. Her legs felt the burn as she stopped often, crouching and checking around her to make sure they weren't spotted. Finally, they came up to the house boat.

There was no sign of Barry, but the engine was purring. The boat was painted sky-blue, the sunshine-yellow curtains pulled across the windows. Not the kind of home Rita would associate with a well-known criminal. Which, she guessed, was the point. It looked in good nick. The small decking area at the front of the boat was clean, the rope securing the vessel to one of the many moorings along the route. A gull circled overhead, and she caught a glimpse of the peaceful life canal boat owners must strive for. Lazy days. Unhurried journeys. No traffic or pollution or noise.

Barry appeared from inside the cabin, scratching his balls, a cigarette in the corner of his mouth. He gave the canal path a cursory glance left and right. Confident that he was alone, he untethered the rope and went back inside.

Was he alone? It didn't matter. Regardless of his company, Barry needed to be behind bars, before the boat moved further from the bank,

Rita gave the signal.

Four officers climbed aboard as the boat began to drift lazily away from the bank, the first man on, offering a helping hand to the others, and tossing the rope to Richard. He worked quickly, looping the rope round and around the post before it grew taut, fumbling with the knot.

Rita's breathing grew shallow, her pulse gathering speed, adrenaline surging through her veins. She heard a yell from inside the cabin. "Barry Alders, you're—" The voice faded.

Thumping sounds followed. Footsteps. The target was trying to escape.

Without second-guessing herself, Rita ran towards the bank and leapt onto the deck, catching her back foot on the safety rail, and tumbling into a roll to break her fall. She silently thanked her PE teacher from high school for recognizing, and encouraging, her athletics abilities. She was good at long jump.

She was back on her feet in an instant, ignoring the ache in her right shoulder from where she landed. Before she could enter the cabin, she heard a sound from above and peered up. Barry was on the roof. He must've climbed out of a window to escape the police officers, and now he stood there, both arms windmilling like he was walking a tightrope rather than a solid expanse of cabin. Behind him, an officer hauled himself through the same window and clambered onto his hands and knees.

Barry spotted Rita on the decking. He was weighing up his options – the cop behind him, or the DI blocking the deck.

Water, Rita thought. He was going to jump.

She didn't waste a beat. The cabin was low enough that she could swing herself up without needing a prop, and she'd maintained her core upper body strength over the years.

She'd caught Barry by surprise. That was her initial thought as she pushed herself upright. But it was too late. He moved towards the edge of the roof, taking his chances with Rita rather than the cop who was already on his feet and running towards him.

Rita lunged at the same time as he raised his arms to dive headfirst into the water. Wrapping both arms around his ankles, she wrestled him to the floor, knocking him sideways as she threw all her weight behind the move. The officer had been joined by a colleague, and both men pinned Barry's arms behind his back, clipping handcuffs around his wrists before he could wrench them free.

Panting and breathless, Rita stood over him. She wiped sweat from her forehead.

"Barry Alders, you're under arrest for the assault of a police officer, possession of drugs, and possession of illegal firearms. You have the right to remain silent. Anything you say can and will be used against you in a court of law."

Barry glared at her while she read him his rights. One officer had his knee in the small of Barry's back, waiting for the signal to move the suspect.

"Where is Andy Robson?" Rita asked.

No response. That's how he wanted to play it.

"Did you kill Sarah Collins?"

Rita caught the flicker of his eyelids, but still nothing.

"Do you know who killed Sarah Collins?" she pressed. "Was it Andy Robson? Karim Ahmadi? Someone else from the organized crime network that you're involved with?"

Rita knew that she wasn't going to get anything out of him, but she had one final question. She wanted to gauge his reaction because, despite his silence, she believed that he at least knew Sarah through Karim or Andy.

"Who is the Keeper?"

The furrowed eyebrows, and confused expression didn't give her any insight into his thoughts.

CHAPTER 32

"I warned you not to interfere." Nicola's voice was like ice crawling down Rita's spine. Rita had been summoned to Nicola's office the moment she returned to the station.

"With all due respect, ma'am," you told me that you wanted to see Barry Alders behind bars after the attack on DC Jaffer."

The Detective Super had said that hadn't she? Rita's recollections of their previous conversation – *altercation?* – was hazy, blurred by the fine red mist of anger and frustration.

"*When* the NCA have sufficient evidence to take him down for a long time. I didn't expect you to completely disregard my orders and bring the man into custody in *my* station less than twenty-four hours later."

"Perhaps you should've been more explicit with your orders." Rita winced, regretting the words the instant they left her mouth and hung in the air between them. Insubordination would lead to a written warning at the very least.

A sinister smile tugged Nicola's lips upwards at the corners. It was not a smile that expected or required to be reciprocated. “Release Barry Alders from custody. Is that explicit enough for you, DI Gupta?”

Rita finally realized how close she was to pushing her luck with the Detective Superintendent. She’d already crossed a dangerously thin line at their previous meeting – she wouldn’t get a third chance.

“Barry Alders attacked a member of my team.” She kept her tone calm and steady, despite the trembling in her arms and her clenched fists, which, thankfully, Nicola couldn’t see from behind her desk.

“He is working with Sarah Collins’ stepdad, Andy Robson. Yesterday, we confiscated evidence of violent sexual activities – including the making of snuff videos – from a garage used by Mr Robson. I have a duty to the family of the murder victim, to bring the killer to justice, and I will not release him without interrogation.”

“Do you have any idea of the resources currently employed by the NCA, DI Gupta?”

“I think so, ma’am.”

“Then I don’t need to remind you that when they want us to back off, we *back off*.” Nicola’s eyes narrowed.

Rita got it, Nicola was getting hassle from above, but this was her murder investigation, and Barry Alders was a key suspect. She wasn’t backing down on this one, even if it made her position precarious. She didn't only owe it to Sarah and her family, but to all the other sad, depressed kids out there.

"I intend to question the suspect first," Rita said firmly. She rose from her seat.

"Sit down, DI Gupta." Nicola gripped the edge of her desk. When Rita didn't move, she repeated, her voice shrill, "*Sit down!*"

Rita sat down. "I need to find—"

"Listen to me, Rita," Nicola ground out, her jaw clenched, using her first name. She thrust a finger at Rita.

"I covered for you with Karim Ahmadi, against my better judgement, and do you know what it got me? It got me an earful of reminders of my role within the police department, and a warning that no one is indispensable. No one. Do you understand?"

"Yes, ma'am." Rita could only begin to imagine.

"I do not want a repeat performance. In fact, I would go out on a limb here and say that a repeat performance will have serious repercussions for you. Do I make myself clear?"

"Crystal, ma'am."

"Barry Alders' presence in my station will have serious consequences for the NCA's case. So, I'm going to wash my hands of them and pass them over to you. Let's see you convince them that *your* case is more important than *theirs*, because that's what it boils down to. You have placed your own needs above those of the NCA's surveillance team, and even when you release their target, it will set them back by God only knows how long."

Rita understood. Men like Barry Alders knew how to fly under the radar. They had connections. It was how they managed to avoid being caught whilst flaunting their criminal activities in plain sight of the cops. The NCA was hoping by watching Barry, they could get sight of Barry's connection to the top boys of the OCN.

"I'm sorry, ma'am," Rita said, "but, his involvement with the OCN aside, I suspect that Barry Alders has information relevant to my investigation. I intend to find Andy Robson with his help, and I will explain this to the NCA. Then, I intend to charge him with the assault of a member of my team."

"Oh, you *intend*, do you?" Nicola's face twisted into an ugly expression. "For your information, DI Gupta, your charges will go nowhere."

"But we—"

"The house your colleague broke into – it isn't in Barry's name."

Rita felt the colour draining from her face. Her head started swimming, and she dug her nails into the palm of her hand to keep her focused.

"The house is rented to council tenants. It's all above board, of course. The housing department has the application to prove that the house is allocated to a Mr and Mrs Jones."

Original, Rita thought, sensing the discussion once again slipping through her fingers.

"The OCN pays the 'tenants'—" Nicola made speech marks in the air with her fingers "—to use the house as a cuckoo nest for their drugs and weapons. The Joneses earn enough to scuttle back to wherever they came from, no doubt under another alias, and everyone is happy. The council gets their money each month. Barry Alders uses it as a drop-off point. And the only people with any connection to the property are a couple who don't even exist, at least in the eyes of the law and as a married couple in need of a roof over their heads."

So, there was no evidence to connect Barry Alders to the assault on Riz. He was attacked from behind and rendered unconscious while the perps made their escape, and Maggie's description, witnessed in the fading light from a distance, wouldn't be enough to convict him. Maggie didn't even get a good look at his face. Even if they traced the Joneses, there would be no evidence to connect Barry to the property.

"I still want to question him over the murder of Sarah Collins," Rita said.

"On what grounds?"

"DNA taken from the property was a match for Andy Robson's DNA sample. Barry Alders knows the whereabouts of my main suspect."

"You have no evidence that Barry Alders was ever at the property."

Rita swallowed. "He was captured entering the house on CCTV. The Ford Focus he rented under a fake name…" she winced, realizing this was another dead end. "The rental car was seen parked directly outside the property when Barry Alders went inside."

"You see my problem with this interrogation, don't you, DI Gupta?"

"Yes, ma'am. But I need to find Andy Robson."

"You have one hour, DI Gupta."

Nicola's chair rocked forward, and Rita had a vision of the Detective Super flying across the desk and hitting the opposite wall with her legs in the air like an upturned beetle. She quashed the image and chewed her bottom lip. A hint of amusement now and she'd be hauled in front of a disciplinary committee before she could blink.

"I will personally listen to the recording, and if I hear a whisper of drugs and firearms, I will have you back on a train down to London before nightfall. Do you understand?" she gritted out the last three words.

"Yes, ma'am." Rita rose a second time.

“DI Gupta,” Nicola said, claiming her attention. “I let our conversation go yesterday. I am this close to breaking point.” She pinched her thumb and forefinger together to demonstrate.

“Yes, ma’am.” One hour. She might as well have nothing – but it was the only chance she had to get Barry Alders to talk.

CHAPTER 33

Barry Alders had the same air of arrogance as Andy Robson. He had pale beady eyes that fixated on Rita when she walked into the interview room with Richard but missed nothing, and plump cheeks scarred from teenage acne. Rita's spine tensed when she saw Peter Watson, the duty solicitor, sitting next to him. Rita sat down, and spoke on the machine, introducing everyone.

"Where is Andy Robson?" Rita got straight to the point, once the tape was running.

A smirk danced across Barry's features. "No comment."

"What do you know about Sarah Collins, the teenager who was murdered earlier in the week?"

Barry's forehead contracted, and a shadow passed over his face, then he recovered. "No comment."

"Did you kill her?"

"No comment."

Rita wondered if Barry was aware that he was under surveillance by the NCA, or if he felt protected by the organized crime network. They'd obviously kept him out of prison thus far, but she wasn't about to let an arrogant drug dealer get away with murder, no matter whose protection he was basking under.

"Why are you protecting Andy Robson? What hold does he have over you?"

This produced a glimmer of a smile, but the same noncommittal response.

"Did you record Sarah's murder for Andy? Is that how you get your kicks - by making snuff videos?"

Rita didn't even wait for the 'no comment' to leave his lips.

"Or did you kill her? Is Andy the one who likes to do the watching without getting his hands dirty?"

Peter Watson didn't even attempt to step in – maybe he recognized a client capable of dodging his own questions when he saw one. But Andy's expression was more watchful now. A frown creased his forehead. He looked at Peter, and had a hushed chat with him.

Peter said, "DI Gupta. My client was relaxing in his boat when you arrested him without any cause. You haven't given us a reason, apart from the fact one of your detectives saw a man matching his description leaving a house where a detective was assaulted. We both know that is not a valid reason to arrest anyone."

Peter gave Rita an evil, lop-sided grin. He was enjoying this, she could tell. With an effort she controlled herself.

“I suggest you let my client go immediately. In addition, what is this baseless and false allegation of murder? You are just throwing names at my client, in the hope something will stick. My client has never heard of Sarah Collins, or Andy Robson.”

Peter settled back in his chair, satisfied. A smirk decorated Barry’s lips, and Rita wanted to reach out and rip his lips off. Yes, that’s how pissed off she felt. She knew she had little to go on. But maybe she could still try.

“Think of all the stash you lost. That’s got to be worth a few million, right? And also, the top boys in the OCN have no idea how much you told us.”

Rita smiled inwardly as the grin faded from Barry’s face. “From now on, every time one of your depot houses is raided, the OCN will blame you.” Rita pointed a finger at Barry. “Surely you’re better off in prison? You’re a marked man now, Barry. You know what the OCN do to men they don’t need anymore?”

Barry’s face had spots of colour and he was breathing faster. Peter interjected. “DI Gupta. Enough of this. Either you charge my client, or let him go.”

Rita ignored him. “Have you heard of the Gathering?”

Barry frowned at her. “No.”

“Which one of you is the Keeper? You or Andy?”

This question produced the same puzzled expression as it had on the canal boat.

“No comment.”

Frustrated, Rita terminated the interview. She stomped upstairs, thoughts churning in her head. She signed off the paperwork to release Barry Alders.

She was still convinced that Andy Robson was their man. Someone was shielding him, and she was determined to find out who it was.

*****

“What do you think, guv?” Richard asked when they were back in the office.

Rita studied the whiteboard. Barry was friends with Andy, but was he the killer? He was far too cocky for her liking. If his body language had been any more relaxed, he’d have been snoozing right there on the table. No remorse, although that was rare in her experience. No teasing them with titbits of information like a bird feeding its chick. He could’ve snitched on Andy, thrown them off his back, but no, he chose the ‘no comment’ route all the way.

Rita had barely sat down at her desk when her phone rang. A number she didn't recognize. She picked it up and answered. "DI Gupta."

"DI Gupta, this is Inspector Nigel Warren. I'm an investigating officer with the National Crime Agency."

Rita's eyes flashed to Richard and Maggie, and she instinctively sat forward in her seat, her spine straight, like a soldier standing to attention. "Hello, sir."

"It has been brought to my attention by Detective Superintendent Perkins that a case you're currently working on has somewhat overlapped with our surveillance team's operations."

"Apparently so, sir."

"I need you to release the suspects with immediate effect."

That was it. No references to the weather, no foreplay, just straight in for the jugular. The man's voice conjured up an image of a too-tight collar, heavy jowls, and eyebrow dandruff. Another golfer. They were a peculiar breed, she'd discovered over the years, rather like salesmen and politicians. Men like him believed they could talk their way out of an erupting volcano.

"Karim Ahmadi and Barry Alders are no longer being detained."

"Glad to hear it." There was a pause in which she imagined he was examining his reflection in the mirror while trying to loosen his tie enough to reduce the appearance of being strangled. "Leave the OCN to us, will you? We've been building the case against them for some time now. I would hate to see your name appear as a reason why we had to throw more resources at it than necessary."

Oh, she'd bet he'd hate that almost as much as he'd hate polishing off a bottle of red wine with his steak dinner. "Of course, sir."

Another pause. Perhaps he'd been expecting a bit more of a fight from the feisty detective. "Well, that will be all."

"However, sir," Rita said, her heart thumping wildly, "if I can prove that either of them is guilty of Sarah Collins' murder, the NCA will surely have some questions of their own to answer to. I'd hate to see your name come up as the reason I let them both go without charging them. Especially given the evidence confiscated from one of the properties known to be used by Barry Alders."

"I-I beg your pardon." Rita smiled to herself as Chief Superintendent Nigel Warren spluttered into the phone. "May I remind you that—"

"No need, sir. Forgive me for being so forward." Her smile grew wider. Not even the NCA could ignore an apology sweetener, not when it was delivered with just the right amount of tartness.

"Apology accepted, DI Gupta." Rita allowed herself a moment of smugness. "I trust we will not cross paths again." He ended the call with a click.

"Whoa." Maggie's eyebrows had almost disappeared into her hairline. "What the hell was that all about?"

"NCA officer acting like he has all the strings in one hand," Rita said. "I wish they'd take a step back and realize that there's room for both of us. I'm not interested in taking down the entire OCN. I only want to find Sarah's killer, and if that means dragging Barry Alders over the coals, that's what I'll do."

"Fighting talk, guv," Maggie said with a smile. "I knew there was a reason I liked you the moment you stepped through the door."

"And I thought it was because I offered to buy you lunch."

"Well, there was that, too."

"Guv, I think you might want to see this." Richard was frowning deeply at his laptop screen. Something in his voice got Rita worried.

She crossed the room and stood behind him, closely followed by Maggie.

"Might be nothing," Richard said.

"But…" On the computer screen, Rita saw a screenshot taken from CCTV footage inside Sarah's school.

Richard clicked on the video footage. Girls were filing out of a gymnasium dressed in netball kit complete with coloured bibs. He pointed to one girl who had her back to them. "Sarah Collins. Just watch."

Rita followed Sarah who hung back from the other girls as they made their way to the changing rooms; she crouched low to fasten the laces of her trainers, but her hands were not moving. Rita's eyes instantly narrowed when Max Drake, the headmaster appeared in the corridor, smiling at Sarah. The teenager straightened, and they stood chatting for about a minute before both heading in opposite directions.

"Stop," Rita said. "Go back a bit."

Richard rewound the footage and replayed it from when Sarah straightened. She still had her back to the camera, but Rita was watching the headmaster.

"There," she said, pointing at the screen. Richard froze it again and zoomed in. "Do you both see that?"

"Yep," Maggie said. "He went to touch her hair and pulled back when he realized what he was doing."

Rita had never mastered the art of flirting, but she'd watched enough movies as a teenager to recognize it in other people. They couldn't see Sarah's face as she walked away, but the girl had an unmistakable spring in her step.

"Anything else?" she asked.

Richard used his mouse to navigate to another recording. It was late in the school day, shortly before the final bell. Students were starting to file into the corridors in dribs and drabs, either from study periods or classes that had been turfed out early. "Along here," Richard said, indicating a door on the screen, "is the headmaster's office."

The door opened as the school bell sounded, and Max Drake appeared in the corridor, hands by his side. He looked as smart as he had when Rita and Maggie questioned him about Sarah, his suit immaculate, obviously expensive, his hair well-groomed. He spoke to a couple of lads as they passed by his room.

A teacher came along, and they exchanged greetings. A regular day in the life of a senior school headmaster. A younger kid came hurtling around the corner of the corridor and skidded to a halt when he saw Mr Drake standing there. He slowed down and nodded to the headmaster when he spoke, probably reminding him to slow down.

Richard gripped the mouse tightly as more students filled the corridor.

Max Drake didn't move. It wasn't long before Rita understood why. Two girls appeared ahead of a group of boys, and she recognized them instantly. Jackie and

Sarah. The headmaster called Sarah over, spoke to her, and gestured for her to enter his office. Sarah must've told Jackie to leave without her, because the other girl shrugged and kept walking.

"How long before she comes out?" Rita asked.

"Close to forty minutes," Richard said.

"He told us that her name hadn't crossed his desk," Maggie added. "On the CAMHS application."

That was what worried Rita. Why did the headmaster lie to them? Unless he had something to hide.

She went back to her desk and called the school, asking to be put through to Sarah's form tutor, Mr Logan. It was several minutes before the teacher came to the phone, having been called away from class.

"Mr Logan," Rita said, recalling the gangly man in his crumpled clothes, "DI Gupta. I visited you earlier in the week with my colleague. I wanted to ask you some more questions about Sarah Collins."

"Of course. I'll answer to the best of my knowledge."

"Do you recall Sarah Collins spending time in the headmaster's office?"

"I … um … Sarah was never in any trouble, if that's what you're asking."

"Not exactly. Mr Drake mentioned that he had to sign off Sarah's CAMHS referral. Did he ever speak to you about that?"

"No. I knew of it, of course," Mr Logan said. "All Sarah's teachers were aware of her mental health problems."

"Is that something Mr Drake regularly gets involved with in his capacity as headmaster?"

"Yes, if the situation is escalated to him." He was being cautious, trying to work out what was required of him.

"Did you escalate Sarah's problems to him, as her form tutor?" Rita asked.

"Yes, I did. The Principal needs to be aware of any student's mental health issues."

Rita changed tactic. "But, you wouldn't say that Sarah was one of Mr Drake's repeat offenders, the students who always end up in his office to be disciplined?"

"No, far from it," Mr Logan said.

"So, can you explain the CCTV footage of Sarah being invited into the headmaster's office after school the day before she was murdered?"

The teacher was quiet for a while. Rita could literally hear the bolts in his brain turning round and round.

"I… I'm sorry, but I wasn't aware of this."

“Are there any other occasions that you were aware of?” Rita pressed.

Pause. Had the teacher suddenly figured out where Rita was going with this? “One or two.”

“One or two,” Rita repeated. “Yet when my colleague and I spoke to Mr Drake, he said that Sarah’s name had crossed his desk. He failed to mention that Sarah had ever been called to his office for a chat about her mental health. Why do you think this is?”

“I-I honestly don’t know.”

Honestly. It was a powerful word.

“Do your other students have regular chats with the headmaster after school, Mr Logan?”

“N-not that I’m aware of.” His voice had lowered, like he’d been cornered by a ferocious wild animal and saw no way out of his predicament.

“Mr Logan,” Rita said gently, “this is a murder investigation. Sarah Collins was murdered, and I can’t bring her killer to justice unless I’m armed with all the relevant information.” She paused, allowing her words to sink in. “Did you ever see Sarah Collins going into the headmaster’s office?”

“Yes,” he said quietly. “Yes, I did.” He cleared his throat. “Just the once. I had to visit Mr Drake to ask him something. Sarah was coming out of the room. I was surprised to see her. She said it was about her

CAMHS referral, and Mr Drake wanted to know how she was."

"And that was the only time you saw Sarah in Mr Drake's office?"

"Yes. I'm positive." Mr Logan now sounded contrite, and Rita believed him. She waited for a few seconds.

"Is that all you can remember, Mr Logan?"

"Yes. I can assure you. I'm sorry, I can't believe this, actually. I thought it was all standard student teacher interaction. I never thought…" His words trailed off.

"Please ask the other teachers, and whatever you can find out, call me or my team ASAP. Is that okay?"

Mr Logan exhaled. "Yes, certainly."

CHAPTER 34

Marissa was waiting for him in the wide hallway of their home when Max Drake got back after dropping the boys off at their swimming lesson. They'd bickered in the back of the car all the way there, stupid arguments over nothing. Damian pulled a face at Liam behind their dad's back. Liam punched Damian in the leg. Max had been an only child, so he had no idea if all siblings fought this much, but he'd reached his limit this afternoon and had snapped at them both, yelling at them to shut up. It had resulted in Damian bawling, but at least it had given him some quiet time with his thoughts.

Not that he had anything figured out. He needed time to grieve, and instead, he was putting all his energy into worrying that someone would find out what was going on between him and Sarah. Marissa, once the font of all his problems, had sunk way down the list of things that were stressing him out.

He tossed his car keys into the bowl on the ornate stand by the front door, his teeth grating when he heard the clank, as they always did. Why couldn't they have a hook on the wall like everyone else?

"The police called while you were out." Marissa folded her arms across her chest. "Didn't you call them back?"

"I've been busy."

His eyes darted upstairs towards his study. The door was still closed, but there might as well have been a sign hanging on the front of it that said: MARISSA WAS HERE. He knew that his wife had been poking around in there. He could tell by the accusatory look in her eyes, the way she leaned against the wall, casually, as if it was far more comfortable than the expensive leather sofa in the living room that he was still paying off.

"Too busy to call the police about one of your students?" Her perfectly plucked eyebrows drew together.

"I forgot. I've already told them everything I know."

He wanted to yell at her to shut the hell up. He needed time to think. How could he plan his next move when she was constantly nipping at him like a bloody piranha?

Twice the cops had called him now. Why? What did they know? Had someone told them about him and Sarah?

He'd been so careful, always covering his tracks, providing plausible excuses when he came home late. Marissa suspected that he was having an affair, but she would never have linked him to a student. Someone else had known then. What other explanation was there? Someone else had known, snitched on him to the cops, and they were closing in on him.

He had to get away.

This wasn't supposed to happen.

"You'll have to pick the boys up from swimming." He turned away from his wife, his numb legs carrying him towards the stairs.

"Where are you going?" Her question was sharp as a stab in the back.

"Manchester. The conference. I told you about it." He didn't look at her.

"You're leaving now? What about the rush hour traffic?"

"Not much I can do about it," he shrugged.

He placed his right foot on the bottom step. Heaved himself up, forced himself not to turn around.

"Max!"

Second step.

"Where are you going?"

Third step. "I told you."

“You bastard.” Her voice had dropped. That was when he knew that there was no turning back. “Who is she, eh? Donna Grant the fucking PE teacher? I’ve seen the way you look at her. She’s going to the conference too, is she?”

Max zoned her voice out of his head.

He had no idea where he was going. All he knew was that he had to get away. Now. Before the police came knocking on the door. The neighbours… His boys… He had to get as far away from here as possible until this all died down.

Max slung some clothes into a holdall, grabbed the phone from his desk drawer, and went back downstairs. Marissa wasn’t even waiting for him. He could hear the telly blasting from the living room. One of the American sitcoms she was so addicted to.

He slipped out of the house without saying goodbye, stowed his holdall in the boot of his car, and climbed into the driver’s seat. His hands were shaking, but his body moved on autopilot. Key in the centre console. Start button. Reverse gear. Check the rearview mirror. Right foot on the accelerator. Go.

Driving down the hill towards the main route out of Scalby, he saw revolving blue lights, flashing headlights, the distinct blue and yellow design of police cars. His heart almost ended up flying through the windscreen as he slammed on the brakes.

He hooked a left at the bottom of the hill. Circled back on himself towards the canals and the long defunct railway route. He knew the area well, often came cycling with the boys when he had them to himself for the weekend. He knew all the shortcuts and off-grid lanes. He could drive around the canals all day and dodge them if he had to.

It occurred to him then that he was a respectable headmaster on the run from the cops. It was like a scene from an action movie, one where he'd be thinking there was no way a guy like him would get himself into a situation like this.

The sirens were louder, and getting closer.

CHAPTER 35

Panicking, Max skidded along a narrow lane and, at the last moment, pulled into a dirt track near one of the derelict station houses along the route. Branches clawed at the windscreen and side windows as he buried the car out of sight. No one would try to come along here – it was so overgrown, it was barely wide enough for one car, and it led straight down to the canal.

The police passed him by, the revolving beacon creating disco lights inside his car as he slumped down in his seat. They'd spread out to catch him. They knew he would do a runner.

His heart was frantic. It was difficult to think. He raised a hand in front of his face and realized that he wasn't driving anywhere in this state. He would have to wait it out. He was safe here. The dirt track was hardly noticeable from the road, and even if they spotted it, they would dismiss it as a pedestrian path to the water.

He would wait until it was dark, wait for the sirens to disperse, and take his chances in the dark. No headlamps. He considered that they might've set up roadblocks to catch him on the main routes out of town. It wouldn't be easy to escape into one of the motorways. But did he even want that? It was easier to find his way along the narrower country lanes that snaked up and down the North Yorkshire Moors. No CCTV in those roads. He could lose the police there, and have some time to think about his options.

Max switched off his phone in case they could track him through that. He separated the battery from the rear case. He didn't have the social media apps that the kids used these days, but he knew that he could be traced through the signal alone.

It wasn't long before he heard the whirr of helicopter blades circling above Scarborough. Was that for him?

He closed his eyes and focused on his breathing, trying to regulate his pulse before he died of a heart attack. That would be no way to go, alone in his car on a dirt track, turning blue, the flies and maggots getting to him while the police carried out an extensive search of the area. They wouldn't find him. Not here.

His mind drifted to images of Sarah. So young. So beautiful. Too young to die. Remorse gripped his heart in an iron grip, and he couldn't breathe. What had he done? He thought of his two sons, and his dead parents. Briefly, he thought of his sister. Along with Sarah, the only people he still loved. How would they feel when they heard about him?

But most of all, he saw Sarah's angelic face, a few inches from his own. The promise in those eyes…Max's eyes grew heavy with grief, and then with exhaustion. He didn't know when he had fallen asleep.

*****

Max Drake's eyes flew open.

He didn't know what had woken him, but his heart was racing again like he'd just completed a few laps of the school track. He didn't even know he'd fallen asleep, but his mouth was dry, his neck twisted painfully into the wrong position.

A groan escaped his lips as he twisted it slowly back in the opposite direction like ironing out a kink in a sheet of folded paper. Time to go. He wished he'd picked up a bottle of water and some snacks before he left.

His heart skipped a beat when he saw someone standing next to the driver's window. He gasped out loud.

The man was wearing a white cloak, the hood covering their face like a monk, or someone from the Ku Klux Klan. His mind drew on every horror movie he had ever watched when he was younger and he and his mates would watch them in the dark, pranking each other to see who would scream first. Had he driven blindly into some kind of ritual ground? Were they waiting for him to leave before they could begin whatever dark magic they believed in?

He tried to swallow and only succeeded in cricking his neck again. His tongue felt as if it had swollen to twice its regular size, filling his mouth so that he couldn't breathe. He should start the car. Get the hell out of here, take his chances on the back routes out of town, because right now, the police seemed like his safest option.

Before he could press the start button, the driver's door was yanked open. Max cursed himself for not locking the car before he dozed off.

"I'm leaving," he croaked. "I-I must've fallen asleep."

"Max Drake, do you want to escape this life?" the man in the hooded cloak asked, enunciating his words carefully.

He knew Max's name. How was that even possible?

Max squeezed his eyes close. This must be a terrible nightmare fuelled by his fear of being caught by the police. That's what it was. Stuff like this simply didn't happen in real life.

He opened them again. The guy in the cloak was still there. Max couldn't see his face, but he knew that the man was watching his every move. Then it dawned on him – he'd left the car unlocked. The guy must've gone through his stuff, found his wallet, got his name from his credit cards and driver's licence.

"Look," he said, angry at the way his voice cracked, "give me back my wallet and I'll drive away. I won't tell anyone what happened. You can—"

"Be my guest." The hooded man gestured to the start button next to the steering wheel with a gloved hand.

Max felt around the centre console – the keys were gone.

Anger surged through him. He went to get out of the car and faltered when he realized that his legs were bound. He reached down to unfasten the ropes wrapped around his legs just below the knees as a flash of white-hot pain sliced through his hand.

His breath came in short raggedy bursts. His hand looked all wrong. Blood was dripping from his palm, circling his wrist like a ruby bracelet, and down his arm. Pain pulsated in his brain. He couldn't think. What was happening here?

Then he spotted the severed finger in his lap and screamed.

Something hard and round filled his mouth. A strong chemical smell stung his nostrils as he fought to breathe through his nose. His clothes were wet. Blood? Had he pissed himself? He tried to speak, and gagged on whatever was forcing his tongue down the back of his throat.

Hot tears stung his eyes. Snot dribbled from his nose, but he didn't care. He had to get away from this maniac. He lashed out with his right arm, but pain flared the length of his spine and the wacko in the cloak dodged him easily.

Something sharp was pressed against the corner of his eye. The hood came closer. "How does it feel to know that Sarah wasn't yours?"

Max couldn't swallow. The words made no sense through the pain exploding like fireworks inside his skull.

"I couldn't let you have her, you see," the voice continued. "She belonged to me."

Max's vision blurred as the pain in his eyes got worse. He was afraid to move, but his brain was telling him to get away from the knife slicing through his eyeball. So much pain. Consuming him… Turning him into a ball of flaming frozen agony.

Please make it stop. He tried to form the plea inside his head, send it out there, pray that someone would listen. *Please ... make ... it ... stop.*

Max Drake didn't even hear the flare of the match. Didn't hear the Keeper telling him that he was offering him freedom from this life, from the terrible things he did to Sarah.

Flames licked his body, and he succumbed to the blackness, Sarah's smiling face the last image he saw before the fire engulfed his car. As the orange yellow flames licked higher, and the burning pain in his feet started to engulf his body, Max screamed. No one heard him as the flames got higher, ravaging his body.

No one but the Keeper, who stood there watching in silence.

CHAPTER 36

The smell of spices hit Rita the instant she opened the door to her flat. She stopped in the doorway and listened to the sound of food sizzling in a pan, music drifting from the kitchen, and another sound: her dad singing along.

"Something smells good."

She turned around to face Jack, whose eyes were almost closed, breathing in the aroma of homemade curry.

Jack had been waiting for her outside the station when she left. She was exhausted after the argument with Nicola and the equally frustrating phone call with the snotty detective from the NCA. Then, Max Drake had given them the slip. His disappearance only reinforced her suspicion that there had been something going on between him and Sarah, but it still meant that she was no closer to arresting the killer.

So, when Jack asked about her plans for the evening, she invited him along to dinner with her dad on impulse. Should she have brought him? Now that she could smell the curry aromas wafting from the kitchen, she realized that her dad might've wanted to surprise her with some authentic Indian cooking. He might be disappointed not to have Rita all to himself.

But then again, did it really matter? They were all adults here, and she acknowledged with a jolt, that she couldn't remember the last time she had invited anyone to dinner.

Jack followed her into the kitchen. Her dad looked at home, stirring the curry sizzling in a small, blackened wok that Rita had never seen before. He turned to them with a smile, his gaze settling on Jack. He set the wooden spoon down on a plate on the counter and shook Jack's hand. "Jay Gupta. I'm Rita's dad."

"Jack Banford." He shook Jay's hand formally, and bumped shoulders with Rita. "I dated your daughter in college."

Jay's smile widened, and Rita could almost see the matchmaking ideas dancing around behind his eyes.

"What are you cooking?" Jack removed his jacket and tie, folding them neatly and placing them on the end of the counter, and inspecting the thick red-brown sauce in the wok.

"Karahi chicken. I thought I'd impress my daughter with my culinary skills." He winked at Rita, who pulled out a seat and sat down, suppressing a yawn. She watched with interest as the two men tasted the sauce and discussed the row of spice jars lined up next to the hob.

Living alone and working long irregular hours, Rita either came home and prepared her own food, or she settled for a packet of crisps and a bottle of wine. It wasn't something she dwelled on. It was simply a fact of life. But tonight, she felt drained by the obstructions piling up in front of her and preventing her from solving this case. So, she sat back, enjoying the feeling of being looked after for once. Jay carried on cooking, and Jack got some advice about making curries from him.

"Your dad's a good chef," Jack said, turning to Rita.

"I wouldn't go that far," Jay said, turning from the hob. "My wife doesn't cook much, so I kind of fill in."

"This is more than filling in," Jack insisted. "The sauce is delicious, and not greasy or oily." He winked at Rita, who smiled back at him. "Now," Jack rubbed his hand. "Where's the wine?"

Rita went for a quick shower and got changed while the men carried on in the kitchen. She smiled to herself as she got ready. She could definitely get used to this lifestyle. When she got back, Jack and Jay had laid the table out, and were sipping a glass of red wine, each.

"I could use a helper for the house," Rita laughed. "Would one of you like to apply?"

"Can you afford me?" Jack raised his eyebrows. "I'm expensive."

They sat around the small kitchen table, a bottle of wine in the middle, beside a dish filled with homemade poppadom, and two smaller bowls containing mango chutney and mint raita.

"Where did you buy this from, Dad?" Rita asked, dipping a corner of crispy poppadom into the chutney.

"I found an Indian shop in town, for the poppadoms. I made the chutney. It's not hard."

"You'll have to give me the recipe," Jack said.

"Do you cook?" Rita arched an eyebrow. The Jack she knew when she was younger was more into football and a chippie than preparing an authentic curry. Had he now learned to cook? Maybe that's what marriage did to you.

"I learned at Uni." He spooned sauce into his mouth and swallowed. "Wow, that's good. My flatmate was into cooking. He taught me everything I know, although I'm nowhere near this standard."

Rita saw the smile on her dad's face and felt warm, fuzzy inside.

"I cook when I have my daughters at the weekends," Jack continued. "My eldest, Frankie, likes to help. Georgie's only ten. She still wants to watch telly when she isn't playing with her friends. I try to make everything from scratch. Apart from pasta. No way I'm investing in a pasta machine when I can buy a packet for less than a quid from Tesco."

Rita laughed. They sat down to eat, and conversation stopped for a while. Rita hadn't realised how hungry she was. The curry was incredible. She caught her dad's eye, and he smiled at her, pride evident in his eyes. Rita grinned at him, then looked away. She still needed time to adjust to him being back in her life.

"You must miss the girls," Rita said to Jack. She noticed her dad following their conversation.

"It was hard at first," Jack said. "It was a huge upheaval for all of us. Georgie would play up for me all weekend, and then play up for her mum when I took her home. It was her way of dealing with change, I guess. But we're getting there now."

"Do they stay with you every other weekend?" Rita asked.

"Pretty much. Unless they have specific plans or I can't avoid a work emergency, which is rare."

Rita wondered what life with children would be like. She swallowed a mouthful of tender chicken and kept her eyes on her plate.

Jack said, "But I try to avoid weekend invitations. It isn't fair on the girls or me. I still want to be there for them as much as I can while they're so young." He stopped and there was a sudden silence in the room. Jay stared down at his plate.

Jack then realized what he'd said and peered at Jay. "I'm sorry. I honestly didn't mean anything by that.

Everyone's story is different, and I… Well, I'm not here to judge."

"No need to apologize," Jay said, sipping his wine. "Not staying in touch with Rita is the biggest regret of my life." He reached for Rita's hand and squeezed it.

"Dad…" Rita began.

"It is, Rita. There were so many times that I thought about jumping on a train and coming to find you, but as the years slipped by, I knew that I'd missed my chance. Why would you want a man you didn't know in your life after so many years? I think the fear of rejection was real."

Here was where Rita should say that she wouldn't have rejected him, but she couldn't in all honesty say the words out loud and mean them. When her mum was still alive, she didn't need a father. They had each other, and that was enough. Then, after Clara disappeared, it was too late for her dad to come back, they'd both known that. She didn't want a father who was only there because she had no one else.

"You're here now," Jack said. He raised his wine, and all three of them clinked their glasses together in a silent toast.

He *was* here now, and listening to her dad talking about his regrets felt like the warm hug she didn't know she needed.

"Maybe you could teach me to make a curry," she said.

Jack spluttered, wine dribbling from the corners of his mouth. "You do realize that will require spending time in the kitchen."

"Hey, I spend time in the kitchen." She frowned at him.

"Seeing is believing."

"Now you're being judgemental," Rita said, swallowing a tasty morsel of the chicken. "How do you know I don't cook?"

"I'll tell you one day," Jack winked at her. There was something intimate in that gesture. Rita felt a heatwave slowly spread up her neck. She was relieved when Jay started speaking to Jack.

The rest of the dinner passed easily, with good chatting, helped by the free-flowing wine. This was good, Rita thought. This was how other people spent their evenings, and she wanted to do this again.

CHAPTER 37

Rita was up early the next morning at 6am. Jack had left around midnight; their conversation had turned to the fun times they had at school, with her dad joining in with his memories. It had been a lovely evening, and she wanted more of the same – but life had taught her not to build up hope. The present moment was enough, and she had to enjoy that as much as she could. Life was fleeting, and evenings such as last night were meant to be enjoyed by being immersed in the moment.

She was on her way to the station when she got a call on the radio. It was the duty uniformed sergeant.

"Morning guv. We found a burnt car discovered near a derelict station house in Scalby. Close to where Max Drake lived."

The uniformed sergeant's voice was sombre. "Guv, I've run the vehicle reg through the DVLA database. It's registered to Mr Drake."

Rita's mouth opened in shock. She thanked the sergeant, told him she was on her way, and hung up. Her skin prickling, she called Richard and Maggie and diverted them to the same location. Maggie planned to drive down from home, and pick her up. Rita took the bus to the town centre and waited for her. Once Rita was in the car, Maggie put her siren on, and made short work of the distance to Scalby.

The SOC team was already there, and they walked along an overgrown dirt track to reach the burnt-out vehicle, pushing thorny branches and brambles out of the way to avoid getting their faces scratched.

Shola was hunched over the remains of the vehicle. The driver's door was open, still attached – barely – to the charred frame.

The detectives donned blue shoes and gloves and proceeded cautiously towards the ruined car. It wasn't until Shola straightened and turned to face them, that Rita saw the burnt corpse in the driver's seat.

The air was filled with the stench of smoke, and charred flesh, which made Rita's nose crinkle with distaste. She was used to horrific sights in her line of work. But she also caught the smell of something else. Something altogether more sinister. She inhaled through her nose, trying not to cough. Fuel. But that would've been caused by the engine catching fire.

"What have we got?" she asked Shola. The SOC team would be able to give her the make and model, but Rita could see that it was a large car.

"Initial findings point to an IC1 male, but forensics will elaborate on that. The fire started here in the driver's seat."

Rita didn't ask how Shola could tell that from the blackened remains of the car and driver. She assumed the corpse was the driver as it was in the driver's seat. Was it suicide? How did someone strike a match and set fire to themselves? She shuddered, remembering Jackie's story about the girl who set fire to her arm live on the Gathering feed.

"I thought potential suicide at first," Shola said as if reading Rita's mind. "Remote spot. Late at night. A single corpse."

"But?"

"But." Shola crouched beside the car and gestured for Rita to watch closely. Parting the blades of dried grass surrounding the wreckage, she pointed at a discoloured patch. "Blood spatters. Until I test the samples, I can't be certain that they match the corpse, but my guess is that they will."

"Do you think he was attacked?" Rita stared at the corpse, at the slack jaw that made her think the victim died screaming. Hardly surprising. She'd seen third degree burns. Not a pleasant way to go.

"The car door is open. He might've tried to get away once the vehicle caught fire, but the footprints we discovered, lead towards the scene. They stop there."

She gestured to the slight indentations in the dirt beside the blood spatters. "There are other footprints, of course, heading away from the scene. Henry is currently taking samples for the forensic boot print database, but whoever approached the car on foot had to walk away, so I think we'll find that they're identical."

"Can we send them to the gait analyst too and check them against the footprints discovered outside the warehouse?" It was a long shot, but Rita couldn't discount the possibility that they'd find a match.

"One more thing." Shola rose and turned back towards the corpse. "You see the way he's sitting here, knees and ankles together?" Rita nodded. "It's not a natural position especially given the cramped conditions in the front of a car."

"You think his legs were bound together?" Rita asked.

"I'll know for certain once the samples have been tested, but I'd say it's a possibility. Survival instinct when the fire began would've been to run, hence the open door."

"We don't have an ID, do we?"

"Dental records should confirm if this is Max Drake or not, very soon. I've sent samples off to the lab," Shola said. "Dr Das is treating them as a priority. No wallet or other ID documents were found in the car."

"Thanks," Rita said. "I think we have to assume this is Max, for now, until we are told otherwise by Dr Das."

Had the car been abandoned here? Barry Alders had dumped a rental car at a disused railway, so it wasn't entirely implausible. The dead guy might've discovered the location while out jogging one day and come back when he was ready to end his life. Or he drove here, parked up out of sight for whatever reason, and was attacked before he could drive away again.

Rita's stomach twisted. Max must've driven here to avoid being questioned. Did he take his own life because he couldn't face being convicted of Sarah's murder? She peered back at the footprints and the discoloured patch of grass.

Max Drake hadn't walked here. He'd driven here in his car, holed up for the night, and then what…? Did he call someone? Arrange a pickup that went wrong? Did someone happen to be passing by when he pulled into the dirt track, or was he followed?

Rita walked back along the dirt track to the road where the police cars were parked in a row like bowling pins. She approached a couple of uniforms from the station, recognizing one as the rookie officer, PC Dixon, who'd been present at the warehouse when Sarah's body was discovered.

She called Dixon over, and gave Max Drake's address and asked the route he might have taken to arrive at the dirt track. It was so well hidden that he must've known about it. But what she wanted to determine was how someone else might've discovered his car in such a remote spot in the dense darkness of an unlit lane.

"Do you know this area?" Rita asked the young PC.

He swallowed, and looked like Rita had asked him about the weather in Shanghai. Then he scratched the back of his neck. "Yes, guv, kind of."

Rita sighed, and looked at a map on her phone. "If he came down Church Hill and hooked a left into Hackness Road, there are lots of old military roads he could've taken to reach the canals."

PC Dixon, peered left as if marking the distance by sight. "Many of these roads don't appear named on Google Maps. But the locals know of them. They're quiet routes for cyclists and joggers."

"And farmers," he added.

"Dog walkers?" she asked.

"Not likely." PC Dixon shook his head. "Too remote. Unless they know where they're going and park up somewhere."

Rita thanked him and went back to Richard and Maggie. "I want an extensive search of the woodland, over a one-mile radius. I mean a fingertip search. I will call in extra units from Whitby and Bridlington." She pointed to the sky. "Get the drones up there ASAP."

"Yes, guv," Rizwan hurried off to make the calls.

"Speak to the neighbouring farmers. Their workers. Find out if they saw Max Drake's car or any other unusual activity in the area."

"Unusual activity?" Maggie asked.

"Like a car on the fields, or anyone they saw. An eye witness description of a suspect would be valuable. Someone did this to Max. We need to find out who."

Rita stared through the foliage at the burnt-out wreckage of the headmaster's car. Max was running scared about his relationship with Sarah, but her gut was telling her that he had been followed, and someone had been watching him.

Barry Alders, Karim, Andy Robson – had all been either in custody or under watch.

To Rita's mind, this seemed like the handiwork of the shadowy person known as the Keeper.

Who was he?

*****

Mrs Drake opened the door to Rita, a look of resignation in her eyes.

"DI Rita Gupta." Rita produced her warrant card. "We spoke yesterday on the phone."

"Come in." Marissa stood aside, and Rita stepped into the neutral hallway as an air freshener sprayed a waft of vanilla behind her back.

The house was large – at least four bedrooms, Rita guessed – a typical attractive new-build, but lacking the character of the grand old houses overlooking the Scarborough seafront. The interior was tastefully decorated in muted shades of beige, ivory, and grey. It wouldn't have looked out of place on the pages of a glossy interior design magazine, but it told her nothing about the family who lived here.

"I'm assuming my husband didn't call you back," Marissa said.

"Mrs Drake, is there somewhere that we can sit down?"

Marissa's eyes narrowed; a gesture so brief that Rita would've missed it had she blinked at the wrong time. Marissa gestured for the detective to follow her through to the kitchen. She filled a kettle and offered Rita a coffee which she declined. She didn't sit down.

"Mrs Drake, did your husband tell you where he was going when he left here yesterday?" Rita asked.

"Teacher's conference in Manchester." Marissa's expression was blank. Unreadable. "Not that I believed him. He has a string of excuses that fly off his tongue whenever he wants to stay out."

"Do you mean whenever he isn't coming home for the night, Mrs Drake?"

Marissa shrugged. "I'm sorry, DI…"

"Gupta," Rita reminded her.

"Max and I… Well, our marriage was over some time ago. The first time I suspected that he was having an affair."

The first time, Rita wondered. Mrs Drake was an attractive woman – it was obvious that she took care of herself and was fortunate enough to be able to do so. She didn't need to explain that they stayed together for the kids, for the mortgage, for the lifestyle. She'd seen it so many times before, but she would never understand why people settled for a life that made them unhappy.

"Can you remember what time he left, Mrs Drake?" Rita asked.

"He'd just dropped the boys at their swimming lesson, so around five thirty."

Around the same time that uniforms were on their way here to bring him into the station. Still daylight. Someone could've followed him down the unmade road, marked his location, and then returned after dark.

"Mrs Drake," Rita said, "I'm afraid I have some bad news. Your husband's car was discovered on an unmade track earlier today."

Marissa swallowed. Rita had her full attention now.

"As far as you know, did anyone else drive your husband's car?

Marissa frowned. "No. I don't think so, anyway. Well, I drove it as I was insured on it, but not recently."

Rita considered that, then nodded. "The car had been destroyed by fire. A corpse was discovered inside the vehicle, and although we are waiting for a positive ID, we think it was your husband."

The woman squeezed her eyes shut and sucked in a deep breath. When she opened them again, they were still dry. "Max is dead?" she whispered. "Do you think he killed himself?"

"We're still waiting for forensics to sift through the evidence. Until I receive their report, I'm unable to answer the question, but I suspect that your husband might've been murdered."

"Murdered?" Frown lines appeared on Marissa's forehead.

"How did your husband seem to you over the last few days, Mrs Drake?"

Marissa thought about it for several moments. "The only difference I noticed was that he was at home." Pause. "We stopped eating together a long while ago. The kids have so many after-school activities, it's easier for me to eat with them when Max is working late."

“Did your husband work late often?” Rita asked.

“More and more frequently. I assumed that his latest conquest must work at the school.”

“Why would you assume that?” Rita had just delivered news of her husband’s death, and she was discussing her husband’s affairs with about the same level of emotion she might reserve to discuss his shopping.

“We’d been married for twelve years. It’s just one of those things that you instinctively pick up on when you know someone as well as you know yourself.”

Rita nodded. “I’m very sorry for your loss, Mrs Drake. I’ll be in touch once we have the postmortem results. I’ll see myself out.”

Mrs Drake didn’t respond. She was staring out of the kitchen window, her shoulders shuddering gently, head bowed.

CHAPTER 38

"Heavy morning?" Jack Banford was waiting for Rita outside the Love Brew Café, two mochas to go and a paper takeout bag in his hands.

Rita accepted the coffee and took a sip, wincing as the liquid scalded her tongue. "You could say that."

Jack smiled. "Lucky for you I know a bench overlooking the beach that's always empty."

He was right. The bench was set up in the hills, close to the Victorian cliff railway with an uninterrupted view of the North Sea. Far below, the water's surface glinted like diamonds in the sunlight.

"I used to ride the tram at weekends with my mum," Rita said wistfully as it passed them by. A little boy had his face, and hands, pressed up against the window, mesmerized by the view as the carriage descended. Rita smiled at him, but she was too far for him to notice.

"I never got bored with it."

"You'd probably still feel the same way if you rode it now."

She nodded. She needed this: coffee, fresh air, Jack. He opened the bag and offered her a slice of banana loaf which she took with a grateful smile.

While they ate the sticky cake, she told Jack about Max Drake. "I'd been so certain that he was the killer, or that he would at least be able to shed some light on Sarah's movements leading up to her death."

"We got positive ID from the dental records," Rita added. "DNA results should be back first thing tomorrow."

"You think someone wanted to shut Max up?"

A crumb was stuck to Jack's bottom lip. Rita dragged her eyes away and licked her fingers to stop herself from leaning across and picking it off. Too familiar. Touching his lip would be like announcing to the world how badly she wanted to kiss him. She stared ahead, and focused on the case instead.

"Seems that way. SOC thinks that his legs were bound so that he couldn't escape. They found fragments of rope by his feet. It's too much of a coincidence that he was randomly murdered in the middle of bloody nowhere so soon after Sarah's death."

"Serial killer?" Jack asked. "Or someone with a gripe about their affair? Have you thought about the wife?"

Rita wrinkled her nose and shook her head. "I did think about it. But I don't think she cared enough to murder him. She had the children at home with her, she wouldn't have left them alone to go and set fire to her husband's car, torture him, and then return."

"What if she did it while the kids were sleeping?"

"We checked the security cameras on the front gate of their house. She didn't leave the home in the evening. The back garden cameras only show a couple of foxes jumping over the fence. Nothing else."

"Fair enough." Jack crumpled up the empty paper bag and stuffed it into his jacket pocket. "What about Karim?"

"I'm more worried now about Karim. Specifically, about his relationship with Sarah. What if Max Drake was murdered because he and Sarah were lovers?"

"You mean you let Karim go, and he tracked down Max and killed her because he was jealous?"

Jack's eyebrows were raised, and Rita pursed her lips together, staring at him. "Doesn't sound right, does it? Unless Karim is a crazed serial killer, and I doubt that."

Perhaps it was just as well that the NCA were keeping tabs on Karim's movements. Rita enjoyed having Jack to bounce ideas off, but her instincts were telling her that the killer wasn't done yet. She had to catch this vicious murderer before he struck again.

***

“Hey, guv.” Rizwan grinned at her as she walked back into the office.

“What are you doing here?” Rita asked, sliding into her seat. “I thought you were signed off.”

“Aye, about that.” Riz winked at Maggie. “My headache’s gone, and I can’t sit around at home listening to my mum complaining that I don’t eat enough vegetables. So, I asked my dad to pull some strings.” At Rita’s frown, he added, “My dad’s a GP. He studied medicine with the doc who signed me off.”

Rita couldn’t help smiling. “Good to have you back. If I see you popping paracetamol though, I’m sending you straight home with a bag full of carrots and broccoli.”

Riz laughed. “Deal.”

Rita’s phone rang. It was Dr Das. “The results of the postmortem are ready,” he said, before Rita could speak.

“I’ll be there as quickly as I can.” Rita hung up – she hadn’t even sat down yet – and nodded at Riz. “Looks like I’m breaking you in gently with a trip to the morgue.”

The grey-haired doctor was still working on the remains of the corpse discovered in the car wreckage when Rita and Riz entered wearing gloves and masks, white plastic aprons covering their clothes.

Rita studied the sooty remains of Max Drake, once again struck by the wide-open jaws and empty eye sockets. The man was having an affair with a student. He'd been a suspect in a murder investigation. But she couldn't erase from her mind his screams when his car went up in flames. Someone heard them. Maggie and Richard hadn't gleaned much information from the neighbouring farms, but the killer heard those screams. What kind of person could sleep at night with those sounds raging around inside their head?

Dr Das smiled briefly, peering sideways at his visitors. "Max Drake. Male Caucasian, age thirty-nine. DNA samples taken from the victim match sperm samples taken from Sarah Collins."

"That was quick," Rizwan exclaimed.

"I leaned on the lab," Dr Das said. "Told them it was a double murder. It wasn't difficult for them, given they had Sarah's samples already."

"How recent was the sexual activity?" Rita asked.

"Within the last five days prior to her death."

"Did you find any other DNA in the sperm samples?" If Max Drake didn't kill Sarah, she needed to know if the killer had sexually assaulted the teenager either before or after death.

"No. I did however take DNA samples from skin cells found on her body."

"What does that mean?" Rita asked. "Someone she hugged or swapped clothes with?"

"Potentially." Dr Das stopped his probing long enough to picture the scenario in his head. "There's nothing sexual about these samples, although the person touched her in some way. I found the same skin cells under her nails which would indicate that she might've tried to fight off this person."

Rita liked the doctor's straight way of talking. He called it like it was, to the best of his professional ability and experience.

"Did you find a match with any of the suspects?" Her heartrate increased at the prospect of finding Andy Robson's DNA on Sarah.

"I'm afraid not. Nothing to match Barry Alders, Sarah's mother, Andy Robson, her partner. No matches on the national police database either." He peered at them both from behind his glasses. "Any other DNA samples you can provide me with will be gratefully received, as always."

"You think they could belong to the killer?" Rita asked.

"With the cells scraped from beneath her nails, I'd say there's an extremely high possibility."

When Rita and Rizwan got back to the office, Maggie had news for them.

"Andy Robson's DNA has matched in sexual assault cases on young girls. The perpetrator was never caught. They happened outside a school in Cornwall, when a girl was returning home. She managed to claw her attacker's face and able to get free. A car spotted her, and gave her a lift to the police station."

"Bloody hell," Rita said. Her suspicions had been correct. She flopped down on the chair.

Maggie continued. "Through the DNA samples, they were able to match Andy to several previous counts of assault on teenaged girls, carried out under various names. It seemed that Andy Robson targeted single women with young daughters. The more vulnerable the better."

Maggie pointed at her screen. "I've been reading up on the reports, along with the skipper." She glanced at Richard. He cleared his throat.

"Not exactly bed time reading," he grimaced. "He had a routine of love bombing the mother so that they didn't hesitate to welcome him into the family, before targeting the daughter as his next potential victim. Three years earlier, under a different name, he'd been reported for sexually assaulting a teenager in Cornwall. The victim had told her friends that she found him creepy, bur her mum was an alcoholic and refused to listen."

“So, two cases where his DNA matches so far?”

“Yes,” Maggie said.

Rita suspected that he was guilty of many other assaults that hadn’t been reported. But the real question that now sprouted sharp thorns in her mind was the same – could Andy Robson be the Keeper?

“We need to catch him, and fast,” Rita said.

CHAPTER 39

Rita and Rizwan returned to the station to learn that Nicola had called an urgent conference in the major incident room.

The Detective Superintendent was seated at the head of the table with some police officers Rita didn't recognize when she and her team walked into the room.

"Ma'am," Rita said, joining Nicola at the front of the room near the whiteboard.

Nicola's eyes barely grazed Rita's face, and her expression was deliberately neutral as she introduced the officers who had been called in from York and Leeds to assist with the investigation. The frost that hung in the air between the two women was palpable, but not to anyone else, and Rita shrugged it off. She had a job to do.

Nicola addressed the table. "Detective Inspector Rita Gupta is the SIO, and leading the case. She'll fill you in on what we have so far."

Rita talked the expanded team through the list of suspects. She elaborated on the equipment discovered in the garage used by Andy Robson, and informed the officers that Andy's whereabouts were still unknown.

"DC Jaffer and I have just returned from the morgue. Dr Das informs me that sperm samples taken from Sarah Collins' corpse were a match with those taken from Max Drake, the victim discovered earlier today in the burnt-out wreckage of his car. Other skin cell samples taken from Sarah's fingernails have, so far, drawn a blank in terms of DNA matches."

She peered at the faces around the table.

"The Scene of Crime team discovered blood spatters on the ground outside of the wreckage that match the victim's DNA. The postmortem revealed that Max Drake was missing the little finger on his right hand which would tie in with the location of the blood samples. They also believe that his legs were bound with rope so that he was unable to escape."

"Does this murder bear any similarities to that of the first victim?" The question came from a uniformed sergeant.

"Good question. No, the MO is not the same. Sarah Collins wasn't tortured, but her murder had all the trademarks of a ritual killing."

She paused. "Sarah was a member of a secret social media group called The Gathering. Youngsters suffering from depression are lured to join in with self-harming videos in the hopes of being reset by someone who calls themselves the Keeper. Max

Drake doesn't fit the criteria for joining the society, but his wounds would suggest that his death was as much about inflicting pain as it was ending his life."

"And yes," Rita continued, "There are elements of a ritual in the way Max Drake was killed. He was tortured slowly, and his murderer watched him suffer."

Rita paused again. The entire room was silent, hanging on to her every word. "Do I think that the two murders are connected? The answer is yes. Max Drake and Sarah Collins were lovers. A headmaster and a student. Perhaps this was his punishment."

"Do we know how the killer escaped?"

"No." Rita spread her hands wide. "Helicopters and a drone were searching the area for Max Drake's car. Roadblocks were in place. The victim's wife told me that he left home at around five thirty p.m. My guess is that he knew we were going to bring him in for questioning regarding his affair with Sarah, saw the helicopters, and holed up on the unmade road until nightfall."

"So, the killer possibly followed him," another officer suggested.

"He had to. The car wasn't visible from the road."

"The killer must know the area well," Riz added.

"No witnesses have come forward following the house-to-house," Richard said.

“If the killer followed Max Drake when he left home at five thirty,” Rita said, “they wouldn’t have risked torturing the victim in daylight with the helicopters and drone in place. Which meant that they waited it out too.”

“The victim might’ve fallen asleep or been drugged,” Maggie suggested.

Rita nodded. “It would explain how the killer managed to bind his legs without alerting him to their presence.”

After answering a few more questions, Rita concluded the meeting. “DC Long is still trying to find a way into the Gathering so that we can speak to the Keeper. So far, he has not fallen for the bait.”

Nicola didn’t wait around to speak to the team once the meeting was concluded, and Rita found herself visibly relaxing. She didn’t need the distraction of the Detective Super breathing down her neck.

Walking back downstairs to the office, Rita’s mobile phone vibrated in her pocket. Sliding it out, she opened a text message from an unknown sender. She clicked on the message’s information, expecting it to be the regular kind of spam from a company claiming to be a recognized courier or insurance agency, and found nothing. No details. No telephone number. No callback allowed. She didn’t know how these bots did it, but they were getting clever, making it virtually impossible to trace back to source.

She opened the message.

How is your dad? Settling in well?

Rita froze. She instinctively looked behind her to check that she wasn't being watched.

"Everything okay, guv?" Maggie asked.

"Aye, fine," she said. It was a prank. The sender had no way of knowing that her dad was staying with her. They just got lucky.

She kept walking, her phone vibrating in her hand a second time.

Your mother was a bitch. She deserved everything she got.

Rita's mouth was dry. Her heart cannon balled slowly against her ribs. A familiar panic was unfurling in her bloodstream. She halted in the corridor, waving the rest of the team to carry on without her. This was no prank. This was personal, and whoever sent it had gone to extreme lengths to cover their tracks.

Her mind spun as she made her way downstairs. The only person who knew that her dad was staying with her was Jack, which meant that someone had seen them together. Maybe at the train station. Or had they seen her dad leaving her flat? Either way, the second message had made her blood run cold.

She saw PC Dixon and Inspector Bennett in the corridor and stopped to show them the messages.

"Inspector Bennett, can you spare PC Dixon to keep an eye on my dad while he's here? This might be a scam, but I'm not taking any chances."

"Rightly so," Inspector Bennett agreed.

Rita felt somewhat relieved when PC Dixon headed directly to her apartment, but the messages had unnerved her.

Who could this be? And why now?

CHAPTER 40

Jay Gupta answered the phone as soon as he saw it was from Rita. "Hi Darling." He smiled as he said the words. How many years had he waited to say those two words? Far too long. Now he had to make up for lost time.

"Dad, where are you?"

"At the flat. Why?" Jay caught a hint of something – *panic?* – behind the simple question. "Is there something you need? I've been shopping, but I can pop back out."

Rita said, "No, just checking you're alright."

"Why wouldn't I be?"

Pause.

"Are you listening to Celine Dion again?" Rita asked.

Jay chuckled. "You caught me out. I am. It makes me feel younger, I think."

"A policeman is on his way to the flat, Dad. His name is PC Dixon. He's going to be keeping an eye on you while you're here."

“Keeping an eye on me? In case I escape while you’re at work, you mean?” The smile faded from his lips. “What’s this all about, Rita?”

“Just humour me, Dad,” she said. “It’s this case. There’s been a second murder and… Well, just be careful, okay?”

“I’m always careful, sweetheart.” He was about to add ‘you know me’ and stopped himself in time. “Is it really necessary to waste resources on me when you’re so busy with this investigation?”

“You let me worry about resources, okay? I’ll see you tonight.”

It wasn’t much, cooking for her, but he didn’t want to overwhelm her with too much too soon. He would love for her to meet Anna and Aaron, when she was ready. He’d even thought about giving her the guided tour of Cardiff and his favourite beaches.

But again, he wasn’t about to go pushing her too far. Not when she seemed so … content having him around. If he was honest, the way that she had welcomed him into her life was more than he had dared to hope for after being an absent father all her life, and he wasn’t going to jeopardize it by outstaying his welcome either.

The instant he thought that she was ready for him to leave, that was it. He’d jump straight on that train and give her some space. Tomorrow maybe, or the day after. But his heart told him he wanted to stay, and that made him smile. Love always guided the heart to its right destination. After years of wilderness, Jay felt he had arrived – back to his little girl.

Jay busied himself marinating meat for the evening meal and soaking cherries in kirsch to make dessert. He was a feeder, Anna always said. He often wished that he'd trained to be a chef when he was younger, but turning a hobby into a career often sucked the joy out of it.

A knock on the door caused him to wash his hands quickly and dry them on a tea towel. He opened the door to find the uniformed policeman that Rita had mentioned. They didn't hang around. He was a young man, and he took his cap off, twisting it in his hand. His dark eyes were still and watchful.

"Jay Gupta?" the cop said. "My name is PC Dixon. I've been asked to watch the flat. I just wanted to introduce myself and make you aware, sir, so that you don't get worried if you see me standing outside."

"Yes, my daughter called a short while ago. Is this really necessary?"

Jay eyed up the young, uniformed copper. He didn't want to make him feel superfluous, but at the same time, he was conscious of wasting the police department's time when there were more important ways to utilise the man's day.

The man smiled. “I’m just following orders, sir. Don’t mind me. Please, just go about your business as if I’m not here.”

“Okay. Well, it’s very kind of you. Would you like a coffee? I’ve just boiled the kettle.” Jay gestured inside the flat, suddenly aware that he hadn’t even invited the young man inside.

But PC Dixon was already walking away. “No thank you, sir. I’ll be outside if you need me.”

Jay closed the door. He walked to the window and watched the policeman station himself outside the building, feet planted squarely, hands behind his back. It felt surreal having a copper standing outside protecting him, like he’d become the obligatory innocent bystander caught up in a dangerous situation in every crime movie ever made.

*****

Jay kept himself busy. He prepared vegetables to go with dinner, cleaned the kitchen, the fridge and the oven, and then peered out of the window. PC Dixon was still standing in the same position. Jay had checked the weather forecast for later in the day – heavy rain – and decided that if he didn’t go out now, he’d be stuck inside, and he would get irritable sitting around waiting for Rita to come home when there were still so many places he wanted to revisit.

Grabbing his jacket and the spare key that Rita had given him when he arrived, he went outside, locking the door behind him.

"Everything okay, sir?" PC Dixon asked him when Jay approached.

"I'm going for a walk. I thought I might wander up the hills towards South Bay and the castle. I haven't been there in years. Is the cliff railway still operating?"

"It is, sir." PC Dixon smiled, and his cheeks dimpled, making his features appear even more boyish.

"I might take a ride on my way back then," Jay said.

He went to walk off, but hesitated when the officer followed him.

"It's okay. No need to come with me. I'll be back in a couple of hours."

"Sorry, sir. My orders were to stay with you, not the building."

Jay could imagine his daughter warning the young man to stay close. Whatever was going on with this case, she was obviously concerned, and he didn't want to add to her stress. Or that of the uniformed policeman – he was only trying to do his job.

“Okay.” The officer’s presence had already cast a shadow over his day, but he realized the young man wasn’t going to be deterred. He would simply have to try to pretend that he was alone and make the best of it.

The walk through the hills was exactly as Jay remembered. Even after all these years. He had never been back to Scarborough. It was too much of a reminder of all that he’d walked away from, but now, he recalled everything that he had loved about it. The wide beaches. The castle standing sentry up above. The clifftop railway which had always retained a sense of nostalgia for bygone days when people strolled along the promenade with parasols and paddled in the sea practically fully clothed.

At first, he was conscious of the police officer strolling along several paces behind him, but when he reached South Bay, and the glorious sandy beach came into view, he immersed himself in Scarborough again.

Memories came flooding back. Sunbathing on the rocks at the back of the beach with Clara like lizards soaking up the rays. Her laughter which lit up the world even on a gloomy day. Bringing Rita down to the sand as a baby, chuckling as she scrunched up her toes because she didn’t like the texture, dipping her feet in the water, her sunhat catching on the breeze and being carried away to sea. *“Hat, Daddy.”* He could still hear her voice.

Pleasant memories. No point clinging onto the unhappy ones. Departures, tears, goodbyes. He had such fond recollections of Scarborough that it seemed a shame to have turned his back on it and his daughter. He'd had his reasons of course.

But they were not for today. He'd long ago made his peace with what happened between him and Clara.

There were dog walkers on the beach, a Dalmatian cantering along the sand like a horse, a terrier yapping at the gulls, a collie chasing a stick into the water. He said hello to the people he passed on his way up the hill to the castle. Everyone greeted him back. People were more generous with their greetings when they had nowhere important to be and the sun was shining.

The castle was deserted. This wasn't the time for holidaymakers to come exploring, and the locals had grown up with the crumbling building perched on the promontory – it had likely become as invisible to them as the supermarket they visited once a week for their groceries. The view across the North Sea with the sunlight's shimmering golden zigzag created a breathtaking pathway to the rest of the world.

Jay stood for a while and soaked up the sea breeze, filling his lungs with fresh air. It was so tranquil. He had always tried to make time for peace in his life, but nothing beat the taste of salt on your tongue and the wind on your cheeks.

He remembered, as a young man, stumbling across Anne Bronte's Grave just beyond the castle, where parts of the outhouses were still standing and reachable by narrow paths. Not many people walked this way – they visited the castle and then headed straight back into the welcoming arms of Scarborough seafront.

The snap of a twig behind him jerked him back to reality, and he turned around to find PC Dixon still shadowing him. He smiled. He'd forgotten about the police officer while he was musing over his youth.

"I'm going to find Anne Bronte's Grave," Jay said. "You can wait here if you like. I won't be long."

"It's quite alright, sir," PC Dixon replied. "I've never seen the grave, and I'm enjoying the fresh air."

Jay wondered briefly at how many locals never bothered to explore the attractions on their doorstep but didn't comment on it. He took some pictures of the grave to send to his wife and kept walking, past the ruins and beyond the boundary wall, to where land sea and sky were untainted by manmade buildings. It gave him a sense of freedom, watching the clouds rolling in. Like he could spread his arms and soar like a bird, up and away, watching the people below scurrying around like beetles.

He raised his phone and set the camera to panoramic view as something hard connected to the back of his skull. He heard a dull crack as pain flared behind his eyes, and tried to figure out what it was. What? How…?

Another thud. This time, Jay's knees buckled, and he went down, his face hitting the ground. More pain exploded in his mouth. He tried to roll over, but the blows kept coming, and it was all he could do to protect his face with his arms as thoughts of the young police officer flooded his mind. Jay hoped that he was safe. Perhaps he had already called for backup.

A rough grip wrenched his arms away from his face. Jay opened his eyes. One was almost closed, his vision blurred with blood. He could taste the iron tang of blood in his mouth and trickling down his throat. But he recognized the face peering down at him instantly.

"PC … Dixon?" He tried to form the words, but his mouth was misshapen and clumsy.

"I am the Keeper," the police officer whispered, his breath warm on Jay's face. "This is my revenge."

The baton came down on the side of Jay's face. He felt his eyebrow split. Felt the spurt of warm blood trickling into his eye. Pain cascading around his brain and finding no release. But he held on to the whispered words as he was dragged away from the castle and dumped behind a crumbling wall. He had lost a shoe along the way. Perhaps Rita would find it if she came searching for hi

CHAPTER 41

Maggie took the call from Jill Collins, Sarah's mother.

A neighbour saw Andy hanging around the flats, and she was worried that he might break in to take his stuff. Not that he'd moved much stuff in.

"She sounded panicky, guv," Maggie said. "Not surprising now that she knows what he's been up to."

Rita couldn't afford to let him get away. She had to release Barry, and although he'd given them nothing, he was their strongest link to Andy Robson. And with Max Drake dead, she wondered if Sarah's stepdad was the killer.

"Stakeout time?" Richard was already on his feet.

It was all the prompting Rita needed. They literally ran to the car, and Richard put the siren on as he picked up speed.

They parked up behind a row of cars with a clear view of the entrance to Jill's block and waited.

"You think he's our guy?" Richard asked.

Dr Das's confirmation that the skin cells detected underneath Sarah's fingernails didn't match Andy's came flooding back. These observations were throwing Rita off-kilter. The samples pointed to a struggle, so either Sarah didn't put up a fight in her final moments, or someone else was holding her down. Someone without a criminal record. One of the other youngsters from the Gathering perhaps.

"Aye," she said without conviction. The forensic results were niggling away at her. She had the overwhelming sense that she was missing something, but whatever it was, it remained firmly out of reach.

They didn't have long to wait.

Andy emerged from another building, hands stuffed inside his pockets, hood raised over a baseball cap. He walked slowly, his eyes darting around like he expected danger. He was holding something that Rita couldn't quite make out.

"What's that in his hand?" she murmured.

Richard squinted in the suspect's direction. "Looks like a hammer." He was already opening the driver's door of the car, but Rita stopped him.

"He's too far away."

She wondered if he had the balls to try breaking into his girlfriend's flat in broad daylight, but her fears were confirmed when he approached Jill's building. His strides were sure. He didn't slow down now, intent on getting inside the flat.

They were out of the car in an instant. Rita couldn't risk him lobbing the hammer through one of Jill's windows.

"Stop, Andy!" she yelled, running towards him.

Andy froze, his arms swinging loosely by his side. It took a couple of beats for recognition to set in, and then, without warning, he threw the hammer at Rita and bolted.

Rita dodged it easily. She heard it land on the pavement somewhere behind her. Richard had run around the outside of the parked cars and was closer to Andy as he crossed the road and hurdled the low fence surrounding the park.

Richard jumped over the fence, a few paces behind him. Andy barged between the swings and hurled one towards the detective to slow him down. But Rita had skirted the park and was almost at the gate on the other side. Andy spotted her and legged it in the opposite direction, but he hadn't counted on the dark-haired man walking a Staffie, who'd obviously observed the chase, and was loitering outside the park. The dog barked aggressively, rearing up onto his hind legs.

Maybe Andy was afraid of dogs, because he hesitated. It was just long enough for Richard to tackle him to the ground and cuff his hands behind his back.

"Get the fuck off me!" he spat, trying to buck Richard off his back like a bull at a rodeo.

"Andrew Robson, you're under arrest for the murder of Sarah Collins. Anything—"

"I didn't kill her." Face pressed to the ground, he eyed up Rita as she approached them, and swore loudly. "You can't even get that right."

"We'll see about that," Rita said. "Let's get you back in custody."

CHAPTER 42

Andy was in the same interview room in which she had interrogated Barry and Karim before him. He wore a white T shirt under his blue jumper, and his hands moved under the desk. He glared at Rita when she walked in with Richard.

Andy's lawyer remained silent, impassive. His name was James Mason, and Rita had never seen him before. Neither had Richard. James wore a navy pinstriped suit and pale blue shirt, which would've looked smart were it not for the pale stain on the bottom of one of the lapels.

Richard spoke for the machine, introducing everyone. Rita didn't waste getting to the point.

"Andy Robson, did you sexually assault Sarah Collins?"

"I didn't." Andy's bottom lip permanently drooped making him appear gormless, Rita thought. He breathed heavily through his mouth, and she had an awful vision of him looming above the frightened teenager before he killed her.

"It isn't the first time you've attacked a female teenager, is it, Andy?"

"Dunno what you're talking about," he said.

"Daisy Thornhill," Rita said. "Name ring a bell? You were in a short-term relationship with her mother Sherry. You went by a different name then, but we've matched the DNA samples from Daisy's crime reference report to the sample we took from you a couple of days ago."

Andy shrugged. "Nope. Still no clue."

"How many other vulnerable girls have you targeted, Andy? Is that what you do? You choose your girlfriends carefully. Roam the council estates searching for a suitable candidate with children?"

"I ain't a paedo."

Rita kept her expression deliberately bland. "I didn't mention that word. You did."

"Sounded like you were suggesting it."

"Sarah Collins was seventeen years old when she died, Andy. Did you sexually assault her when she was underage?"

"I never touched her." He slouched back in his seat and wiped his nose with the back of his hand, while his lawyer kept his eyes firmly fixed on the plastic cup of tepid water in front of him. Something about his attitude told Rita he didn't want Andy as his client. She focused back on Andy.

"Sarah shouted at you in the street to leave her alone. Didn't she?"

"Not my problem. Kid had a complex." Another shrug.

"A complex?" Rita asked.

"Thought the whole world was out to get her."

"The whole world, or just you, Andy?" Rita held his gaze.

His pupils were enlarged, his eyelids heavy. She saw no emotion in his eyes. She'd seen none in Barry Alders either, but this guy was different. It was almost as if he was flaunting his previous record in her face, confident that she couldn't pin anything on him, and that he'd walk free within twenty-four hours.

"Dunno what you mean. I steered well clear. The kid was trouble."

"Trouble in what way?" Rita asked.

"Drugs. Boys. Slicing up her fucking skin. Only a matter of time before she ended up pregnant."

"Well, she'll never have the opportunity now."

Rita had more respect for the criminals who owned their crimes and expressed some remorse. But guys like Andy, sitting there accusing their victim of causing trouble…she despised them with a passion. Her jaws ground together as anger jolted in her blood. She remained calm externally.

"Tell us about the equipment we found in the garage you've been using, Andy."

"Dunno nothing about a garage."

"Two days ago, my colleague and I followed you to a garage on the housing estate north-east of the town centre. After you left, we entered the unit and confiscated equipment to make films of a violent sexual nature along with instructions on recording snuff videos."

"No comment."

So, that's how he was going to play it now.

"Have you ever made a snuff video, Andy?"

"No comment."

"Did you record Sarah's murder with the intention of posting it online?"

His nose wrinkled, but he refused to make eye contact. "I never killed her." James Mason looked up sharply at the mention of the word murder.

"Did someone else kill her while you videoed it?" Rita sat forward; fingers entwined on the table in front of her.

"Nope."

"No, you didn't video it, or no, someone else didn't kill her?"

Andy's face scrunched up in confusion. James Mason spoke slowly. "DI Gupta, are you accusing my client of murdering the victim?"

Rita stared back at him. "Your client has to answer the question. He has a history of violence against teenage girls, and he lived with the victim, Sarah Collins, also a teenage girl."

"No comment," Andy said. Rita turned back to him.

"Then who killed Sarah Collins?" she asked quietly.

"I don't know." Rita caught the note of impatience in his tone and was reminded of Dr Das's report, and the skin cells under Sarah's nails.

"Did she struggle to get away from you when she realized that you were going to kill her?"

"I told ya, I didn't kill her." His eyes moved sideways, and he didn't look Rita straight.

"Why the warehouse, Andy?" Rita persisted. The cracks were starting to appear – they were still faint, but that belligerence was wearing thin, and panic was seeping through.

"What do you mean?"

"Why did you kill her in the warehouse?"

"I didn't—"

"How did you shift the lighting and the video equipment up there? Did Barry Alders help you?"

Andy blinked several times. It was the most animated Rita had seen him, his facial muscles struggling to remain neutral. "No. I don't know what you're talking about."

"Or was it Karim Ahmadi? Did you use Karim to lure Sarah to the warehouse?"

"The kids use the warehouse," he said.

"For what?"

"Smoking, shooting up. Why are you asking me?"

Rita needed to rotate her shoulders, ease some of the tension in her neck caused by his attitude, but she didn't move. Not when he was on the backfoot. She glanced at Richard, who shook out some photos from the brown envelope on the desk. They showed the material collected from Andy's garage. She showed them to Andy, whose eyes widened. Splotches of colour appeared on his cheeks.

"As you can see, we confiscated drugs from your garage along with the sex props. Did you supply Sarah with drugs, Andy? Was she using the night you murdered her?"

"I never murdered her."

"I think you got her high on cocaine in the warehouse and murdered her while someone else filmed it. What did you do with the video, Andy? Has anyone else seen it or are you saving it for when things settle down?"

"There ain't no video." Andy's voice climbed a notch.

"Did you get scared and destroy it?" Rita was firing the questions at him now, leaving him no room to worm his way out.

"What video? I don't know what the fuck you're talking about."

"Why did you kill Max Drake?" Rita watched him carefully. There wasn't a DNA match to Andy found at the crime scene, but she wasn't discounting Andy's role in the second murder. Not yet.

The blinking resumed. Andy shook his head as if trying to clear his thoughts. "Who?"

"How did you find out about him and Sarah? Did you follow them? Is that why Sarah warned you to back off?"

"No idea what you're talking about." The sneer on his face told Rita otherwise.

"Were you jealous, Andy? Is that why you killed them both?"

"Jealous!" he scoffed. "You're clutching at straws, lady. I didn't give a damn who she was screwing. She could've shagged everyone for all I cared."

"That's your girlfriend's daughter you're talking about." Richard's tone was cold. It was the first time he'd spoken during the interview – he'd been choosing his moment wisely.

"Not anymore."

Rita's thoughts crashed together into one violent tidal wave.

"You do realize that we have evidence that implicates you in both murders," she said. "We have witnesses who saw you arguing with Sarah shortly before she was murdered. You have a previous history of violence against vulnerable teenagers."

"And the equipment and drugs in your possession," Richard added. "Just wait till the DNA results come back tomorrow."

Andy wriggled in his seat and hunched forward, wrinkling his nose from side to side like he had an itch he was too embarrassed to scratch. "You can try," he said, "but I'm not guilty. So, who's going to look stupid then, eh?"

He was worried though. This was just the façade he was used to hiding behind. But she saw the fear in those bulging, watery eyes.

"Okay," James Mason said, tapping his fingertips together. "I think my client has had enough for now. Despite your threats, we both know there is no evidence tying my client to either murder. May I suggest that we stop for a break and resume questioning later?"

Rita agreed begrudgingly. She wanted to see this man locked up … not only for Sarah, but for every other youngster he'd assaulted over the years. Men like Andy Robson didn't try their luck once and then give up. They became repeat offenders, their crimes becoming increasingly violent with the knowledge that they'd gotten away with it so far. Sometimes, it even resulted in murder. At least she could hold him for 24 hours, and start again tomorrow.

*****

The sky was ominously dark when she left the station to head back to the flat. Despite the earlier sunshine, they'd been given a weather warning for rain, and she was looking forward to getting home and eating whatever meal her dad had prepared.

The first heavy raindrops caught her as she let herself into the building. Shivering, she was glad to be home. She hadn't inherited her mum's love of the rain, especially when it was torrential, and would much rather be listening to it through the window than out and about in it, her clothes sticking to her skin.

She didn't see the squad car outside. She thought Dixon might be out on a patrol.

No lights were on inside the flat. There was no music coming from the kitchen. No sizzling sounds of food being tossed in her dad's wok. Only darkness and silence welcomed her. It felt strange.

"Dad?" Rita called out. She turned on the hallway lights. Still, no sound came from the kitchen. The bathroom and bedroom doors were shut. Rita kept her jacket on, and walked forward.

"Dad, are you here?" Jay didn't call her to say he was going out. And where was PC Dixon?

Rita's hackles were up.

She slid her phone from her pocket as a text message popped up on her screen.

Looking for your dad? I know where he is.

Her phone rang and she answered almost before the sound had reached her ears. "Who is this?"

"*Oh no, no, no. You don't get to ask the questions*." The voice was tinny, mechanical. "*Come to the abandoned farmhouse in the hills behind the castle. If you want to see your dad alive, you'll come alone*."

CHAPTER 43

Rita's heart was in her mouth. She couldn't control the thud-thud of her heartbeat, the blood gushing through her veins, the bile rising in her throat.

But through all this, her brain insisted that she remain focused.

Calm. Remember your training, she told herself. She clutched the phone so hard she feared she might break it.

"How do I know that my dad is there?" She heard the tremor in her voice. Was it obvious to the caller, or would it get lost in transmission?

"*Here, listen.*"

There was a pause. Rita concentrated on the sounds coming through the phone. Was that rainfall? The wind gusting in the background? Then she heard a groan, and her stomach lurched.

"Rita…" The voice so faint she had to strain to hear it. "Rita." Barely enough to pick up on the accent, but it was there. It was her dad.

“Rita, don’t listen to him. Don’t-

There was a wrenching sound, and Rita could tell there was a struggle. Then it was suddenly quiet.

“Dad? Dad, are you hurt? Can you tell me where you are?”

The man’s voice came back on the line. He breathed heavily.

“*Enough! You know where to come.*”

The call ended with a click that was so final, so despairing, that Rita was left staring at the blank screen in the gloomy twilight of her entrance hallway. Frustration burned in her heart, and with that, a sinking feeling.

The caller had used a voice modifier to distort the cadence, of that she was certain. They’d called her from the same untraceable source. IT would probably be able to track it, but there was no time. She should’ve spoken to them sooner, but there was no time for what ifs and maybes either.

How had they got to her father? What had happened to PC Dixon?

Fingers trembling with rage and frustration, Rita called the station and asked the duty officer to place a call through to PC Dixon while she stayed on the line. The wait was interminable. The seconds ticking by inside her chest, tick-tock, tick-tock, tick-tock. Then she heard the officer's voice telling her that there was no response from PC Dixon.

She thought of trying Inspector Bennett, but she didn't want to alert the constable's boss to a potential breach of his orders. What if her father had dismissed the officer? She didn't know her father well, but she'd learned enough about him over the past couple of days to recognize the same stubbornness of which she had often been accused.

He'd laughed off her suggestion that he needed protecting. She could imagine him marching outside and sending PC Dixon packing. Perhaps the officer tried calling her while she was interrogating Andy Robson.

She could alert her team, but they would want to come with her, and she couldn't risk that either. She wasn't gambling with her dad's life. He had a wife and a son in Wales. She'd only just welcomed him back into her life – she wasn't going to lose him again, not to a crazy who was using him to get to Rita. If they wanted her, that's who they were going to get.

Arming herself with a knife from the kitchen, which she slid inside her sock, and a spanner from the basic toolkit supplied with the flat – the heaviest thing she could find – it occurred to her that if this perp was the killer, it couldn't be Andy. She shoved the thought aside. She'd get him on the other charges, regardless.

Rain battered the living room windows. Rita hadn't visited the castle since she came back to Scarborough – she'd had no time for touristy stuff – but she knew that a brisk walk up the hill on a good day would take her around thirty minutes.

She wanted to call Jack. But even as her hand hovered over the phone in her pocket, she knew that she wouldn't risk another innocent life. Whoever had her father knew about her mum. This was personal, and that on its own, sealed the deal: she was going alone or not at all.

Peering all around her as if she knew that this would be the last time she saw her cosy flat, Rita found the food that her dad had prepped for dinner. Tears prickled behind her eyes. He was trying. He was trying so hard to make his time here seem normal, to do what any other father might do and take care of her for a short while, that the unfairness of this situation hit her like a punch to the gut.

As anger swirled around her veins, gathering momentum with the adrenaline kicking in, she opened the kitchen drawer and picked up the wine corkscrew. She added it to the pocket with her penknife and shut the drawer, remembering the scissors in the next cupboard along. If this guy thought she was going to arrive quivering and bowing to his demands, he was going to be in for a shock.

Rita locked the front door behind her. There were no signs of a break-in, so either her father opened the door to his attacker, or he was taken by surprise outside the building.

The rain lashed her face the instant she stepped outside. The world was so dark, the moon and stars smothered by the dense cloud cover, that it felt like the middle of the night instead of early evening. The streetlamps came on as Rita walked, following her like some eerie inexplicable trail shadowing her every footstep.

She was drenched before she reached the end of the street. Jack had taken a shortcut to drive her home the evening before, and she walked it now, following her nose as if the storm raging up above was guiding her towards the hills overlooking the sea.

Her mind was now surprisingly empty. She'd never been one of those people who could stare at the telly or a book and while away the time thinking about nothing. Not daydreaming as such – daydreaming normally produced pleasant thoughts – but literally emptying their minds completely and starting afresh with a clean slate.

But heading towards the castle, she made no plans. She didn't figure out her next move. She didn't even try to picture her dad broken and bloody on the floor of the abandoned farmhouse. She needed this emptiness so that when she finally came face to face with this wacko, her brain would function without fear or inhibitions.

She would kill him if that’s what it took.

CHAPTER 44

Scarborough castle was barely visible in the grim grip of the gusting rain. Rita followed the shadow of the immensely high ramparts - that had been there for centuries, guarding the town like an ancient stone sentinel fulfilling its life's mission.

She climbed higher, her thigh muscles burning dully. Her clothes were soaked through, her skin clammy and bobbly with goosebumps, but still she put one foot in front of the other, driven by what she must do when she reached her destination.

Skirting the castle walls, she followed the steep narrow path that most tourists only walked as far as Anne Bronte's grave, the curtain wall offering some little protection from the stinging rain. The caller had mentioned an abandoned farmhouse. She had no idea what lay on the other side of the castle, but she hoped that the building would be prominent enough for her to find in the wretched stormy twilight.

Emerging from the path like a mole abandoning its subterranean crypt, Rita found herself exposed to the elements. Her cheeks felt raw. The rain was even more aggressive here, taking advantage of the wind blowing in off the sea and blurring her vision. She scanned the horizon and saw the lumbering bulk of a building, a smaller crumbling barn to its right.

The abandoned farmhouse.

Sticking as close to the castle ruins as she could, she approached the dark building, the wind trying to sweep her up and away. She no longer felt the heavy weight of her saturated clothes. She could no longer hear the thumping of her heart above the howling wind. Adrenaline burned in her veins, filling her with a new energy.

She sprinted the final stretch – no one inside would hear her footsteps over the rain hammering against the windows. The element of surprise was out of reach, but at least they wouldn't hear her coming.

Closer, and Rita saw a flicker of lacy light from a window. The doorway was set in the middle of the building, and ducking low, she made her way around the back, taking in the missing roof from the crumbling barn, the rusting tractor, the fenced off yard that must've once house a chicken coop.

She tried the back door. Tentatively. Her slippery fingers wrapping around the handle. It turned, and she released a shaky breath.

Pushing the door slowly, she waited for it to be wrenched from her grasp. When nothing happened, she peered inside.

The room was pitch-dark with the lack of natural light from outside. It smelled musty, the results of an unloved home, damp, and mildew. Rain followed her inside, pooling on the floor at her feet before she closed the door behind her, shutting herself in with the gloom.

Rita stood still, listening. She could hear nothing. No subaudible sounds of the electrical equipment, no buzz of energy entering the building from the outside cables that would've once fed the property.

Slowly, she stepped inside. The old floorboards creaked under her boots. The granite darkness was impenetrable. She took out her torchlight and flashed it around.

She was standing in the kitchen. The grey square shape to her immediate right looked like a fridge. The butler sink was like a lone tooth in a gaping mouth. A pine table stood in the middle of the room, lino curling around its legs. No chairs. Grubby curtains were pulled across the window, black veins of mould creeping across the raggedy cloth.

Rita stood in front of the back door surveying her surroundings. It occurred to her that the previous owners might've left some equipment behind. She flinched as her boots squelched across the linoleum covering and she tried a cupboard. Something moved. Rita stifled a scream as a rat ran across her feet and disappeared inside an invisible hole behind her.

Her pulse was racing a marathon. Crouching, Rita went to the cupboards on the wall, and opened one. She saw that there were cartons of food on the filthy shelves and shut the door again softly. The cartons were not old. Someone lived here. She slid open a drawer. She found some cutlery, but no knives.

Rita crossed the room and opened the interior door leading to the rest of the house a fraction. The entire building was in darkness like a cave. It felt oppressive, the dark pressing heavily on her shoulders, the shrieking wind outside raising the hairs on the back of her neck.

Deep breath. Her hand closed around her extendable baton, and she stepped into the hallway. Rita listened. Still no sounds of movement, but she sensed that she was close.

A doorway appeared in the gloom like an apparition. Rita gripped the handle tightly and pressed her ear to the door. She couldn't hear anything, but then these old farmhouses were built to withstand the elements, and the door was more solid than the plasterboard ones in her flat. Resting her shoulder against the door, she shoved it open and burst into the room, baton raised.

It was empty. This must've been the living room. Two small sofas covered in once-white sheets were arranged either side of the hearth. Mould-covered ornaments sat haphazardly across the mantelpiece, and rotting paintings hung limply on the walls. Again, the curtains had been drawn before the farmer and his family moved out, giving the shadows ample opportunity to take root and form their own alliances against intruders.

Rita was about to turn around and leave when she caught a whisper of movement from the corridor. Whirling around, she went to the door and peered both ways as a door clicked shut on her right, in the opposite direction to the room where she'd glimpsed the sputtering light from outside. Had she imagined it? She didn't think so, but all her senses were screaming at her to follow the sound.

Something inside her clicked, and she ran. She covered the distance between her and the closed door in three long strides, barged inside, and stood in the middle of the room, waiting for her eyes to adjust to the even denser darkness. No furniture in this room, but there was a strange smell vying for attention with the mould and damp.

A click behind her made her whirl around. The door was shut. Had she left it open? She couldn't remember, but the prickling sensation down her spine made her question her movements. She ran back and yanked on the handle, but the door didn't budge. She tried again. It gave a little, but it was stuck fast. That's when she noticed the metal lock beneath the handle.

Rita rattled the door. She thumped on it with both fists, the vibrations reverberating in her skull. She yelled, "Let me out!" But no one came.

Then she saw the smoke curling through the cracks between the door and its frame.

Rita swallowed. She'd fallen for the oldest trick in the book. She was trapped, and now the man had started a fire somewhere in the building. Panting heavily, she banged on the door again. "Let me out! Is anybody there?"

What did she expect – someone to open the door and say, "There you are!"

Rita coughed. She had to get out of there. Smoke inhalation would kill her before the flames did. Running her hands across the walls, she skirted the room looking for a way out, but there wasn't even a window. She was only getting out of there one way – through the locked door.

Crouching in front of it, she removed her coat, dragged her shirt over her head, and wrapped it around her face, knotting the sleeves at the nape of her neck. She shrugged her wet coat back on and found the penknife in her trouser pocket. It slipped through her wet fingers, and she had to feel about for it on the damp carpet, the smoke already making her eyes sting.

Rita suppressed a cough and tried to regulate her breathing. She extended the slim metal pen knife and poked it into the lock. It got so far, and then hit the key that had been inserted the other side. She would have to push that out before she could pick the lock, but her fingers were so wet and cold that each time she thought she had it, the tool slipped, and she had to start again from scratch.

The smoke was drifting through in steady clouds now that swirled around her knees and made it difficult to focus on the lock that swam in and out of her vision. She was taking too long. Her throat felt scratchy, and she succumbed to the heaving coughs trying to expel the smoke filtering through the wet shirt to her lungs.

Sliding the penknife back into her pocket, Rita stood up and gripped the steel baton with both hands. She raised it above her head and brought it down into the thinner centre panel of the door. The baton made a dent. But it wasn't enough. Rita tried again, aiming for the same spot and missing the mark by a centimetre. Swallowing, bile irritating her raw throat, she raised the baton and swung again. A splinter flew towards her and bounced off her collarbone. It was all she needed to spur her on.

Rita brought the baton down again and again, putting all her weight behind each blow until, finally, the wood caved, and she could see through a narrow gap in the cracked wood to the darkened hallway beyond.

Without a thought to what might be lurking on the other side, she shoved her arm through the gap and felt around for the key, gritting her teeth against the shards of wood penetrating her coat sleeve and slicing her skin. If she dropped it, she would have to pick the lock, and she was running out of time. Already, her brain cells were spinning, and she still had to get out of the house. Finally, her fingertip brushed metal, and she froze, feeling her way gingerly around it until she could grip it tightly.

Holding her breath, she twisted the key to her right, praying that she wouldn't cough and jerk it from her grip. Tears stung her eyes, and she squeezed them shut, concentrating on the key in her hand. Rita heard a dull click, and her shoulders sagged with relief.

But there was no time to congratulate herself. She still had to find her dad.

Holding the shirt in place over her mouth, Rita staggered into the smoky hallway and stared through the dirty-grey smog towards the closed room at the far end, the one where she'd seen the light from outside.

Gaudy orange flames licked at the doorway, spitting embers into the dingy narrow space. The room was on fire.

CHAPTER 45

Rita froze. Tears trickled from her eyes and into the makeshift mask she'd wrapped around her face. Her dad was in there. She could feel the heat from where she was standing, and realized what it was she'd been able to smell inside the room she'd just vacated. Some kind of fuel. Gasoline. Petrol. It was only a matter of time before the whole house went up in flames along with everything – *and everyone* – inside.

She knew that trying to open the door would be the biggest mistake she could make. The flames would consume her instantly, and she was probably already covered in fuel from kneeling on the floor and touching the walls.

But she couldn't leave without saving her dad.

She was probably too late. The thought ripped a hole in her chest and gripped her insides, twisting them violently, but she didn't come here to stand back and watch him die at the hands of some sicko with an imaginary grudge against her.

The window!

That room had a window. She'd seen the light – had it been the first flames erupting?

It wasn't important. Rita dashed back through the kitchen, praying that the back door hadn't been locked behind her. It hadn't. She darted outside, almost crying with relief when the rain drenched her face and plastered her hair to her forehead. But she had no time to waste.

She skirted the farmhouse until she reached the window. Her breath left her lungs with a whoosh when she saw the fire crawling around the room and swallowing everything in its path. The glass was cracked but still in place. Rita gripped the baton again and swung it towards the window, turning away and covering her face with her arms when it exploded outwards, sprinkling glass shards all around her.

The rain pelted the open space, fighting the flames trying to use the wooden frame to escape. She could see a well of smoke in the middle of the room, surrounded by fire. This was probably the craziest thing she'd ever done in her life, but Rita tightened her shirt at the back of her skull, raised both arms as if preparing to dive from the highest board at the swimming pool, and plunged through the open window space.

She immediately threw herself into a forward roll to break her fall. The fire extended clawed hands towards her, searing the skin on her forehead and hands, and singeing her eyebrows. Rita remained on her knees. She turned three-sixty, scanning the room for a glimpse of her dad, and realized a beat too late, that he wasn't there.

Another empty room. Another trick she'd fallen for.

Something cracked above her, and a burning chunk of plasterboard tumbled down from the ceiling, narrowly missing Rita. She was back on her feet, swaying unsteadily as the fire roared angrily around her and the smoke claimed her lungs.

She had to get out… She had never been this close to a wildfire before, and the flames were mesmerizing, holding her gaze and not letting go. Blisters formed on the backs of her hands and the exposed skin on her face, the searing pain penetrating the hypnotic state, slowly consuming her.

Rita tried to blink, but her eyes were dry.

Move, she told herself. *Move!*

She hadn't checked the ground outside and didn't know if she would land on grass or paving slabs, but it was too late to worry about that now. At least if it was grass, the rain would hopefully have softened the soil enough to cushion her fall. Rita ran, and then dived through the window.

She landed awkwardly on her left wrist. She heard a crack, but instinct kicked in, and she curled herself into the foetal position, to protect her head and face. She landed on a soft surface which cushioned her fall.

Grass. Rita lay there panting, the rain soothing her scorched flesh as she stared up at the heavy clouds.

He wasn't in there. Her dad wasn't in the house, which meant that he was still alive somewhere.

She heard a faraway sound snaking through the rainfall to reach her and rolled her head sideways to stare out towards the sea.

"Rita!" There it was again.

She wasn't sure if she was hallucinating, the smoke having affected her more than she realized, but then a figure came into focus through the slanting rain. Her eyes were sticky and dry, and she couldn't quite make out the distorted shape, but the voice sounded familiar.

Hauling herself upright, Rita stumbled across an open expanse of land towards the figure, realizing how close they were standing to the edge of the cliff. It was like a silhouette against a backdrop of stormy sky. Only that wasn't the worst part. As she grew closer, she realized what she'd been unable to make out from the farmhouse. The figure's arms were outstretched at right angles as if it were hanging from a cross.

A groan escaped her lips, and she started running.

She couldn't see the person's face. The head was lowered, chin resting on their chest, but even through the rain, she recognized the blazer her dad had been wearing when she met him at the station. He called her name again. He had seen her tumble out of the window.

“Dad!” Rita cried as she ran forward.

Rita was a couple of metres away from her dad when another figure stepped out from behind the cross, wearing a white hooded robe.

CHAPTER 46

Rita skidded to a halt, her boots sliding across the muddy ground, and cartwheeled her arms to keep her balance. Anger consumed her as she stared at the odd figure, standing there with his head bent.

She shouted. "Who are you?"

The man didn't answer.

"What do you want?" she asked, dragging the saturated shirt from her face.

He spoke for the first time. "Revenge, Rita. What else would I want?" The man's face was hidden by the hood, but she was certain that she recognized the voice, only she couldn't attach it to a name.

"Revenge?" She shuffled closer, a few centimetres at a time, her feet barely moving. "For what?"

"You killed the only person who'd ever looked out for me."

Okay, the guy was a lunatic. The chances of him having followed her here from London were slim, which meant that he was obviously confusing her with someone else. But that voice…

"Why don't you show me your face? I'm not talking to a hood."

She thought she heard a chuckle as the guy raised both hands and pushed the hood away from his face. Rita's breath caught in her parched throat.

PC Dixon? She shook her head and waited for him to come back into focus.

Her brain wasn't cooperating. Words formed but didn't fully materialize. "I… Why… I don't … understand…"

"You stole Robert McFarlane from me. Because of you—"

But Rita wasn't listening. *Robert McFarlane.* Her mother's ex-boyfriend, who turned out to be her killer. What did he have to do with PC Dixon?

"…I lost my best friend because you put him behind bars," Dixon spat the words out viciously. "You took him away from me."

Words penetrated her cloudy mind, jolting her back to the stinging, burning pain of reality, of seared flesh and lashing rain, and seeing her dad strung up like Jesus on the cross.

"…the Brotherhood…"

The robe. The Brotherhood. The Gathering. *The Keeper*.

Suddenly it all collided in her head like incendiary ingredients tossed into a mixing bowl and exploded. Like lightning in the sky, her mind cracked and illuminated, exposing a fearful picture. Some of the jigsaw came together.

"You're … the Keeper?" She could barely hear her own voice. She watched as a maniacal grin spread across his face. A smile that sent ice cold spasms of fear reverberating around her body.

An evil pride shone from PC Dixon's face – she didn't even know his first name – as if he'd finally achieved the recognition he deserved.

"Yes. You thought you killed the Brotherhood when you locked up the Master. But we don't give up that easily, Rita."

He continued, a note of reverence entering his voice. "Robert was the Master. He was our Guardian. He looked after me."

Rita thought of the horrible crimes that group, the so-called Brotherhood, had committed against the children in that care home, and how Robert had killed her mother in cold blood.

Confusion ebbed away from her and was gradually replaced with anger. Hot, seething rage that splashed against her heart like the rain pelting her face. "He killed my mum," she spat.

"She deserved to die."

Rita clenched her fists, willing herself with every ounce of control that she possessed not to lunge at him. She needed to assess the situation. Safety first. Her training was urging caution, walking her through the scenario step-by-bloody-horrific-step. She had to figure out her next move.

Her father was bound to the makeshift cross by his chest, wrists and ankles. Thank God the wacko hadn't used actual nails. The rain was making it difficult to check his wounds, although she thought that she could see dried blood congealing above his left ear and on the back of his head.

The biggest problem she faced was that they were standing right on the edge of the promontory. One wrong move, and they would all go crashing over the edge. She had to take down PC Dixon – *the Keeper?* – first, and then deal with her dad.

But how?

Keep him talking, her brain told her, while her teeth chattered. Her body was starting to freeze. It was the cold, the rain, the trauma of her burns and seeing her dad strung up like some kind of sacrificial offering.

"Why did you kill Sarah?" she asked. "Did she deserve to die too?"

"I wanted more time with her before her reset." His voice was eerily calm.

Rita flinched at the way he said it, like he was switching a computer off and on again, not ending a life.

Dixon continued. A steely note crept into his voice. "But she was planning a new life with that man. A new life away from the Gathering."

"With Max Drake? Is that why you killed him, because Sarah loved him and not you?"

She watched his expression falter momentarily through the rain blurring her vision. Had she hit a nerve? Did he want all those kids he lured into his evil trap to love him? To worship him like a god?

"It wasn't part of the plan."

"What plan?" Rita's voice rang out.

"They come to me for help. They come to me because they need me. Life treats them badly, and I fix them."

"By murdering them?" Rita picked up on a shimmer of movement in her peripheral vision, but kept her eyes fixated on the Keeper. She needed to keep him talking, buy more time. Maybe Jack had called her and got worried when she didn't respond. She wished for that now, desperately.

“Only in this life!” Dixon’s voice was shrill, angry because Rita was questioning his methods. “They are born again into a new life because of me.”

“And then what?” Rita shuffled closer to her dad. She thought that she’d seen him move. If he was conscious, he could help her set him free once she’d dealt with the Keeper. “You meet up again in some glorious Utopia?”

“They come back to me in the next life because I’m their Keeper.”

Rita was grateful for the rain. Her eyes flickered to her dad, certain now that his legs were twitching. She noticed that one of his shoes was missing. He was still wearing a sock that was half hanging off his foot, and the sight of his bare ankle made Rita’s stomach twist.

“And these kids buy your crap?” She forced herself to look at Dixon. “You’re not their Keeper. You’re a coward who preys on vulnerable youngsters, kids who are weaker than you are.”

Her dad’s foot twitched again. Don’t look, she told herself. Stay focused.

“Don’t call me that!” Dixon shrieked. “You don’t know anything about me! Robert was the only one who ever knew me. My own parents left me in that care home. Robert and the Brotherhood picked me up from there. They gave me a life.”

A horrible picture was starting to emerge in Rita's mind. Dixon had been raised by that gang of abusers, and his life must've been hideous. She blinked.

"They raised you? You mean…"

"They took me away from there," Dixon roared, his face red, a vein throbbing on his temple.

"What did they do to you?" Rita shook her head. They had turned a poor boy into a monster through their abuse. She felt it in her bones, and it made her sick.

"Shut up!" Dixon shouted, but she now saw he was unsure, a mask slipping from his face.

"They hurt you, didn't they?" Rita was creeping forward slowly, her eyes fixed on Dixon.

"No," He whispered, his eyes bulging.

There was something in his hand. Something small and metallic. He kept flicking it, and a shudder travelled through Rita's body when she realized that it was a lighter.

She changed direction. "Let my dad go. He hasn't done anything wrong."

Dixon's chest heaved with emotion, then the macabre smile was back. "You took my family from me, now I get to do the same to you."

Rita's ears keened. What could she hear?

The Keeper was still toying with the lighter. Still waiting for her to respond.

"You've got it wrong. He means nothing to me," she said, her words clogging her throat. Her dad would understand. She just prayed that she would get the chance to explain to him that she had to say this. It was the only way. "He has never been part of my life until now."

The Keeper's laughter rang out, but the other sound was still drifting through the rain towards her, so subtle that she half imagined it was inside her head. The Keeper hadn't noticed. Yet. But the harder she strained to listen the clearer it became.

It was the wings of a bird. A seagull. It was interested in their spectacle, because it thought there might be some food here. Seagulls were predators after all. They had strong beaks. The bird was in the air behind Dixon's head, circling above. She kept her eyes off it as it swooped down, heading towards him. She had to time this to perfection.

She noticed her dad's shoe was missing – perhaps he'd lost it when the Keeper dragged him here. Rita's boots were thick-soled, but she could feel the water seeping through her socks, and even she had skidded across the grass.

Her eyes flicked to the Keeper's boots poking out from beneath the white robe. Standard police issue? If so, they would be too thick to plunger her corkscrew through.

She had to attack him from below rather than head on. Get him away from her dad because if they slipped on the saturated ground and went over the edge, at least her dad would be safe. Someone would find him.

"You don't fool me, Rita. I heard you on the phone to him. I saw you." He waited for her to process his words. "That's why he has to die first. Pity he won't get to watch me kill his precious daughter."

A spark erupted from the lighter in his hand. The seagull swooped down low, and Dixon finally felt the bird, and he turned his neck, momentarily distracted.

Rita didn't wait. She dived toward him; her fingers wrapped around the corkscrew in her pocket. She plunged it into his ankle, just as her shoulders slammed into his legs.

CHAPTER 47

The Keeper lurched above her, caught off-balance with the pain in his foot. He howled in agony. Rita shoved him hard, sending him toppling forwards. He landed face-first in the muddy grass. Enough time for Rita to scramble to her feet and jump on him with the baton in her hand.

She clobbered the back of his head, but he rolled over, his legs somehow twisting around her middle and trapping her beneath him. The baton flew from her hand. She clawed at the grass behind her and found the bottom of the wooden cross. Grabbing it with both hands, she held on tightly and bucked her hips upward, her knees connecting with the Keeper's diaphragm.

He was winded momentarily. Enough time for her to drag her knees up to her chest and lash out with both feet. She caught his jaw with her heels, and he reeled backwards. Rita sprung to her feet. Her plan was to run away, make him chase her, hope that her boots would find more purchase than his. If she could make it as far as the curtain wall, he'd have to search for her, buy her some time to call Richard and alert the team.

But before she could go anywhere, she realized that he wasn't even watching her. His fingers were scrabbling about in the grass for something.

The lighter!

Rita lunged forward and kicked him in the head. The blow glanced off his ear. But he had the lighter in his hand. She watched as the world slowed down… and the lighter flipped from his fingers towards her dad.

She tried to catch it mid-arc, but she was in the wrong position, a beat behind the tiny spark. Rita heard a scream and realized that it came from her. She was back on her feet diving towards the bottom of the cross, hoping to grab the lighter before it could do any damage. The smell of fuel was strong, even with the rain pelting her face and trickling into her mouth.

The lighter hit the bottom of the wooden post, and nothing happened. Rita crawled towards it; arms outstretched. She could get it. Her fingers were almost there when iron fists grabbed her ankles as the flames caught. Delayed reaction. The post was wet. She'd told herself that the fire wouldn't travel anywhere, but the fuel was too potent to be diluted by rainfall no matter how torrential.

Anger surged through her. She kicked and bucked, writhing her hips and raising her pelvis until her leg muscles screamed at her to stop. He was dragging her away from the flames and back towards the burning farmhouse. Away from her dad.

Rita tried to grab hold of the soil either side of her, but he was moving too fast for her to get a grip of anything solid. Until her hip caught the side of a rock. She didn't waste a beat. Ignoring the pain, she twisted her upper body and grabbed it with both hands. It wasn't too heavy. *Great!* She was only getting one shot at this.

The Keeper wasn't even watching her. His demonic expression was fixated on the burning cross, and this only fuelled Rita's rage further. Calling on everything she'd learned in high school about throwing the shot, she aimed the rock at his midpoint, and released it.

She got lucky. The rock hit him square in the forehead with a dull thud that was drowned out by the rain. The Keeper dropped Rita's ankles as he spreadeagled backwards.

Rita rolled onto her side and pushed herself upright. Her spine and the back of her head throbbed, but there was no time to think about it. She ran back to the cross, thanking God and the universe and every other spiritual being for making it rain tonight. Flames danced around the bottom of the post, travelling slowly upwards towards her dad, but they hadn't reached him yet.

Rita took her coat off, barely conscious of the fact that she was only wearing a bra, and trousers, and smothered the flames. She hoped that the rain would continue to be on her side. Sliding the knife from her sock, she sawed away at the rope binding her dad's ankles.

"Dad, can you hear me?" she muttered.

Jay groaned, his legs still twitching as she sliced through the first strand of rope. But he didn't raise his head. She tore the rope away from the post, tossed it aside, and reached up to start on the rope around his right wrist.

"Dad?" She peered up at him as she worked with the knife. His face was grey, all his natural colour sucked from him during his ordeal. The rain pelted the back of his head, and she wanted to wrap him in a waterproof blanket and carry him as far away from here as possible. Your parents should never be this vulnerable, and it broke her heart.

"Dad. It's me, Rita. Blink if you can hear me."

Her dad's lips parted. Water trickled from his mouth, his nose, his hair, but she almost whooped with joy when she saw his eyelids tremble.

The rope gave. She dragged it away from his wrist and tossed it aside, draping his arm across her shoulders to support his upper body weight. The flesh around his wrist was raw and pulpy, but he didn't even seem to notice.

“I need you to lean on me, Dad, while I free your other arm.” Rita kept her face close to his chest, trying to shelter him from the rain as well as support him while she worked on the rope.

Jay understood. He gripped Rita’s shoulder, and helped her to free his other arm. Then he was on the ground, on his knees. They hugged each other, panting. Rita felt the strength in her dad’s arms. He was a strong man. Jay had kept himself in shape over the years – thankfully. Even after being strung up like that, she could feel the strength flowing back to him.

“I’m okay,” he whispered, gripping her shoulders.

But Rita didn’t hear the Keeper sneak up behind her. A hand snaked around her shoulder and wrenched her backwards. The bottom of her spine hit the ground, sucking the oxygen from her lungs and causing pain to flare in her kidneys.

The Keeper came at her. He reached down to grab her arms, but she rolled aside, taking him down with her legs at the same time. She tried to get up. To run. To get him away from Jay, but he grabbed the waistband of her jeans and dragged her back on top of him. The back of her head collided with his face. She was clawing at the rain to get away from him, then she was underneath him, and he was raising her shoulders and bashing her skull against the ground.

Pain mushroomed in her head. Dull, sickly pain, clouding her vision. Blackness started to roll in, sucking the stormy muted colours from her line of sight.

"Do you want freedom, Rita?" His spit landed on her face.

Had she never looked at him before? Really looked at him? If she had, she surely would've seen the darkness behind his eyes, the cruel grin, the lack of emotion. Or would she? The uniform had made him invisible. Hidden in plain sight.

"Tell me, Rita," he snarled. "Beg me for freedom."

Rita couldn't swallow. Couldn't breathe. Had to tell him… For her mum… Before he won…

His hands were around her throat, squeezing hard. She forced her lips to part, formed the words, and stared at him through the black clouds swirling across her vision. "Fuck you," she managed as darkness claimed her.

But even as her vision turned to black, she saw a shadow loom up behind the Keeper. The shadow bent lower, and suddenly, the pressure on her throat released. Dixon's hands went lax, then she felt him getting dragged off her.

Rita's body went into autopilot, her lungs sucking in great gulps of oxygen as her airways opened. Her vision was still blurry, her eyes filled with hot, stinging tears. She instinctively rolled onto her side; knees drawn to her chest. All she could hear was the blood gurgling in her ears. The Keeper was being dragged away now, by her dad, his right hooked around the Keeper's waist, the other bending his neck forward.

Jay hit the Keeper on the back of the head, and the man stumbled to his knees. Jay hit him again, and the Keeper collapsed. Rita watched her dad stagger to the cross. The ropes that had tied him now lay on the ground. He picked some up, and then tied the Keeper's hands and feet securely together. The man wasn't moving anymore.

Jay trudged back to Rita, and sank to his knees beside her.

"Rita." His strong arms wrapped around her. She was cradled against a warm chest, rocking back and forth, while her dad murmured, "It's all right, sweetheart. I've got you. It's all over now."

Tears erupted from her eyes, but the fear and adrenaline remained. She gripped her dad hard, and couldn't speak.

Jay's voice was surprisingly clam. "He was weak from fighting you. You were strong." He gripped her harder, and she clung on to him like she would never let him go.

CHAPTER 48

Two Days Later

The Major Incident Room was hushed and quiet. Rita stood in front of the projector, and faced the room full of police officers. She pressed a button on the remote, and PC Dixon's face appeared on the screen. It was his police ID image, but she averted her eyes quickly, her skin crawling.

"Joshua Dixon was raised in Scarborough, at a care home that got shut down in 2000. He lived in a succession of care home afterwards, and finally he was adopted by Robert McFarlane. Mr McFarlane was the man who murdered the 32-year-old woman Clara Winters in 2003, a crime that was finally solved last year."

Rita described how Dixon had formed the online group called the Gathering, and how he had groomed several vulnerable teenagers.

"Dixon made a mistake when he abducted Jay Gupta. His desire for the revenge of his mentor, Robert McFarlane, overrode everything ese. Which is lucky for us." Rita looked up at the darkened rows, and smiled once.

"He was finally apprehended by myself and Mr Gupta. He is now incarcerated in HMP Wakefield, a Category A prison. Dr Das confirmed that Dixon's DNA was a match for the skin cells recovered from beneath Sarah's fingernails."

Rita stopped to catch her breath. She faced the assembled room, the rows of faces in darkness. In the front row, she could see her team, the D Sup Nicola Perkins, and right at the end, only his dim outline visible, sat Jack Banford.

Many here knew about Clara, her mother. The news had percolated, like water between sand. Did that make it easier?

No. Nothing would make it easier.

She breathed again. "When Dixon entered the police force, he didn't have a record, obviously. There was no reason to suspect him. We're lucky, in fact, that he was posted in Lancaster, and not in Yorkshire. He could've caused serious trouble with the Winters investigation."

Rita continued. "We must remain vigilant as to who enters our Force. This is true of all Forces, up and down the country. We now know Dixon had a history of petty crimes. Arson in his neighbourhood that he was a suspect in, sexual assaults on underage girls in his school. His name came up in investigations, but he was never reported. There were no PCNs. And these were never looked at when he applied to enter the Force."

Nicola cleared her throat at the front row. "Do we know if there is any more of the gang still around? Last year you caught McFarlane, and now Dixon. What about Edward Salt and Lord Northallerton?"

"Salt and Northallerton are serving long jail sentences. Allegations of historic abuse are hard to prove, but many former residents of the care home came forward after the Winters case was made public. But with Dixon, the problem is he had an online following. Thousands of sick and depraved people adored him – and I don't just mean his fans, I mean others like him, who would kill without thinking twice. We don't know how big that group is. But with the help of the NCA and Interpol's Cyber Crime Division, we're starting to track them down."

Rita smiled to herself. Nigel Warren, the DI at the National Crime Agency, had been very helpful when he heard of Rita's ordeal. Without Nigel's help, she wouldn't have been able to mobilise the NCA's vast supercomputers to track down the criminals who followed Dixon, The Keeper and his Gathering.

Rita said, "Hopefully, none of them will be left to cause any more trouble. But we must remain vigilant."

Rita's recollections of what happened on the promontory were patchy – and the nightmares still bothered her. She remembered PC Dixon revealing himself when he lowered his hood. Remembered him telling her that he wanted revenge for Robert McFarlane, and what followed after. She shuddered now as some of the visions cut into her mind like sharp knives.

Maggie, Rizwan, and Richard had filled her in when they visited her in hospital. The emergency services had received a call regarding the fire in the old farmhouse near the castle and the duty sergeant at the station had been alerted. Richard was just leaving the office when the call came through. He'd tried calling Rita, and when he got no response, told Maggie and Riz that he was concerned about her. They got Traffic to triangulate Rita's call location, and it was by the castle. It didn't take them long to put two and two together.

By the time they arrived at the castle top, Rita and Jay were slowly trudging down. Maggie found Rita first, and didn't waste any time calling an ambulance.

*****

Rita took some questions from the floor. Her feet were hurting, her ankles had been twisted badly. Her back and shoulders also ached. It had taken her two days to recover from the harrowing events on the Castle's hillsides. Jay was well, and resting at home, thankfully. His wife, Anna, had joined them.

The lights came on, and Rita blinked. The gathering started to file out, and some officers stopped to congratulate Rita. Nicola came up to where Rita was chatting to Richard, Maggie and Rizwan.

"Well done," the D Sup said in a rare show of praise. "Do we have all the DNA evidence to tie Dixon to the murder?"

"Yes," Rita said. "The DNA under Sarah's nails, and on her clothes belonged to him. There's enough to prosecute him. The CPS are happy with the evidence."

"Good." The ghost of a smile appeared on Nicola's lips before it vanished. Was there a softening in her stance, or was Rita imagining it? The latter, most likely, she thought.

"See you later," Nicola said, and the others nodded. She walked away, her back straight, the high heels failing to raise her petite frame much.

"Even the iron lady spoke today," Maggie murmured, and Rita grinned at her.

"I'll see you at the pub, in case you're coming tonight," Jack's voice came from behind her. "There's a celebration after the case is over, right?"

Maggie said, "Can you keep up with us coppers drinking? We normally put you lawyers under the table."

Everyone laughed, apart from Jack. He said, "Sounds like a challenge. Accepted." He did a mock bow. "Pints at 7pm?"

"Deal," Rita said.

CHAPTER 49

Three Days Later

"You will come and visit us soon, won't you?" Anna, Jay's wife, stood outside Rita's apartment building the clear, blue Autumn sky providing the perfect backdrop for their departure.

"She already said she will." Jay wrapped an arm around his wife's shoulders and smiled.

Anna was petite, bubbly, brunette, and much shorter than Rita. She drove to Scarborough as soon as she heard what had happened to Rita and Jay. Rita was in hospital when she arrived. She didn't have time to psych herself up for the visit, to mentally prepare herself for meeting her dad's wife, but it turned out that she didn't need to.

Anna was sitting in the visitor's seat by Rita's bed when she woke up the next day.

"Hey." She perched on the edge of the bed and stroked Rita's hair away from her face. It was a curiously intimate gesture from someone Rita had never met. "I'm Anna, your dad's wife. I came as soon as I heard. How are you feeling?"

"Groggy." Rita was shocked at how hoarse she sounded. Her throat felt as if it had been scoured with sandpaper. Her eyes were gritty. Her face and hands were sore beneath the sterile dressings. "Dad?" she croaked.

"He's fine. They kept him in overnight to monitor his vitals, but he's been along to see you."

Rita had nestled back against the pillow. Her dad was okay.

"You saved his life." Anna had said. "I will never ever forget that."

"He saved mine too," Rita had whispered. Then she fell asleep again.

***

Rita had enjoyed having Jay and Anna stay with her in the flat. Anna talked relentlessly about their life together, and by the time they were due to leave, Rita felt as if she'd always been a part of their lives.

Jack carried their bags outside to the car and Anna hugged Rita.

"Your eyebrows are starting to grow back already," she said, standing back and studying Rita's face.

"Probably not my best look." Rita rolled her eyes. She'd forced herself to look in the mirror earlier that day and had recoiled from the shiny pink skin and patchy scabs.

"You're exactly as I always pictured you from the baby photos your dad kept." Anna smiled at her, and Rita's heart swelled with the unexpected rush of affection for someone she'd only known a few days. "I was worried that he'd wear those pictures out. I don't know what I'd have done if he had."

"I never knew."

"Sometimes I think that not knowing is how we deal with the important stuff in our lives, Rita. You had enough on your plate, honey. The last thing you needed was worrying about your dad."

They both glanced at Jay, who was closing the car boot, the car all packed up ready to leave. His eyes narrowed as he and Jack joined the two women outside the entrance to Rita's building. "What have I done?" he asked.

"Nothing, Dad." Rita threw her arms around his neck and hugged him tightly, breathing in his spicy, citrussy scent.

It was a rare display of affection, and Rita buried her face in her dad's shoulder to hide her flushed cheeks. They'd visited her mum's grave a few days earlier. As morbid and sad as it sounded, it seemed to have cemented the fragile relationship they'd begun to rebuild between them, and Rita had the strange sensation that Clara was smiling down on them now.

Rita knew that Clara would be happy she'd played her own part in bringing them back together again.

Warm saline moistened her eyes. She had achieved closure for the regrets in her life. But the loss remained, and it sharpened when she thought of her mother. When she finally pulled away, she said, "Thank you. For everything."

She saw him struggle to hold his emotions in check. He took off his glasses, then put them on again.

"You never have any need to thank me, Rita. You'll always be my baby, you know."

Anna smiled at them both like a mother duck counting her chicks. "Ready?"

"Ready." Jay nodded. To Rita and Jack, he said, "Don't forget – Christmas. Aaron will be home from Uni. We'll have stuffed turkey, homemade Christmas pudding, crackers, carol singing, the works."

"Games," Jack said. "I'll bring the games."

"We'll be there," Rita said. She meant to say *I will be there*...but Jack was finding a way to segue back into her life. She didn't know what to do about it. She was enjoying it, for now. And Rita had learnt to live in the present – not the past, or the future.

She usually spent Christmas watching old movies on the telly – *White Christmas, It's a Wonderful Life, Miracle on 34*th *Street* – eating pasta and mince pies, and stuffing herself with chocolate until she fell asleep on the sofa. She didn't have the heart to tell Jay and Anna that she normally couldn't wait for Christmas to be over. She got the feeling that Anna was a Christmas freak, the person who shopped for sparkly baubles and tinsel all year round and started gift shopping in January.

If Rita was honest, she was looking forward to her first proper family Christmas in almost thirty years.

She and Jack watched her dad and Anna drive away, waving until they were out of view. She'd spent ten days with her dad, but it felt as if he'd taken a tiny part of her with him, and she already felt the brush of cool air on her healing skin from the spot where he'd been standing moments earlier.

She was going to miss him. It seemed odd now, that the father she almost never had, and hence not really missed, was suddenly such a big part of her life.

She walked back inside with Jack.

"You don't have to stay, you know," Rita said. Jack hadn't stayed overnight – but he'd arrived on cue every morning as Rita emerged from her bedroom and hadn't left until he'd seen her curled up on the sofa in her pyjamas with a cup of hot chocolate and a mountain of biscuits. "You must have work to catch up on."

"Why don't you let me worry about that?" Jack murmured as they went back inside the building.

“Because I know that you don’t.”

“Precisely my point.” Jack followed her back inside the flat and closed the door behind them. “I can do video calls, and work from home. Besides, work will still be there tomorrow, and the next day, and the day after that.” He smiled at her. “It’s a beautiful day, and you have a rare day off. So, what do you want to do?”

Visions of her childhood, floated into her mind like white clouds in a blue sky. Riding the choo choo train with Clara, giggling with excitement.

“I want to ride the clifftop railway,” she said.

CHAPTER 50

Joshua Dixon was seated in the stiff, green plastic chair at the visitor's chamber in HMP Wakefield. Dixon didn't have any contact with the outside world, apart from a couple of highly selective visitors. These visitors were vetted deeply. Only close family members were allowed. When they attended the prison, they went through airport style security. Every movement was captured on CCTV from the moment they parked their car in the prison car park.

One of these visitors now sat in front of Dixon. His sister, Janice. She had wisps of black and white hair trailing down her face. Her cheeks were fleshy and flabby, and eyes red rimmed from drinking and lack of sleep. Janice was an alcoholic, amongst other things.

She glanced at the guard who stood at a distance. He wasn't able to hear what they said. But he kept an eye on them, making sure there was no physical contact.

"He came to see me," Janice whispered.

"You can speak up," Dixon said, allowing himself a smile. "That's one thing they can't record."

"Alright. Anyway. I didn't believe him at first. He approached me in the park, when I took Billy for a walk."

"What did he say?"

"That he worships you. He followed your website, and he knows about Robert McFarlane. Who's he?"

Dixon smiled again. "My mentor. What did he say about Robert?"

"Just that he looked after you, after you left that horrible children's home. He said Robert's a great man."

"What did you say his name was again?"

Janice told him. "He contacted you on the website. The Gathering? His screen name was Wolf Watcher."

Dixon narrowed his eyes, but couldn't recall. He had thousands of followers. Besides the website had now been taken down. Janice continued.

"He wants to stay in touch. He says he's got plans, and he wants your blessing. Whatever that means."

"Excellent. We need to find a way to get my messages to him."

"How? You're not allowed a phone. I can't even bring my own phone inside. Bloody ridiculous, if you ask me. I can't show you photos of Billy."

Dixon bent his head, thinking. “I’ll think of something, don’t worry. Until we have direct contact, you can be our go between.”

“No problem.”

Dixon placed his elbows and leaned closer. “Tell him I want revenge for what they did to me. He can unleash hell.”

Want to read more? Book 3 –*Little Voice Lost* is out soon!

AUTHOR'S NOTE

Thank you for reading this book, and I hope you enjoyed it. Would you please mind leaving a review?

That would make my day. Please visit Amazon in your country of choice and leave a review. It takes 2 minutes of your time.

Book 3, *Little Voice Lost*, will be out very soon, so get ready!

Kind regards

Sam Carter.

Printed in Great Britain
by Amazon

61900372R00231